Praise
Jane

MW01136304

"Jane Lindskold is one of those hidden treasures of American letters; a true gem of a writer who simply gets better with every book."

-Charles de Lint

"Lindskold is a writer with strong world-building skills and a knack for intricate yet comprehensible plots."

-Romantic Times BOOKreviews

"Lindskold writes everything from contemporary to mythic, from wonder-filled science fiction to epic fantasy to thoughtful whimsy. She can be dark, hopeful, adventurous, funny, disturbing, insightful, and piercing, often within the same work."

-Julie Bartel, literary critic and librarian

"Her characters live – and the world they live in lingers in the mind: heroic, squalid, exotic, everyday. I was convinced that it went on by itself when I turned the last page. Bravo!"

-S.M. Stirling on *Through Wolf's Eyes*

"The author's ability to create complex tales involving believable human and animal characters makes this a standout fantasy saga."

-Library Journal on *The Dragon of Despair*

"An exotic historical fantasy. The action [shifts] to high gear and the supernatural spookiness carries the story to a satisfying conclusion."

-Publisher's Weekly on *The Buried Pyramid*

"The characterization is superb, the plotting swift, and the prose a pleasure to read."

-Publisher's Weekly on *Child of a Rainless Year*

ASPHODEL

Other Books by
Jane Lindskold

The Artemis Awakening Series
Artemis Awakening
Artemis Invaded

The Firekeeper Series
Through Wolf's Eyes
Wolf's Head, Wolf's Heart
The Dragon of Despair
Wolf Captured
Wolf Hunting
Wolf's Blood

The Breaking the Wall Series
Thirteen Orphans
Nine Gates
Five Odd Honors

The Athanor Series
Changer
Changer's Daughter (aka Legends Walking)

Captain Ah-Lee Short Stories
Endpoint Insurance
Winner Takes Trouble
Here to There
Star Messenger (the box set of all three short stories)

ASPHODEL

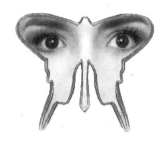

Jane Lindskold

Obsidian Tiger Books

Cover and interior design by

emtippettsbookdesigns.com

For Jim, who understands the value of dreams and visions.

Acknowledgements

Asphodel owes its existence to Paula A. Paul who, at a meeting of First Fridays when business not creativity was dominating the discussion, asked "Isn't anyone *writing*?" Her words haunted me. I went home and started this book soon thereafter.

I'd like to thank my husband, Jim, for his encouraging me as I entered onto the very odd creative journey that was the writing of this novel. He also was my first reader. His overwhelming enthusiasm for what to that point I had just thought of as creative self-indulgence made me begin to wonder if maybe *Asphodel* was a story other people might enjoy reading.

My second round of readers – Julie Bartel, Paul Dellinger, Sally Gwylan, Alan Robson, Jan Stirling, Steve Stirling, Emily Mah Tippetts, and Bobbi Wolf – convinced me that a widely varied group of people could find something appealing in this tale.

Asphodel's final audition occurred twenty minutes at a time over several months as I read the manuscript aloud to my friends Rowan Derrick, Melissa Jackson, Cale Mims, and Dominique Price. Tori Hansen was there for the beginning of the reading, and encouraged us to keep going after she moved. Jim listened to the reading with unflagging interest, despite the fact that he'd already read the manuscript twice.

Rowan Derrick supplied the cover art, drawing on her vision of the novel for the imagery.

Thanks also to Emily and the staff of E.M. Tippetts Book Designs for helping create the finished book.

And thanks to those of you who took the gamble of reading *Asphodel*. I most sincerely hope you enjoy.

sphodel. The word echoes in the quiet within my mind as I awaken. I have no idea why. I'm not even certain what it means. A flower? A place? Both. Neither.

I look around me, hoping for understanding. All I find is more confusion. I am in a bed in a room. The coverlet on the bed is soft-rose and deeply quilted: individual, somewhat rounded shapes like squished marshmallows or mushroom caps.

I am in a bed. The bed is in a room. Like the shapes on the coverlet, the room is also vaguely round, a soft octagon that is walled in seven windows and one blank panel. The windows show light and occasional clouds. These clouds are also rounded and lumpy: sky sheep. Cumulous, as innocuous as the full stop that makes the end of a sentence.

Outside can't hold my interest long, not with only light and fluffy white against a pale blue. Fine. I will look elsewhere. Without leaving my bed I do this. What do I see? The bed does not hold my eye long. The sheets (when I lift and peek) are as pale pink as the coverlet. No. Even paler. That is rose. This is blush. A maiden's blush, so lacking character as to fail to hold the eye.

I swing myself to one side so I might see the floor. It is carpeted in some dappled pattern: pale green on paler green light. I think of water in a still pond beneath the thick cover of early spring foliage, fully leafed out and yet not darkened by strong sun, roughened by wind, by weather. Rose leaves about a bud, but no rose bud was so without perfume, without, without… character?

I look to one side of the bed, note my back, my shoulders, are propped against fat, fluffy pillows, not two or four, but six, eight, ten, more, all of various sizes, all of shades of pink that go with the blush, the rose, without argument, complaint, even contrast. Cotton candy, carnation, early dawn, rose-quartz, rosy dawn, rose-diamond, rose…

I rise. Swing my feet to the floor where they discover the carpet is very thick, soft as dreams, as kitten fur, as down.

Down I come from the bed, discovering that it is very high, coming to my waist. Getting back will be a challenge if I don't wish to be discovered out of it.

Discovered? By whom? I have no idea, and the vague sense of dread that touches me vanishes.

I look around, wonderingly. When I had been in the bed the heaped pillows had so walled me in that I had not realized that a small nightstand stood just to one side of the bed. Upon it rests a small cut crystal glass and an enameled box the size of the palm of my hand. It is shaped like a ladybug, its dark red and black spots a shout in the pastel of this place.

(The nightstand is a faded white, lightly veined, an ivory white, though something in me says that ivory is often yellowish and, being made of tusk and tooth, is very rarely pure.)

The ladybug box fascinates me. I take it up, wondering why I was so certain it was a box, for I can't open it, nor do I see hinges or latch or anything to indicate that it should open. I hold it to my ear. Give it a slight shake. Is that a rattle I hear? Again. Maybe? Maybe something so tightly padded it can't move. I turn the box in my hands, noting that what is not red or black is gold. Strong colors, all a shout in this pale, restful, easy place.

Reluctantly leaving the puzzle of the box – or of the ladybug figurine that might not, after all, be a box – I step away from the bed. My feet are small, dainty, pinky-peach, each nail tipped with a tiny crescent so clean and white that it is nearly luminous. Although they work perfectly well, there is something unusual about these feet. I can't imagine them in mud or squeezed into shoes. They seem to have no purpose but to lie abed or perhaps to pick a dainty course across the dew-dappled pale green of this carpet.

I am so disturbed that I look no more at myself except to note that I am clad in something of palest lavender, almost a cobwebby grey. It is silken soft and does not cling. There might be adornments but, having been so disturbed by my feet, I don't query further. Instead I resolutely turn my attention to everything within this rounding chamber that is not me, as if in not looking I can somehow dismiss all that disturbs me.

Ivory nightstand. Pink upon pinkness of the bed. Green dream of carpet beneath my... no! I will not think of beneath. I almost climb into the bed again, for each soft step I take threatens me with questions I don't want to even shape, much less enhance or try to answer. But climbing seems a greater threat. I will look more.

There is no nightstand on the other side of the bed (I had dismounted on the right) as I had half-expected. Walking around, I see that the bed is set near the center of the roundish room. Two of the seven windows are behind the headboard, yet I had known they were there. There is a space between the bed and any of the windows, space enough for me to lay myself down full-length and have room to spare.

This is true even behind the headboard, where I find set out as if awaiting a doll's tea party a neat little table, oval-shaped, softened with a ruffled cloth in a blue paler than the sky. Only one chair waits at the table and there is no setting, only a box in a blue slightly darker than the tablecloth. The box is as large as my two hands set side by side, fingers outstretched.

To avoid looking at those hands for fear they will worry me as do my feet, I rush to open the box, grasping by an edge and pushing to one side. The top slides off and reveals a blaze of strong colors, twice as long and yet slightly more slender than the fingers I still will not look at. I can't seem to count the colors, but I know them as all those of the rainbow and more. I know them as pens.

Now I see that next to the box, in what I had thought its shadow, rests a book. The cover is like the box – a shade of blue, although both darker and less substantial than either box or tablecloth. Not worrying about whether I will see my hands, I hurry to open the book. Here, surely here, will be the answers I have sought without knowing I am seeking.

The first page is blank but for the rough texture of handmade paper. I want to scream but reassure myself, even as I know I am doomed to disappointment, that surely somewhere within there are the answers I seek. The pages – cream-colored except for occasional flecks of color as if dried flower petals had been mixed into the pulp before the paper was made – remain stubbornly blank.

I bite down on my lower lip with my front teeth, momentarily registering their strength when I feel the throb of my pulse in my bruised flesh. I don't weep, just close the book, close the box of pens. Their brilliance disturbs this tranquil pale haven. I leave the useless table, the solitary chair, behind me and make my way to the nearest window.

For the first time, I register that although there are indeed eight panels, none are precisely the same size. If this chamber is an octagon, as I had thought upon my waking, it is a lopsided one indeed, a poorly cut gem set… where?

I have not yet tried to see. Now, as I pace closer to the pane that directly backs the bed, I study the window with such care that one would think I was approaching a dragon's den, a lion's lair, a wolf's warren, not a simple construction of glass meant to let in light and banish weather. It is a tall window, rising from the floor but for the negligible width of its frame. It reaches nearly to the ceiling, like the window of a great cathedral, but tapers at the top, interlocking with other panes of glass, these opaque and opalescent, that transform the light, not into the strong bars of the rainbow, but into the quieter yet no less gaudy fires of an opal.

I don't let myself be distracted by this overarching firmament of pastel gleams, but study the window. Its center is as clear as need uncomplicated by morality, but the handspan width where it meets the pane beside it is full of facets and Jack Frost's flowers. These give the view less the sense of being "real" and more that of an image framed for presentation. Each window is alike in this, although all differ in their width. The largest is the one I first approached. The smallest is off to one side, left of the bed, if one uses the bed for orientation as for now I must, having no sense of east or west, for the light has held steady, unmoving, and unchanged in brilliance since I came to myself in this place.

All the panels are alike except for the one that foots the bed. This is not clear but dark. If I had thought about it at all, I had thought of it as a door. Now, walking quickly on the soft pale green, I see there is no door, only a panel where the glass is dark and sharply broken, as obsidian breaks. No door and, as surely as I am there and fighting lest my breath burst into sobs and drown me, not one of those windows will open.

I sink down onto the floor in front of the dark panel, my gaze caught by the translucent blacks and deep greens, veined with rusty reds, all holding a sharpness that would cut without pain. I stare into their darkness that yet is not, seeking patterns that are not there. I drift for who knows how long, for I feel neither heat nor cold nor hunger nor any bodily discomfort. I wait, although for what I have no idea, nor does the waiting end, but when I cease to wait.

Waiting changes nothing. Am I nothing then? For waiting changes me. Unsteady on my feet, I rise, walk the edges of the room, stopping, finally, before the window that backs the headboard of the bed. Why here? No reason except, perhaps, that it is farthest from that betraying not-door, dark panel. The light without has not yet changed, nor has the view from even a few feet away. This argues that I am very high up indeed. I have, thus far, seen nothing but sky, light, clouds. Perhaps I need to get close enough to look down.

I do, finding that the window's sill is deeper than I recall from my hasty inspection when all I had sought was clasp or latch or other indication that the window could be opened. Now I press my palms against the sill and look down. As I had surmised, I am very high up, so high that I look down upon clouds. Yet, as I gaze, my vision seems to sharpen and I can make out details. Even my perspective seems to shift so that it is not so much that I look down upon the view, but that I view a scene in miniature, my perspective only slightly skewed by height, as if I look upon a painting and, as I look, that painting slowly comes to life.

First, I see a glade, tree-framed, at the center of which is a pond, clear and bright, fed by a spring at one edge, spilling into courses that ripple and dance – halfway between babbling brook and tiny waterfalls. I believe the glade to be untenanted, but a flash of red announces a cardinal flitting from green-leafed limb to green-leafed limb in the busy way of birds.

And then I see it, stepping lightly, stately, but with a gaiety that robs it of pomposity. Snow white, ice white, pearl white, dainty hooves chased in gold, silken mane threaded with silver, even to the lion-tip of its tail – a unicorn. Impossible yet possibly perfect. Its horn is colorless, taking color from its surroundings – one moment the pale blue of a part of the sky, the next the bloody red of the cardinal, most often the vibrant green of leaf and sward.

In this borrowed color, I glimpse the secret that hides the unicorn's existence from those who would not see it even if it walked right in front of them. They would see a long-tailed goat or an unusually delicate pony. Without the horn to force the issue, they could continue not to see and so be comforted. But I do see and delight in the sight.

For the first time since my confused awakening in this glass-walled tower I smile, nay, I *grin*, cheeks plumping to burst with incredulous joy.

I watch, un-hungering, un-thirsting until my eyelids close with a weariness that I don't feel until it sets upon me and I topple, still smiling, onto the thick green carpet and sleep, protected from even a glimpse of the dark shards of the door that is not, the blank barrier that promises the freedom it also denies.

When I next wake, it is again daylight or should I say "is still" for I have not the least proof that there has been any darkness but that which I keep within my closed eyes. Shoving myself to my knees, getting tangled in the long dress I had been wearing upon my first waking, and which I think of as a nightdress, although I now consider that might as well be thought of as a daydress for, as of yet, I have not experienced night in this place.

Untangling myself, I get to my feet and hurry to look out the window through which I had seen the unicorn and cardinal. The glade is there – at least I think it is the same glade. But of the unicorn, the cardinal, indeed of any living thing that is not a subject of the vegetable kingdom, of any motion that does not owe its action to the elemental forces of wind or water, I see nothing.

Disappointed, I sink down again onto the carpet. I might have given myself over to unthinking despair, for without the prompts of hunger or other bodily needs, I have little else but mood to prompt me. Then I think that I should look out another window. The unicorn might have wandered only a little way while I drowsed.

I creep to the window to the right of the one I had first looked out, choosing right for no reason other than that is where my crawling hand had taken me. I rise upright, brushing my skirts straight with inattention, for my attention is riveted by what I see or – rather – what I don't see.

The glade is entirely gone – gone entirely – although I feel certain I had seen it through this very pane when I had stood at the window adjacent. But no, this is no glade, no brook, no hint of any vegetation. This place is shimmering brightness, gem-bedecked, the light the yellow blending into green into blue of some phosphorescence.

Or is it? Forgetting – or rather deliberately putting aside the dilemma of windows that don't show what I expect, I look – really look – at what is before me. What I had taken for the phosphorescent glow of some eldritch light now resolves to indirect illumination from a panel set like a window in a closed space. The gem-like shimmer is harder to resolve, for the room is so oddly lit.

Then I realize that it is the shimmer of light off of water droplets, and that this enclosed space has one wall – like my own chamber – which is walled in glass. Water – raindrops, spray, splash, I can't tell – has dappled the glass and now gives back the indirect light, giving the illusion of solid form.

Frightened, I cast my gaze back, right, left, but none of my windows show any sign of damp. Reassured from what fear I don't dare shape, I set to study this new vista.

As I do, I notice that in this space, empty as I had thought it to be, something does dwell. It is a monster of some rare sort: bat-eared, with long, slanting eyes, an enormous mouth stretching, even as I watch, in a soundless (to me) shout or roar or bellow.

Uneasy, flabbergasted, I turn away. Frightening as that creature is, I feel a flicker of sympathy, a surge of kinship that troubles me more than I want to admit. What have I to do, me here in my rosy tower, with that monster? Surely I am as sweet and delicate as my surroundings. That is when I realize that, other than my barely glimpsed hands and dainty feet, I have no idea at all what I look like.

I glance around me, but none of the windows are lit so as to give me back a reflection. Hurriedly, I race to the bed. There is no polished surface that might give me even a distorted reflection such as I might have found in a brass knob or rail.

Next I go to the nightstand. The tiny ladybug box is no help. The drawer yields a comb and brush, but no mirror. The little cabinet beneath offers a neat pair of shoes with ruffled socks tucked within, as well as an assortment of ribbons and bows in a rainbow of colors, if rainbows were ever pastel. Further search – under the bed, within the heaped bedclothes – offers nothing that will give a reflection.

Then I think of the dark panel. Its surface might give a reflection as the clear window does not, but do I really wish to learn my appearance from such a broken, distorted mirror? I don't. How would I know what is the truth, what the altered vision?

I have left one option. I can remove my gown and inspect what lays beneath. Surely this is a good idea for, despite our attachment to them, our faces are only a very small part of ourselves. Yes. I could learn much, but I feel curiously loath. I don't even want to reach behind me and discover the color of the braid I now realize rests its weight between my shoulder blades.

I delve deeper. I don't feel amnesiac. I know things. I even know the lack of things – of hunger, of thirst, of a need to loose my bladder – that I don't feel. No. I am not lacking a memory. I have information and to spare. What I lack is identity and, again, I don't feel as if such has been taken from me. I feel – new? No. That isn't quite right. As if I have many selves and none at all.

Frustrated, I decide I will go look out a new window. That, at least, is amusement, stimulus, of a sort. I have just awakened. Give me time and I will have the answers to my puzzles.

For variety, I choose a window adjacent to the dark panel – daring myself, as well I know, by my proximity to its shadow. Pointedly ignoring it, I gaze out at a prosaic scene: two girls, one light-haired, one dark, are washing dishes in a kitchen. The floor is tiled in intricate patterns that yet show wear, scuffed as if from the passage of many feet. The sink at which the fair-haired girl stands, up to nearly her elbows in foamy water, is of a material as white as snow, yet about the edges, above the waterline, I can see scratches and chips.

Clearly, then, this room had once seen better days. The girls seem happy despite their menial tasks. The dark-haired one alternates between drying the accumulating dishes and, when her sister – for I feel sure they are indeed sisters, no matter the variance in their coloration – slows to scrub a stubborn pot, takes up a broom with a green metal handle and dense black bristles and begins sweeping the floor.

The pot must have been very dirty, for at last the fair one – her hair has something about it of the color and texture of dry straw – drains her water and runs in more from a shiny yet water-spotted faucet. She lets in more steamy water and adds liquid from a bottle near at hand. This liquid is the brilliant green of emeralds, but the water it touches remains mysteriously clear, only bursting into clouds of iridescent bubbles where the running water beats it.

Straw-hair cups a handful of the bubbles and blows them at her sister. Sister Brown, in turn, catches a few and blows them free of the froth to float like fairy orbs over the worn tiles of the floor. I can see their laughter, although I can't hear it, and long to join the frolic.

My solitude overwhelms me at that moment, but I will not be defeated. Pursing my lips in a thoughtful frown, I consider my options.

I have no one to talk to, not even a doll or a teddy bear. The ladybug box is too hard, too cold, too mysterious to serve as confidant. Am I to be balked before I even begin? Dolls… The idea wakes something in me. I run to the table set behind the headboard. There, as I remembered, rests a box of brightly colored pens and a blank book.

Hastily, lest my sudden inspiration flee or – worse – seem too stupid to be worth pursuing, I pull out the chair and seat myself at the table. Opening the book to the first page, I grope blindly in the box of pens, stirring them with my fingers until the digits close upon one. I pull it out and find it to be pale blue, a color that goes so well with the book cover and box and table ruffles that for a brief moment it almost seems to be no color at all.

This somehow seems fitting. Lips tightly pursed, I set myself to draw a very simple shape: rounded head, two arms extended, a somewhat chunky torso, and two legs. It only is the idea of a person, but that is all I need and too complicated a shape would defeat my goal. Carefully, I give it two eyes and an upturned smile. It needs hair, so I extend the head with two rounded curves.

A few lines gives my new friend a tidy outfit: trousers; long-sleeved, vee-necked shirt; shoes. I lightly shade the pants in blue, the top in pink, and the hair in yellow. I can feel my smile widening, but now I must free her from the page. I can't leave this strange room, but I will not leave my new friend equally trapped.

Whatever provided the pens and book did not provide scissors or knife. Briefly, I consider breaking the cut crystal tumbler that sits on the nightstand, but that seems a waste and, anyhow, shards of glass might get into the carpet and I would be forever cutting myself. I remember someone saying with laughter in her (?) – yes, her! – voice that broken glass multiplies so that if you could gather up all the pieces you would discover that you had enough to create the object originally broken and half again.

However, I am very determined and soon hit upon a plan. First I bend the book so that the page on which I have drawn my figure rests against the table. Then, taking the pale blue pen, I trace around and around the figure, pressing down hard with the steel nib until it cuts through the paper. This takes a long time and much patience, but time I have in abundance and patience seems wise to cultivate.

Where am I going in any case?

At last, I succeed and can gently push the doll free, leaving a doll-sized hole in the page and, surprisingly, not much in the way of a mark on the tabletop. The paper is of a sturdy sort, and Muriel, for this is what I decide to call my new friend for no reason other than that this strikes me as an elegant and artistic sort of name, seems in no danger of ripping or folding. After turning her over and giving her back side the necessary details, I consider what we should do next.

"Shall we see if the unicorn has come back?" I ask her, and since she has proper enthusiasm for unicorns, we go over to the appropriate window. As it happens, the unicorn has not wandered back, but there are three cottontail rabbits involved in a very elaborate game of tag. Later, not precisely tired, because I never seem to get tired or hungry or thirsty, but ready for a change, I climb up on the bed. Muriel and I have a grand time making a garden of the sheets and blankets, with the abundant pillows for mountains.

Eventually, I feel sufficiently restored to try another window. Thus far I have tried three: the glade, the monster's den, and the one with the two girls. I choose one on the opposite side of the room from the girls and, setting Muriel where she can watch, too, move where I can get a good look out and down.

At first, I am deeply disappointed because all I see is a wide stretch of a blue frothed with white. Although it is darker than the sky – a bit more turquoise – I think we're looking down at the sky. After being surrounded by it, that seems like quite a cheat.

Then something that never happens in the sky happens: a great stone-grey rock rises through the sky, pushing aside the blue, which runs off its surface, bubbling white and clear as water. Water!

I shout happily and realize what I'm looking at. This isn't the sky, it's a bit of ocean, so far from shore that land is less than a memory. What has breasted the blue is a whale, a huge monster, I can tell, even without anything to measure it against. It has a rounded head with eyes set so far apart that they must think what the other eye sees is some sort of idea or dream. Though, maybe not, if all there is to see is open water and opener sky.

The whale leaps nearly out of the water, apparently for no reason other than the fun of it. When it crashes down, Muriel and I wait for it to come up again, but it does not. Eventually, even its ripples fade. I wonder where it has gone, what those wide-set eyes are seeing. Mermaids, I bet, and shipwrecks, mysterious fortresses guarded by long-tentacled squid with beaks like hawks and the ability to shroud the depths in clouds of purple-black ink. Seahorses, too, both the odd fragile ones that look like coral come to life and those beautiful ones that are half land horse, and half some sort of fish, the natural steeds of merfolk.

I wish that I was seeing what that whale is seeing, wish and wish and wish. As I do so, my brain does flip-flops inside my head and I am seeing sideways!

One eye sees one thing and the other, just as I had expected, sees another, but neither of those eyes sees anything that I want to see. On one side there is a merman – or maybe a triton – I never was quite sure if there was any sort of difference. He has a long spear in one hand and is threatening my eye – I mean the whale's eye – with it.

I don't think a spear, even if it was shoved directly into my eye, could kill me, but I am absolutely certain it wouldn't feel very good. In any case, I don't think the merman with the spear thinks that he could kill me either. He is hoping to distract me so I won't pay any heed to what is happening on my other side.

Over there, set back behind a wavy forest consisting of some green and yellow water plants with wide, flowing, translucent leaves, more merfolk are busy with a contraption that is being hauled on a chariot without wheels, drawn by a pair of those magnificent seahorses – hippocampi, as I now remember they are called. The details of the device are hard to make out through all the frothy foliage, but of one thing I feel sure – it has lots of long shafts pointing from it, each tipped with a sharp head cut from some razor-edged shell.

The shell is pretty stuff, shimmering in nacreous pink to green waves as the light hits it, but soon enough it would be reddened with blood. *My* blood. If I don't want that, I need to do something and fast.

My left eye vision tells me that there are now several mermen with spears seeking to drive me closer to that spear-firing contraption. They are unpleasant and frightening. Where they have nicked me with their spears it hurts, but no blood flows. After a moment, I realize why they cut so shallowly. Blood would bring sharks and sharks are friends to none but their own eternal hunger.

At that moment, I know how to save myself – but in doing so might I be creating a new, more certain, danger?

I consider but not for overly long. I can remain beneath the surface without breathing for hours, true enough, but eventually I will exhaust my air and I will need it if I hope to make good my escape. Then, too, to delay would be to give my enemies time to put their own plan into action. I don't doubt that it include some safeguards for themselves when the sharks come to rip my flesh from my bloodied body.

No, I can't wait. I must act!

I slam sideways with my huge, solid rock of a head, swinging it like a battering ram into the brave – or rather imprudent and brazen – merman who had come up closer than wisdom would dictate.

Slam! Again I hit, this time rolling all my huge body sideways and over onto my more proximate attackers. On land, I would have crushed them, but here in the giving realm of water, I must do more. Squealing my rage, I snap, severing a spear – and the arm that grips it – in half. Blood fountains forth in heartbeat jets, but will it be enough?

The mermen clearly think so, for they are scattering, leaving their bleeding comrade to pump his shark call into the sea. My right eye sees the confusion of the army – for it can be called nothing less – that had been preparing to operate the spear-throwing device. Confusion transforms to rout and panic.

I don't wait to see if they retrieve their gear or if they leave the harnessed hippocampi to share the injured merman's fate. With a beat of my tail, I thrust myself upwards, to light and air, away from blood, death, and desperation.

I find myself kneeling on the floor in front of the window that had revealed the undersea. My hands are shaking. My limbs ache as if the transformation I had experienced had been real rather than imaginary.

I reach to grasp Muriel from her perch, taking some reassurance from her reality, flimsy and two-dimensional as it may be. In the unchanging light of my tower room, I contemplate my experience.

Frightening? Yes. But exhilarating, too. Already, even though my palms are damp and my pulse is only beginning to slow, I know I will try again to enter into one of these worlds – places – realms – dreams? Whatever it may be that I seem able to view through the seven windows.

But first, before I venture out again, I will see what the remaining windows offer. I tick them off on my fingers: the unicorn glade, the shadow monster, the two sisters, and the ocean deeps. That leaves three unknown. Three? Well, four if one counts that stubbornly shut, highly irritating, obsidian panel.

The next window Muriel and I inspect shows a silvery-white landscape, apparently without many features of interest other than a deep, rounded valley and curiously jagged mountains etched with sharp lines of inky shadow. I might have given up on it in disgust except that Muriel reminds me how boring the sea had seemed until we chanced to see the whale and the secret of the undersea was revealed to us. Heartened, I agree that we should look a while longer.

As we study the shiny whiteness, I realize that not all of it is still. Some of it *moves*, and not in the manner of windswept sand or blowing dust. This movement is that of creatures that perfectly match their surroundings except for occasional glimpses of eyes or noses. The eyes are usually dark brown, the noses pink – and I soon come to realize – so are the linings of long, floppy ears.

"Rabbits!" I say excitedly to Muriel and am so astonished by the sound of my voice that I swallow the next words and resolve to speak more softly henceforth.

Muriel doesn't chide me for being uncouth. She agrees and agrees again when I point out how the rabbits are lop-eared, their ears hanging down like a girl's long hair.

Now I wonder if the whiteness of the landscape might be that of snow, rather than dust or sand, but my initial impression won't be shaken. This is a world of pale dust, drifting sand, and sharp-edged rock. I wonder what the rabbits eat and drink for, now that I can sort them out from their surroundings, I see that they are quite satisfyingly plump.

Then I shrug. What does it matter? I feel neither hunger nor thirst nor sleepiness. Perhaps these rabbits are more like me than I am like those horribly bloodthirsty mermen.

The rabbits are a great deal of fun to watch as they gambol and play, sliding otter-fashion on their bellies and jumping up and down like fat balloons with ears and bright, shiny eyes. Where earlier I had longed for a glimpse of something interesting – by which I now realize I had thought closer to human or dramatic like the unicorn – now I feel a flash of disappointment when the farthest ridge is crested by a slim human figure.

She – for at once I know her as female – wears what at first I take for a bathrobe, then realize is a kimono, such as grand Japanese ladies wear. This kimono is particularly elaborate, with a trailing hem and sleeves so long that they fall below the lady's knees, nearly to the middle of her calves. The kimono is made from a pale golden silk, subtly patterned with flying birds and bushy-needled pine trees.

The woman's upswept hair is white as the sand, held in its elaborate coiffure by pins of the same pale gold as her gown. Despite the whiteness of her hair, she is not old. Nor is she young. Rather there is a sense of timelessness about her.

The rabbits don't flee at her arrival, but bound up the slope to greet her. She greets some formally, others more exuberantly. A few of the littlest ones she rolls down the hillside as if they are fat, fluffy balls, this to their evident delight, as well as her own.

The woman looks so nice that for a moment I consider seeing if Muriel and I can join her and the rabbits. But the lesson of the whale is still with me, and Muriel agrees that for now we will limit ourselves to watching.

This we do until the lady and the rabbits depart on some business of their own. Muriel and I turn away, disappointed but agreeing that now is not the time to follow. As we consider what to do next, my gaze falls upon the useless bed that dominates the chamber – most particularly on the heaps of fluffy pillows.

An idea comes to me then. Bouncing up, I seize one of the medium-sized pillows, then strip off the pink pillowcase to reveal a white undercase beneath. Next, I hug the pillow so tightly that it is squashed into two sections.

Now, how to preserve this? I consider various options: tearing the hem of my nightdress, seeing if I can pick one of the ribbons loose from my bodice, shredding the now useless pillowcase. Then Muriel reminds me that there are ribbons in the cabinet at the base of the nightstand. Thanking her, I select a white one about an inch wide. With this, I tie off the pillow so that I have two puffy sections, one slightly larger than the other.

Punching and pulling at the upper segment, I create the semblance of ears. These I tie off with white ribbons, so they won't easily meld back into the whole. Now for a face! Carrying both the pillow and Muriel, I trot over to the little table. From the box of pens, I remove dark brown, black, and several shades of pink.

I'm almost scared to start, but Muriel reminds me that there's no way I can make a mistake because I'm probably the first person ever to do this. Buoyed by her confidence in me, I find just the right place to draw two round, dark brown eyes. They don't look quite right until Muriel suggests that I draw a round outer eye around the brown middle. This works! With more confidence, I add a few fluffy eyelashes, a triangular pink nose, and some pink whiskers.

After molding the fabric with my fingers to give the ears more shape, I shade the insides pink. When I add a tiny mouth, my hand slips a little, but when I look at the result, I decide I like it. A perfectly straight mouth might have made my creature look placid. This face is just a little impish.

After consideration, I add two little curved lines to the body to suggest front paws. I don't bother with back paws because, as Muriel points out, if the bunny was a bit plump – as our bunny definitely is – then you wouldn't be able to see the rear feet anyhow. I do add a tail by squishing more pillow and using more ribbon to tie it off.

Experimentally, I give the bunny a hug, worried that my ties will pop loose, but everything stays in place. With a bit of judicious squishing, I can even get the bunny to sit upright, though there is a little tendency for him to lean to one side.

I'm about to close the cabinet under the nightstand when I see a nice pale green ribbon about two inches wide. With it, I give the bunny a festive, floppy bow. He needs a name, though. Muriel and I discuss several options, finally settling on "Puck" because that seems like a good choice. If I'd known what trouble Puck would get us into by being well, puckish, I might have picked a different name. On the other hand, maybe I wouldn't have.

On some level, I know I should be tired, but I'm fresh as ever – fresher even, as if shaping Puck from the pillow made me even more energetic. Taking out a pale grey pen, I carefully trace Muriel, then adapt my tracing to make her a pretty, flowing dress. I'll admit. I started out trying to make a kimono, but that proved too difficult. Anyhow, as Muriel notes, those long sleeves would be a real nuisance.

Even with the vast selection of colored pens, I can't manage anything as nuanced as the elaborate pale gold patterned fabric the kimono lady had been wearing, but I spend a long time with a wide selection of colors and sooner – or longer – time doesn't seem to matter...

Anyhow, soon enough, Muriel has a really lovely dress with sweeping tiered skirts that remind me of rainbows. I make her a floppy sunhat and, after I have slid it into place at a jaunty angle, I'm ready to check another window.

After all the wonderful and exotic locations we've seen to this point, I must admit I'm seriously disappointed. We're looking down over a perfectly normal cityscape. I would have walked away and gone to see if the unicorn was back, but Puck has apparently never seen anything like this. I guess that, being a moondust rabbit, he wouldn't have.

So Muriel and I start explaining what we're seeing, about fences and gardens, about dog houses, gazebos, bus stops, parking lots, and car dealerships.

When we focus on a particular detail, the window cooperates, zooming in on whatever is our current point of interest. It turns out there's a lot more interesting stuff than I would have guessed. Just one example...

There is a house, nice but completely normal, no turrets or gables or gingerbreading or anything. However, whoever lives there loves flowers. The garden is overgrown with all sorts from irises in every shade from deep indigo to pale yellow. Their petals are all fluttery, so the flowers remind me of a girl in prom dress or a fairy princess ready for the ball.

There are roses in every color from pale yellow to deep red to delicate lavender to purest white. There are bachelor buttons, blue as a summer sky. Zinnias multi-colored and with stripes and spots, with long petals and short. Some are as tall as me; some are so tiny Muriel could have carried a bouquet of them. There are hollyhocks, peonies, and dianthus, begonias, portulacas, alyssum, and as well as many other flowers I couldn't even begin to name. There is a fountain out in front of the house in which the goldfish are swimming ballets with the bubbles. There are bees as big as my thumb but so relaxed I want to pat one.

I settle for hugging Puck instead. Muriel is a wonderful friend and very smart, but I can't hug her. She doesn't mind, and neither does Puck.

Eventually, a huge, stripy hot air balloon drifts by, its colors rivaling the flower garden and confusing the bees. We follow it, watching as it passes over fields and strip malls. The pilot is on a cellphone and I guess she is relaying information to the chase crew whose vehicles, complete with a gaily-painted trailer, can be glimpsed below.

When the balloon lands, its bag collapsing slowly like some dying beast falling to earth, Puck glimpses the edges of the city's skyline. After that, nothing will do but that we go along and show him that the tall buildings are houses stretched narrow and thin, not at all like the lunar mountains he had taken them for at first glimpse. We explain to him that the bumps on top of the buildings are heating or cooling units, that those odd things protruding from the brick walls are old-style fire escapes. That the floral explosions are window box gardens. That the reflections giving back the skies are swimming pools. Until Puck expresses his disbelief at this last, I realize I've never thought about how crazy it is to put thousands of gallons of water twenty or more stories in the air just so people can splash around if the weather is nice.

A column of greasy grey and black smoke pulls our attention down to a high-rise that's on fire. We halt our skyline tour to watch as people jump from windows, hoping to be caught on huge trampoline-like nets held by the frightened people far below. Despite the fact that almost certainly the fire will be put out and everyone saved, I feel uneasy and suggest we move on and look at something else. Puck complains a little – he really likes the excitement – but Muriel takes my part and we move away from the fire.

We might be leaving the fire behind, but it isn't so easy to forget. Its influence ripples out through the surrounding area. We had shifted our course to what appears to be a quiet shopping district, only to find it more than quiet. It is nearly completely deserted. The fire has drawn away most of the customers, transforming them into gawkers. A fair number of the shopkeepers have locked up and gone to see the inferno as well.

Nonetheless, the stores are well worth looking at. They have great bay windows, each of which is a miniature world of delights. Most highlight very costly items: clothing made from silks and satins, elegant jewels, exotic imported treasures. The shimmer and glitter amazes us with its variety and vivid colors.

I find myself fighting an impulse to think of the entire shopping district as an elaborate stage set awaiting only the players – maybe a better comparison would be a set for a classic movie with Cary Grant and Katherine Hepburn. I'm musing over this, enjoying myself in thinking up the right sort of story. It would need to be something clever and witty but with room for some physical action…

We round a corner and see just the sort of story I've been considering. A burglary is in process. It's easy enough to guess what must have happened. The thief – thieves, I correct myself, for I see at least two – had seen the general exodus in the direction of the fire and had decided to take advantage of it. This particular shop is around the corner from the main shopping drag, but in no way does this mean it is a poor establishment. Rather, it is one so exclusive that customers would come to it without the need of being lured in.

The thieves have not bothered with being in the least subtle. They had clipped the alarm wires, then used a heavy ladder as a makeshift battering ram to break out the center pane of the window. When we – or rather, our observing selves – arrive, the thieves are grabbing the display items. These are so elegant as to make what we'd admired on the main street seem like cheap gewgaws.

One thief hefts a bejeweled crown worthy of a king, the points topped with rubies, the cushioned band padded with ermine. The second thief is focused on a velvet tray holding various pendants, each with at least one large precious stone as a centerpiece. The thief grasps the pendants by their heavy gold chains and drops them into a sack. Earrings are dumped into sacks by the glittering trayfull.

As we watch, I find myself troubled. Surely the shopkeeper is insured, but is there any way to replace such unique treasures? A car is pulling up to the curb. Only the voracity of the thieves is keeping them from making a quick and easy getaway.

Yet, what can I – we – do? We are observers only, watchers from behind a very strange window. On the other hand, there *is* the example set by the whale – and the sharks and the mermen, I remind myself. I had barely escaped that time. In what danger might I find myself if I force my way into the scene?

But these are the thoughts of only a part of myself – the safe, thoughtful element. Another part of me is already looking about to see what I might be able to do to stop the thieves. The getaway car strikes me as the first problem. If we stop that, then…

I think very hard, envisioning myself not *at* the wheel of a long, dark blue sedan parked just across the street, but *as* that lean, long blue creature. I thrust myself into it, becoming oil and metal, plastic, chrome, and rigid rubber. I shake my body awake and rumble into life.

The thieves freeze, thinking themselves discovered. Then the coward at the wheel of the getaway car steps on the gas, surging away without even waiting for his share of the loot. The remaining two, a man and a woman, gloved and with bandanas tied over their faces in the best fashionable "crook" mode, start running. Each holds a bag with enough treasure to assure they won't need to do another such job for a long time to come.

What to do? What to do? I don't think that staying part of the car would be a great idea. All the thieves would need to do in order to escape would be to dive down a narrow alley or even dodge out into traffic where I can't follow.

Following is my problem. They know these streets. I am a stranger. Or am I? Sure I am a visitor, but I am a visitor with some very interesting advantages. I rip my perspective out of the still-idling car, stalling it in the process, which makes me feel bad. I assure myself that my so-briefly used body will be all right. Cars stall all the time.

I force myself to resume the more generalized perspective, watching from on high and slightly to one side so I can read my target's body language and use it to judge where and how they might choose to flee the scene. For now they choose to stay on foot. Unsurprisingly, they avoid the main streets, the shopping areas where – the fire in the high-rise now subdued – pedestrians are returning to their interrupted shopping and storekeeping.

Unconcerned – perhaps unaware – the thieves continue to make their escape. If they dive inside a building, I will lose them, but for now they seem to be intent on putting distance between them and the scene of the robbery. That makes sense. If they had a local hideaway, they wouldn't have needed a getaway car. Even so, I am losing hope that I might be able to catch them. Watching is not enough. I will need to enter the scene, and I can't figure out how I will manage this.

Then, from my elevated perspective, I see what the crooks don't: the alley down which they are running empties into a small plaza that would usually be quite busy but today is deserted except for a pair of stray dogs who are taking advantage of the lull to scavenge for scraps near a café whose patio is adorned with red and white striped umbrellas over cozy round tables that would seat no more than four.

The larger of the dogs is a rangy, long-bodied creature with a hound's jowly face and droopy ears. His coat is a medium brown and very short. The hound's companion is a prick-eared, brown and black spotted bitch with a white ruff. She looks like a collision of several breeds of shepherd, none of which had scored a decisive win in the genetics competition.

Perfect! I think. I dive into the bitch as I had into the whale. She accepts me with a full-tummy grace, ready for a romp now that she has eaten. I am hoping that the male would follow if I urged his mate along when, to my surprise, Puck assures cooperation by diving into the hound dog. Although this transfer of forms has taken no time at all, still we don't have much time if we're going to stop the bandits. They'll be emerging from the alley at any moment.

With a satisfied yap, I trot over to the alley, Puck-hound at my shoulder. We're just about to turn into the alley when the thieves come creeping forward, evidently slowing to see if the coast is clear. When they see it is except for a pair of stray dogs, they make as if to edge by. The man even reaches out as if to offer a friendly pat.

We aren't having any of it. Curling up my lip, I growl. My shepherd-self adds some moves meant to urge a much larger animal into line. I am quite impressed and resolve to give her as much lead as possible, since she knows what she's doing. The Puck-hound takes his cue from his mate. He doesn't manage as threatening a snarl and his droopy ears can't pin back in threat, but he is very much larger and his deep chest produces a very impressive growl.

"Easy! Good dogs. We don't have anything here you'd like." The male burglar apparently fancies himself a "dog-person," but neither the shepherd or me are fooled. He smells sour with fear, acrid with barely contained tension. His mate – partner, I correct hastily, aware that my canine self is becoming too dominant – is terrified and angry, probably at being balked so close to getting away with her loot.

She feints a kick. Puck-hound backs up a pace, all too familiar with kicks, but my shepherd-self is not taking any such nonsense. Poor urban stray she might be, but in her veins runs the proud heritage of several lines of herd dogs, dogs who would face down an angry ram or a cow many times their size. She isn't going to be intimidated by a mere human, much less one nearly crazed with fear.

We snap, coming close to the tempting muscles at the woman's calf, but settling for ripping the fabric of her trouser leg. She backs away unsteadily, unable to decide whether she wants to kick again or try to escape. When both of us dogs growl deep in our chests, she opts for flight. The male hesitates only for a moment before joining her in a dash back down the alley.

Now Puck-hound is in his element. Letting loose a single deep bay, he joyfully gives chase. I dart after, feeling pleasure as my legs open into a full stride, as my paws strike the damp pavement. Even as most of my attention is on the chase, on the yap and snap that will drive the two awkward bipeds precisely where I want them to go, I am aware of my surroundings as I never am as a human.

Certainly, I've recoiled from the sour stench of a trash bin, but have I ever been so aware of the layers of scent that go into that odor cocktail? This one holds spilled milk and tuna fish as high notes that even my human nose might have detected, but never would I have caught the subtle aroma of a molding loaf of white bread or the fat, organic odor of the grubs that are transforming a slab of rancid bacon into ooze.

My ears are a wonder as well, moving with independent agility to catch sounds both ahead and behind, detecting the whir of pigeon wings as a roosting flock abandons their perch on a fire escape five stories above – a ridiculous precaution, but then since when have pigeons been other than ridiculous?

Now we have nearly reached the point where the crooks first entered the alley. Puck-hound and I have been aware of activity ahead for some time, but it takes the flashing of lights (their colors curiously flattened) against the walls for the thieves to realize that what is ahead may be worse than being bitten by a couple of stray mongrels. They begin to slow, looking above, assessing their chances of grabbing hold of a low-hanging fire escape ladder, of pulling it down and joining the pigeons above.

Puck-hound and I are having none of this. He bellows his best bay yet: a deep, throbbing note that I feel in my whiskers and in the guard-hairs of my coat. I can't make any noise to come close to its impressiveness, so I crouch into the herd dog's crawl, a posture that many humans find deeply unsettling because it combines a low profile – normally associated with abasement – with fierce snarls and deliberate snaps.

Heralded by the Puck-hound's sonorous howls, I herd the two thieves forward, directly into the arms of the astonished police officer who had been filling out a report on behalf of the shaken store owner.

I like the owner of the store at once. He is an older man with an honest receding hairline, rather than the thuggish shaved head just about every man who is edgy about losing his hair tries out, as if he's fooling anyone. The man's nose is a bit hooked and fleshy, and he has jowls like Puck-hound's. His eyes have faded to somewhere between blue and grey, but are keen nonetheless, and the lines on his face seem to indicate that when he isn't shocked, he smiles a lot.

The police officer is so stunned by our arrival with the thieves that he almost lets the crooks get away, but we dogs are having none of that. I bark high and shrill – a "Look at what I've done" bark – and Puck-hound moves to block the alley, his long, heavy tail thumping side to side like a whip.

The crook who thought he was good with dogs is the first to fold. He drops the bag of loot and holds up his hands. A moment later, the woman – with a sour look at us and a wiggle of her boot-toe as if she's considering a final kick – also surrenders. On impulse, I pick up one of the bags and bring it to the shop owner, who takes it from me and pats me on the head. The shock is draining from his features and the smile I knew belonged there blossoms.

The police officer gets himself under control, handcuffs his prisoners, then gets on the radio to report in. Meanwhile, people are starting to mill around, asking questions and marveling at me and Puck-hound. We eat up the praise, as not long before our canine selves had gobbled up scraps of pizza and sandwiches from the café's garbage bins. Food for the soul, to go with the food for the tummy.

I know we should leave the dogs. I feel certain they will be given a home, their choice of homes, even – but the joyful mood, the flow of appreciation, feels so good that we linger.

The shop owner – Bob – gives us water and each half of a roast beef sandwich. We're still pretty full, but we eat out of good manners. I can tell that the shepherd-mix feels relaxed and comfortable, as does the hound. Reluctantly, I pull myself away and drift back to where Muriel greets us with loud congratulations. Even so, the tower room feels barren after the bustle of the streets.

I know that before long I will want to escape out a window once more.

Escape. The word clings to me. I'd all but forgotten my awakening in the room of eight windows (or seven windows and one maybe-door), how strange it had seemed, never mind that I could not remember any other place. Now I give attention once again to the dark portal with its surface of cracked and broken obsidian, at the crazy-quilt reflection of myself it gives back to me. Not so long ago, I had been terrified when that maybe-door would not open. Now I fear that it will…

To distract myself from my fears, I look back over my shoulder at the seven clear windows: unicorn glade, undersea, shadow monster, cityscape, moondust, and the last, unknown. That unknown vista beckons, awaiting revelation. Then I find myself quickly counting off on my fingers. I have only listed six – six including the yet unknown. Which window have I forgotten?

I sit on the carpet, scratching my head, ticking memories off on my fingers. Nothing. It is not until my gaze falls upon where Muriel sits on the edge of the bed that I remember. The unremembered window is the one that had shown me a kitchen with two girls doing dishes. That's it! I wonder how I could have forgotten for, despite its utter mundanity, this scene had strangely touched me. It had been after looking at the two sisters that I had realized how much I wanted a companion and had found a way to bring Muriel to break my solitude.

For a fleeting moment, I consider that perhaps it is *because* the view had so touched me that I had put it from me, but I scoff, dismissing the idea. Surely I had forgotten because the sight of such dull domesticity could not compete with unicorns or mermen or even the mystery of weird shadowy monsters. Yes! Surely that is the reason.

Putting the momentary confusion from me, I decide that I will take Muriel and Puck out through the window with me into the world in which I had seen the unicorn grazing in the peaceful glade, where later I had watched birds, and playful wild creatures. I had been very disappointed not to see the unicorn when I had taken my subsequent glances, but those had been before I had realized I could venture beyond the glass and enter the scene.

Now we would go a-unicorn hunting – or at least unicorn seeking. Why then, as I rise from the floor in front of the dark panel, as I hurry to gather my friends to me, why do I feel as if I am running away, rather than towards?

As I position us before the correct window, Muriel tries to speak to me, but I'm not interested in listening.

"Hush!" I think to her. "You don't want to frighten everything away, do you?" And, of course, she doesn't, so she gives me a bright smile and presses her finger to her lips.

Diving through the window into the view on the other side is getting easier and easier. As when we had visited the city, we begin by taking a tour, rather than anchoring ourselves into isolated perspectives. When we have a sense of our surroundings – the glade is surrounded by deep forest, so the overview we had used in the city is less useful, we decide to find ourselves shapes. In the city, we had slid into the perspective of creatures already there.

This time, as I study a butterfly and wish that it was actually a fairy with butterfly wings, I find myself becoming what I desire.

My wings are iridescent blue, etched with patterns that shift with the light, less patterns than holographic textures: light on water, sky in the sea, deep sheen on the skin of a ripe plum... Muriel becomes a fairy, too, with wings like those of a monarch butterfly: orange and black, delicate as breath. Her dress – including a short, frilly skirt perfect for flying – takes up the theme. I assume that my outfit also coordinates with my wings, but find that I am powerfully afraid to look too closely at my fairy self. It is enough to be part of this beautiful landscape, to dart freely among the trees, to dive down to inspect a perfect rose or a pale lily with wide, curving petals in pale pink or yellow or white, each dusted with golden pollen.

Puck has taken a woodland rabbit form, a cottontail with a wriggling nose and enormous brown eyes. He darts here and there, nibbling at clumps of thick green grass or juicy dandelion leaves. He has a trick of nipping the dandelion flowers off at the base of their fat, tubular stems, then eating his way up to the blossom. These are too large for even him to engulf, but he tries, looking as if he is trying to eat a small fuzzy sun.

As we fly over it (Puck bouncing below) the forest looks completely unsettled. No bridges span the myriad rivers. Neither do the many fruit trees show any sign of tending, other than the natural pruning offered by those who eat their bounty or the ravages of wind or storm.

Some small part of me wants to protest that this is – if not impossible – at the very least improbable. Trees don't bear large, unblemished apples such as those we see on an artfully gnarled tree that overhangs a stream – not without someone to cull the fruit, to put up nets to keep away the birds, to spray against insects.

I might have puzzled more over this if I didn't view this landscape from a body graced with iridescent butterfly wings. Unlocking the secret of the too ideal apple trees might unlock the puzzle of my fairy form, and I am enjoying that far too much to give it up. Indeed, as Muriel and I flutter from flower to flower, share giggles at Puck's silly antics, I even find myself forgetting that I have come here desiring to find the unicorn.

When a flash of pearlescent white below (it turns out to be the plumage of a startled bird) reminds me, I find myself wondering if it is even possible to find the unicorn unless it desires to be found. I remember how it can cause its horn to be overlooked. Perhaps it can simply vanish. Rather than hunting about, looking for mysteries that wish to remain mysterious, surely I should simply enjoy the moment. Just enjoy, not worry, not seek, relax and take pleasure in the impossible possibility of being able to fly.

We are near a stream as these thoughts touch me, insinuating themselves into my drifting progress. The splash of a large fish – a salmon? – causes me to start in mid-air, jumping as if bitten. I give my wings a hard flap that sends me nearly into the branches of one of the willows that leans out over the stream.

After I have managed to dodge between the trailing fronds and regain my balance, I feel as if I have been asleep although – to the best of my memory – I have only slept once since awakening in the tower of seven windows and no door. Hadn't that also been after an encounter with this place? I had been thinking of the view from this window as that of the unicorn's glade, but now I wonder. What else is said of fairyland? Aren't there tales about people stolen away, only to find upon their return home that they have been gone for years and years, that their own children have grown to become grey-haired adults?

I feel even more troubled, but can't say precisely why. Surely I am not giving into some seductive dream. Hadn't I climbed out of that fluffy bed? Hadn't I learned the secret of the windows? Hadn't I made friends, even though everything about the tower seemed set to make this as difficult as possible? No! I am *not* giving into some Lotus Eater's dream of ease.

I am simply going about my quest to find the unicorn all wrong. Fairy wings are great fun, but I don't seem to be getting anywhere on them. I will need to find another option. Briefly, I consider taking on some hunting beast form – a wolf or a cheetah or a clever fox or even a dog, such as Puck and I had been in the cityscape. I discard the idea. I want to find the unicorn, to befriend it, not to make it my prey.

Muriel reminds me – very delicately – of the legend that unicorns are supposed to be susceptible to the allure of a maiden. This makes me acutely uncomfortable but, as with anything to do with my body, I put the discomfort from me. After all, even if I can't claim a virgin's mantle – and I have no idea whether I can or not – surely Muriel can, and she has indicated her willingness to serve as bait.

Again, I shake my head. Is it the act of a friend to entrap another? Is it the act of a friend to reduce a friend to the role of cheese in the mousetrap?

No! I need some magic of my own, some reason that the unicorn will let me find it or it will come to me. As I cogitate, I come to rest on the grassy bank of one of the many brooks that babble beneath the spreading trees of this lofty green forest. Even with Puck's eager nibbling, the grass remains thick with flowers. Idly, my fingers pluck a long-stemmed daisy, white with a golden center. I smile as I remember that these flowers take their name – "day's eye" – from that bright center.

As if remembering some long-lost spell, I pluck another daisy and set it next to the first. Within moments, my fingers are agilely weaving a chain of flowers. There are daisies aplenty in the meadow, some with white petals, some kissed with pink or, improbably, with blue or purple. Muriel has come to rest beside me, and I don't think it at all odd that we are now the same size. After all, hadn't we been fairies together?

Hands moving in comfortable concert, we both set to weaving flowers. My chain is made from daisies, accented with an occasional wisp of some brighter colored flower that Puck brings to me. Occasionally, he will have eaten off the stem, making the flower too short to be used for weaving. These I set all higgledy-piggledy in my hair, enjoying their perfume, though even in this peaceful place I avoid the temptation to catch a glimpse of my reflection, never mind how distorted it would be in these fast-running waters.

Muriel has found a stand of flowers with petals of a blue paler than my wings, although not given over to insipid pastel hues. Each flower has five petals and a tiny splash of almost metallic gold for a center.

"Forget-me-nots," she says, her fingers busy. She drops the completed wreath about my neck where it lays tickling my skin, beauty to adorn a queen.

In turn, I offer her my daisy chain, but instead of ducking her head so I can drop it over, she smiles mischievously and points with her chin to where, peering from a thick tangle of green shrubs and honeysuckle vine, the unicorn is watching.

Muriel's motion was subtle and non-aggressive but, even so, the shy creature starts back. I nod to let Muriel know that I have seen, then continue to gift her with my garland. Do I hear a disappointed nicker from the shrub? Perhaps.

Moving slightly, so that I will have more daisies close to hand, I begin a new chain. Puck immediately catches my intention and begins hopping enthusiastically about, bringing me so many long-stemmed flowers – not only daisies and dandelions, but clover blossoms, anemones, violets, and other flowers I struggle to name. The variety is such that I lose myself in the weaving and selection – not going off into a daze as I had when we were flying about on fairy wings, but instead becoming hyperaware, noticing tiny differences in color or number of petals, becoming more richly myself as I create an ornate garland.

Once the garland becomes long enough, Muriel adopts a free end and adds her own selections. These don't mirror mine, but rather demonstrate how many ways the same elements can be used harmoniously. In wordless concurrence, we bring our two ends together, looping and splicing until the garland becomes a wide wreath.

As we had worked, the unicorn had not remained still, but had observed us, first from hiding, hardly more than blue eyes peering from the green leaves, then flaring nostrils taking in the blend of floral perfumes, accented with the slightly acrid – but not at all unpleasant – odor of sap.

As if the unicorn needs it to sense fully, the next element to emerge from concealment is the horn. In this light – or perhaps through the unicorn's desire – the horn is shining silver. This is not a harsh, hard, and metallic silver, but ethereal, like starlight given a solid yet shifting, sparkling form.

Does the horn sense no malice or trickery from us? I think it must have done so, for the rest of the unicorn emerges more quickly. On dainty cloven hooves, golden – but sunlight, flower-heart golden, not the heaviness of metal – the unicorn picks its way over the greensward, leaving less impression upon the bending blades than does Puck as he bounces about with his bunches of blossoms.

Eventually, the unicorn is leaning over our shoulders, watching as we weave. Its breath is meadow sweet, holding the scent of new-mown grass, spiced with the crisp odors of various leaves, and just a hint of cidery apple. That the unicorn is attracted by the wreathed garland there is no doubt, but I wonder what it hopes? – expects? – I will do with it.

"What do you want, pretty one?" I ask, speaking soundlessly to the unicorn as I do to Muriel and Puck.

"If you give me that," comes the reply in drifting dapples of light and swallow-darts of breeze kisses, "I will show you something you need if ever you choose to be free."

"Choose to be free?" The thought panics me. Does that mean I am imprisoned? If so, who is my jailer? Unbidden, the image of the obsidian not-door comes to me. For the first time, it seems less a barrier than a...

I struggle for a word, an image – a bulwark? a bulkhead? A protection between me and the unknown. After all, imprisonment is never a kindness, is it? What would happen to me if I were to find a way to open that door? I tell myself that I have not the least idea, but I suspect that I do.

All of this rushes through me more quickly than I could have spoken even one question. I feel tempted and, for the first time, begin to wonder if the unicorn is as good as it is lovely.

Muriel is looking at me curiously and even Puck has stopped his silly bouncing and stands on rabbit hind legs, chewing on the long stem of what I realize is a four-leafed clover. I watch the lucky token vanish into his pink mouth with a trace of regret, yet I could not have stolen luck from him, no matter that I would have liked to press those four leaves between my palms, then wish for wisdom and guidance.

Tentatively, I smile at the unicorn. "I will give these flowers to you freely," I think/speak, "wishing nothing in return. I did not create them, after all. They came from the goodness of the Earth. All I contributed was some cleverness of fingers. Me and my friend."

If I expect the unicorn to be impressed by my generosity, I am to be disappointed. The unicorn's ears – longer than those of a horse, although not as long as those of a mule – twitch and I sense not so much disapproval as sorrow. Yet what is there to be sorry about?

"Here," I say, rising to my knees, then to my feet, so that I can put the wreath up and over the silver horn, then to rest upon the slender neck. "We made it for you. All we want is to see you up close, to know that you're not a dream. Isn't that right, Muriel?"

Muriel agrees and, if from the unicorn I sensed sorrow, from Muriel I sense something of the same emotion, touched with relief. Does she, too, dread what we might find behind the dark not-door? I reach and squeeze her hand, feeling it both dry and papery, yet warm and supple in perfectly harmonious contradiction.

The unicorn accepts the garland, but not without a soft breath. "My offer stands," comes the gentle impulse, "also freely given." It raises its head, shaking its neck to settle our floral tribute over its mane and down to rest upon its withers.

Then, with a leap that makes Puck squeak in unfeigned admiration, the unicorn vanishes soundlessly into the surrounding green.

When we return to our tower, I have much to think about. I settle myself at the little table, letting the high headboard shelter me from sight of the dark, fractured slab of obsidian. This seems newly ominous now that I feel certain it can open and, that when it does, it might not be at my bidding. For the first time, I feel relieved that I don't seem to need to sleep.

I begin drawing a new frock for Muriel, one inspired by her monarch butterfly costume. As I shade and color the bright reddish-orange and elegant, powdery black dress, pale orange stockings, and dainty little slippers, I consider how I might provide myself with guards or at least watchers for those times when I choose to venture beyond a window.

For the first time, I fear that I might find my citadel breached in my absence. Yet my delight in these explorations has only intensified with these first attempts and I don't wish to give them up. Nor would that be fair to Muriel and Puck, who enjoy our outings as much as I do.

I carefully consider my limited resources. Puck suggests that we push the bed over to block the obsidian panel. I'm not sure. Not only do I doubt that we could move the bed, even with all three of us pushing, but there is no guarantee that it will provide any sort of barrier. If the door swings into the room *and* we manage not only to move the bed, but to turn it around so that the high headboard faces the obsidian panel, *then* the bed might prove an effective barrier.

But what if the door swings outwards into whatever corridor or room or staircase that awaits on the other side? What if the door slides sideways or even goes straight up? Then the bed would provide no more than an inconvenience.

Puck is still all for it, reminding me that, with whatever delay the bed would provide, we could flee out the window of our choice. I doubt this. I'm still not exactly certain what happens when we go "through" the window. It seems possible that we "go" nowhere at all, but instead are performing some sort of astral projection. If so, we remain vulnerable even then – more so when we are "gone" than when we are here.

No, moving the bed is not the answer – at least not in and of itself. The more I think about it, the more certain I become that a guardian who will warn us in case of invaders is what we need. The question is, what sort of guardian? It should be someone large and strong, else I would worry that he would be overpowered before he could give the alarm. I recall a story about an orchard guarded by a giant covered in eyes. Honestly, that seems very creepy, but the basic idea isn't bad.

Pressing two fingers against my lips, I consider whether I have enough pillows to make a giant. Exploration shows that I do. Two bolsters make sturdy legs. A fat pillow set atop makes a torso. Two more pillows, these originally intended as some sort of neck rest, make good arms. The end result isn't quite as gigantic as I had wished, but Muriel points out that a couple of throw pillows as feet add several inches of height. I tie the lot together with a bunch more silk and satin ribbons, this time opting for the thickest ones, unknotting some sassy bows meant to be worn on top of the head or to accent the waistline of a dress.

When this is done, I contemplate the head. There is a nice round pillow that will serve admirably. Taking this over to the table, I carefully draw on large wide-awake eyes, framing them with lashes so that they look very alert, almost like miniature suns. I color them the most brilliant blue I can find in the pen box. Then I add a strong nose and a mouth perfect for bellowing.

Remembering the tale of the giant with a hundred – or was it a thousand? – pairs of eyes, I turn the pillow over and repeat my artistry on the other side. Then I draw ears on the edges of the pillow, making them very large, so the giant could hear the faintest sound. Pleased, I finish by giving the guardian some curly hair in a bright red that goes well with the blue eyes, although it clashes some with the blush pink of the pillow.

I fasten my giant's head on, then position him where he can watch the obsidian door and most of the windows without have to tire himself out walking a constant patrol. He seems very pleased with my consideration for his comfort and tells me that he will do his very best. His name, he says, is Horatius.

I tell him that when we are in the tower he can consider himself off-duty, so Horatius settles into playing a combination of tag and fetch with Puck, who is absolutely delighted to have a romping partner. This gets me thinking. Horatius clearly enjoys company and I am loathe to leave him lonely when the rest of us go on adventures. That would be too cruel. There are still many pillows, as well as bedclothes I certainly don't need, since I am not about to get back into that bed and not sleep.

After consulting with Muriel, I decide that between us we can certainly make a dragon. Dragons and giants are both traditional guardians, so they should enjoy each other's company. I set to work sculpting the body. At first it reminds me rather of a caterpillar or centipede, but once Muriel and I start drawing on details it shapes up very nicely. Because it has such a long, low body, we style it more along the lines of an oriental dragon. I artfully tie off fabric to make both ears and horns.

Next, I set to work drawing feet and toes, making the latter long enough that the dragon can use them as fingers. I can't see that there would be any harm in the dragon and Horatius passing the time playing board games. Checkers would be easy enough to make, and chess not all that much harder.

We give the dragon a big mouth, so he can join Horatius in bellowing and wide eyes for watching. Taking an idea from that giant with thousands – or was it millions? – of eyes all over its body, Muriel draws on scales and puts an eye in the shelter of each curve. This does not look nearly as creepy as eyes all over a human-style body would have. Indeed, when the dragon – whose name is Eyebright – opens them, they glitter like dewdrops or gems. We make them every color in the pen box, so the effect is like a fragmented rainbow.

With Horatius and Eyebright to keep guard, I feel confident about going forth through the windows again. The only question is where next?

Know how it is when you look under the Christmas tree and realize there's only one more package with your name on it? That all that sparkly potential is soon going to be reduced to known objects – objects that may be wonderful in themselves, but have lost the allure of maybe being anything at all?

Well, that's how I feel about the seventh window, the one I haven't looked out of yet. I didn't want to know what was there – I want one more glittery bundle of potential. Even so, I feel like seeing something new and not much explored. Considering, I realize that there is one window that I haven't looked out through for much more than a couple of minutes – the one with the strange perspective and the creature that had looked like a bat-eared, big-mouthed monster.

I pinch the tip of my nose, worried. Yes, I had not been precisely afraid of the monster, but still it *was* a monster. As I consider this point, I look around the rosy confines of my tower room. Puck is romping with Horatius and Eyebright – a moon-rabbit with a giant and a long-bodied dragon. What do I have to fear from monsters?

Gathering Muriel and Puck, I go to the appropriate window. To my mild astonishment (it's taking a lot more to astonish me lately), I see that the scene has changed from my first view. Gone is the screen of water droplets, gone, too, the bat-eared monster. Instead, I look down and across a plaza framed by fantastical Gothic buildings. Muriel thinks that "Gothic" isn't the right term, since these structures lack a heavy, stone-slabbed stolidity she associates with the form.

I agree, but indicate the touches that say "Gothic" to me: flying buttresses, crenellations, tall windows that narrow at the tops, ornate carvings that swarm over border panels and, most telling of all, the grotesque gargoyles that crouch high and low: leering, silent watchers over the vacant air.

Muriel wants to disagree – she knows a lot more about architecture than I do – but Puck takes the situation from our control. He's spotted something that catches his fancy and, with a cheerful squeak, bounces over the windowsill and drifts like a fat, round, rabbit-eared balloon down towards the plaza. After that, Muriel and I have little choice but to follow. Grabbing each other by the hand, and shouting to alert Horatius and Eyebright that we're going after Puck, we jump.

I feel the skirts of my nightdress billowing around me, puffing out into an improbable parachute. Muriel's shorter skirt pops out around her waist, catching her like an umbrella and bringing her to land safely beside me on the stone paving of the gloomy plaza.

We have landed next to a huge ornamental fountain: two girls hand in hand. Puck had bounced off as soon as he landed, and we strain to catch some indication of where he might have gone. For a long moment, all we here is the splash of water from various parts of the fountain. Then a voice that sounds as if it is gargling around the words speaks. At first, I can make no sense of the sounds. Then they resolve into a sloshy sort of meaning.

"Over there, by the cathedral. Hurry! Before the clock strikes!"

Anyhow, that's what I *think* I hear. As the words resolve into something like sense, a burst of white and grey wings over by the many-steepled edifice that dominates the far side of the plaza draws our attention. Something is going on over there and, knowing Puck, he is likely at the heart of it.

Still holding hands, Muriel and I run across the plaza. My bare feet slap against the slightly damp stones, accompanied by the sharper tapping of the pretty flats I'd drawn for Muriel. As we run, I try to get a better look at the winged creatures. I don't know what I'd thought those wings belonged to – if I'd thought at all, I would have said pigeons or doves or some other common urban avian.

Now, as we draw closer, I realize that they belong to angels – and not to the elegant winged creatures of Art or of school Christmas pageants – those humanoid figures that might as easily be elves or some other more-than-human ideal.

These angels – and I have absolutely no doubt that this is what they are – have the features of slightly chubby, round-cheeked toddlers. The colors of their skin range from warm dark chocolate to pale pinkish white, the sort of skin that sunburns as soon as the sun peeks out from behind the clouds. Their eyes are rounded child's eyes in all the colors possessed by humanity, but somehow brighter and more vivid. To a one, they are framed by the sort of thick lashes the desire for which makes the fortunes of cosmetic manufacturers.

Cute, right? At the very least pretty, especially when framed by thick-feathered wings, coordinated to go with the characteristics of the cherubic face in between. That "in between" is what rips a shriek of shock from my throat, for each one of these diminutive darlings consists of a head and wings – that is all. No body. No arms. Not even feet, just the smiling head of a child framed by wings. Childish laughter and cries of innocent delight rise and echo off the chill stone of the towering cathedral.

When the swirling flock of angels parts, I see what has so delighted them. A terrified Puck is encircled by the angels. Despite their lacking hands or arms, they are trying to pick up my overly adventurous ball of fluff in the only way they can – with the pearly white buttons of their infant teeth. It is evident that they have grabbed hold at least once, for Puck's floppy ears are dotted with bright bloody crescents. Splashes of crimson dot the pavement.

There are dozens of these cherubic horrors in the flock. As best as I can tell, their numbers are working as much against them as for them. The massed flock makes it impossible for Puck to break free, for no matter which way he darts, the flock can swirl to block his escape route. On the other hand – wing? – these creepy cherubs tend to get in each other's way, wings blocking and ensnaring those of their nearest associates so that every so often the mass must break and fly in a wide arc to realign itself. This realignment is what Muriel and I had witnessed right after the gargling voice had uttered its cryptic warning.

Even with how they keep getting in each other's way, it seems clear that soon enough one or more members of the angelic host must seize hold of hapless Puck. I have no idea if they intend him any harm or if they simply want to carry him off as a new toy. No matter. The cat crushed by the passionate embrace of the child who "Wuvs Kitty" is no less injured – or dead.

Nearly tripping over the trailing hem of my nightdress, I rush forward, waving my arms and yelling "Shoo! Shoo!" I can tell Muriel is scared and would rather hide by the fountain, but she darts after me. While I shoo away the momentarily startled angels, she scoops up Puck and does her best to stanch his bleeding ears.

To my relief, she seems to be having some success, although the dark crimson fluid stains her fingers so deeply I fear that they will never come clean again. Although I manage to keep the creepy cherubs from harming us, they force us step by step across the stone-flagged pavement until we are backed against one of the cathedral's carved wooden doors. These are so massive that they might as well be walls, and I despair of my ever getting one open.

How did the priests or sextons or deacons or whoever had the job of opening these doors so that the congregation could enter and leave for services manage? But opening is only part of the problem. Even if the doors had been normally sized, I didn't think I could spare a hand to get one open. I need both hands, as well as the intervention of my body, to shoo the vicious little angels back from their intended toy – and with every moment they are becoming more bold.

When I glimpse the flutter of heavier wings behind the flock of cherubs, my heart sinks to the level of my bare soles against the cold pavement. Are these the parents of the winged horrors? Are they something even worse – perhaps the bodies or limbs lacked by the cherubic-featured creatures that continue to besiege us?

My first clear view of the newcomer does nothing to alleviate my apprehension. Although the creature I now see clearly for the first time possesses a full complement of body parts – with the addition of a large pair of leathery bat wings – those body parts are grotesquely misshapen, the visual definition of "horrific." This creature has a wide mouth and flaring ears that peak at points over the crest of a head that owes equal parts to a fruit bat and a human of uncertain age and sex. Its skin is rough grey, flecked with black, much like certain types of granite. In brief, as if a single word could *ever* substitute for the reality, this new arrival is a gargoyle, though one as alive and supple in motion as the waters of the fountain on the plaza.

With that thought, hope blossoms in my breast. That strange gargling voice which had warned me and Muriel to seek Puck might have been a gargoyle speaking – a gargoyle overlooked because it was engaged in channeling the fountain's waters. I strike out with renewed vigor at the heads and wings that dart in at me. Certainly the angels are not reacting as if the newly arrived gargoyle is an ally, but they aren't treating it as an enemy either. Instead, they seem to view it as an unanticipated complication in their game.

A sharp pain at the back of my head makes me cry out in shocked astonishment. One of the creepy cherubs has made a daring dive and grabbed hold of the braid that hangs felt, if unseen, down my back, between my shoulder blades. Tears welling in my eyes, I swat upwards, but I can't reach the creature. Within a few moments, others have joined it in its game. I'm honestly worried I'm going to be lifted right off my feet. The overarching portico of the cathedral doorway limits the number of cherubs that can get into the space but, even so, I know I'm in trouble.

Remembering the sploshy voice that had given us that initial warning, I cry out, asking the gargoyle for help.

"We just need a distraction!" I beg, "Just enough so that I can somehow get Puck and Muriel to safety." The sound of my voice shocks me, so I don't add what I'd wanted to say, how Puck and Muriel wouldn't be in this position if my restless nature hadn't taken us outside of the tower. How was silly Puck to know that some of the areas outside the windows could be less than safe? He hadn't seen the sharks, nor the mermen.

Wordlessly, the gargoyle accepts my appeal. Flapping its leathery wings like musty curtains, it draws attention to itself. Several of the creepy cherubs drop their toothholds on my braid, others slacken their grips enough so that I can reach up and jerk my hair free. I can feel how horribly tattered my braid is, but this isn't the time to worry about a bad hair day. I drop the braid inside the collar of my nightdress, then swivel to take advantage of the opening the gargoyle has won for me.

"Is still winning for me" would be a more accurate description, for it has not limited its assistance to flapping its wings. Opening its wide mouth even wider, the gargoyle lets loose a throbbing, hooting call. This startles the angels – not so much because the sound is unpleasant, for it isn't at all, holding in it the notes of a bassoon and oboe, with something of a flugelhorn on the edges – but because, as I see a short time after the stone and air have ceased vibrating with the sound, they know (as I do not) that this is a summons from the gargoyle to others of its kind.

Numerous gargoyles fall toward us, not in a flock as the angels had done, but by ones and twos, and occasionally threes. They drop from the high ridges of the fantastical Gothic architecture. They rise from the basins of the fountains and the downspouts of the gutters, water sheeting off over-sized ears or out of the flaring nostrils of their improbable noses. Some drool or spit, but what comes from their mouths is not tainted slime, but instead the purest rainwater. Nonetheless, the cherubs react with revulsion. Their adorable baby mouths cease to smile and laugh, instead puckering up as if preparing for a proper infant wail.

I admit, I'm nearly as transfixed as my distracted attackers. (The angels seem to have forgotten us for the moment.) The gargoyles are so fantastically varied. Although most are colored after types of stone, they only prove how preposterously varied stone can be. Every shade and hue of the grey tones is there, as is purest midnight black and a crystalline white that would put newly fallen snow to shame. There are gargoyles of dark blue, of rose pink, of every red imaginable, from brick to ruby to the rich purple-kissed tones of garnets.

Not one gargoyle is like another, so trying to describe them would be impossible. Some, like the one I had first glimpsed, are quite large – nearly as big as I am. Some would have made fit romping partners for Puck. Others are so tiny they could serve as mantelpiece knickknacks. These last are often jewel brilliant, and I find myself wondering if they are the souls of gemstones.

The shapes the gargoyles wear are even more varied than their colors and sizes. About the only things they have in common are their grotesque fantastical shapes, which might place a cat's eyes on a rat's face, then give that the ears of an elephant. Most of the gargoyles have wings more akin to those of a bat – or a dragon – than of a bird, but that rule is not absolute. Nothing about them is absolute except that they are as real as I am and they are coming in response to their fellow's call.

My heart bounces with ebullient joy verging on jubilation. My relief grows when Muriel tells me that Puck is no longer bleeding and seems to be regaining some of his usual energy. Although, she adds, he doesn't seem nearly ashamed enough of the trouble he has gotten us into. Trouble, I am reminded when a panicking cherub nearly falls on top of us, that we are still in the thick of.

The gargoyles have definitely distracted the cherubs, but apparently the horrific little angels have friends, too. Maniacal giggling heralds the arrival of more of the weird, baby-faced avians. While they don't have much in the way of an attack unless they can close to bite, I fear that they might smother us within their feathered embrace. Then, too, the gargoyles might be injured if a flight of angels forced them to fall onto the flagstone pavement.

I must get us out of here. Then the gargoyles will no longer need to protect us, and can return to whatever quiet pursuits they had been about before. Somehow I doubt the winged baby heads have much in the way of an attention span. If we are out of sight, soon we should be out of mind as well.

What to do? Although I still shrink from looking too closely at myself, I realize that in our eagerness to chase after Puck, Muriel and I had not eased ourselves into a local resident or shaped ourselves a locally appropriate form. This time we are not whale or dog or butterfly-winged fairy. Therefore, we can't simply desire to be back in the rosy haven of the seven-windowed (and one maybe-doored) tower. We are stuck here and must find our way to some sort of safety before finding our way home.

In front of us is a maelstrom melee of wings, feathered and leathered. Behind us is the unyielding cathedral. Yet… Unyielding? Perhaps I am too easily defeated. We have come to rest against a door and, no matter how intractable this one seems to be, doors are, by definition, meant to be opened.

Although fearful of turning my back, I must turn so that I can better examine the massive portal. At first and even second and third inspection, it offers little. Then, just as I am considering that maybe our only option is to take one of the little winged toddler heads hostage – a slim hope indeed, for the violence with which they are slamming into each other in their eagerness to be first in the fray does not seem to indicate that they value each other overmuch – I see what the doors' intricate carvings had concealed to this point.

Set into one edge of the huge panel that makes up the left side of the greater door is a smaller door, similar in size to the front door of a more usual house. This smaller door is concealed within a carved depiction of a garden archway in a scene that is probably meant to be Eden or maybe Babylon. However, once spotted, the small door is obvious.

Crowing with pleasure – even as I bat away a cherub that has taken advantage of my distraction to seize the puffy sleeve of my night dress in its teeth – I hurry over to the smaller door, calling to Muriel and the re-bounded Puck to hurry. Feeling along the convoluted carvings, I seek the latch or knob that I know must be concealed within. My fingers, rather than my eyes find it, well-hidden, the bronze in which it was cast stained or tarnished so that it nearly matches the material – wood or stone, I can't tell – from which the door is crafted.

To my shock, when I press down on the latch it moves only the slightest amount. The door is locked! My fingers seek and find a keyhole but, no matter how desperately I search, I can't find a key. No lazy sexton has stashed one under a rock. No prudent deacon has hung a spare on a concealed hook against future forgetfulness. The door is locked against us and without the key, it might as well be yet another stone in the walls of the cathedral.

I sink down in despair, my hands over my eyes to push back tears – of fear or anger, I don't know, nor do I care. We are lost. I have failed. Then I feel Muriel's hand press against my wrist. I peek up at her and see her smiling at me. Her little hands are still incarnadined with Puck's blood, but she is actually smiling!

"At last," I hear her say in that wordless way we have, "I can be useful. My flimsy weakness will be our salvation!"

She pushes Puck into my arms, then, turning sideways, she slips through the tiny crevice between the door and its frame. Her dress – the thickest part of her – catches, and I hear a faint ripping. Then she is gone. I am left hugging Puck close to me, hoping that my little wisp of a friend can indeed manage to get the door open before enough of the creepy cherubs can press past the wearying gargoyles and overwhelm us.

Letting Puck keep watch for us over my shoulder, I press my ear to the keyhole, keeping my hand on the latch so that I will be prepared to pull or push at Muriel's least signal. I don't hear her voice, but what I do hear makes my blood rush hot and terrified in my veins.

From somewhere far overhead, the cathedral clock is beginning the musical introduction that will conclude with the counting off of the hour. What had the gargoyle in the fountain said about the clock striking? I can't remember, but clearly the creepy cherubs know. Ignoring the gargoyles, the host of baby-headed angels refocuses their assault on us.

"Mine! Mine!" they shriek in the voices of angry toddlers denied a favorite toy. "Give me! Mine!"

I reposition Puck over my arm so that he can press one of his long ears to the keyhole, but I keep my hand on the latch. With my free arm, I fend off the angels, augmenting our defense with butts of my head and kicks, though my long skirts make this last nearly ineffective. Puck catches on though, and – while keeping his ear to the keyhole – he kicks out solidly with his big bunny feet, chortling and squeaking with delight whenever he makes contact with smiling face or downy feathered wings.

Overhead, the clock has begun to chime…One. Two. Three.

I have no sense what o'clock it is. My heart beats a violent counterpoint to the chimes, expecting each to be the fatal last. (Four. Five. Six.) So absorbed am I, that I nearly miss when the latch moves under my hand. Frantically, I shove down, then push my whole body against the door. (Seven. Eight. Nine.) To say the door moves easily would be an exaggeration, but I force it inward just enough that (Muriel scampering out of the way) Puck and I can tumble inside, pushing back one last frantically protesting cherub.

As I shove the door shut, I overcome my aversion to the sound of my own voice to shout as loudly as I can, "Thank you! We're safe now!"

I'm not certain if we really are safe, but the gargoyles have done all – indeed far more – than I could have hoped when I made that initial desperate appeal. As I accept the key from Muriel and lock the door, I hear the clock finishing its rhythmic tolling of the hours, going on for what I could swear is a count of thirteen.

What had I expected on the other side of the door? I suppose if I'd thought at all, I'd expected one of those rooms that in a more usual building would have a name like "mudroom" or maybe "foyer" or "lobby," one of those rooms that exist so that outside and inside shall never directly meet. Those rooms probably have some sort of fancy name if they're in a church, maybe "vestibule"? But whatever the space is called, that was what I expected: a room framed on one side by the outer doors and on the other by a matching set, just as big but made of highly polished wood that would never directly face weather and so could be polished to the highest of shines.

If I'd dared hope for anything other than shelter, then I think I would have hoped to find us back in the rosy tower room, with Horatius and Eyebright looking up from some game, vaguely inquisitive as to where we had gone and how we had returned.

But what I encounter as I turn from closing and locking the door behind us is neither vestibule or tower, nor even the main body of the cathedral, which would have been my third choice. Instead, we face a deep, verdant jungle, thick foliage interspersed with enormous wildly colorful flowers, creating a barrier nearly as impenetrable as the cathedral's stone outer walls had been.

Vines drop down, living ropes starred with white or pale green orchids. Insect buzz, bees and dragonflies and butterflies with wings of all sorts of improbable colors, like ice rose or evening sun-splash or rising storm. There are larger creatures out there, too, for I catch a glimpse of ink-spotted honey that just might be the pelt of a leopard or jaguar. Surely that swinging motion is not merely wind-tossed foliage? I guess it to be a monkey of some sort – a long-armed gibbon or fluffy-eared spider-monkey or a tamarind with a ridiculously huge mane framing a wide-eyed, serious face.

Yet... Yet... There is something not quite right about this jungle. In a moment, I realize what it is. There is no wind, no sense of damp or of any weather at all. There is a pervasive humidity, true, but the temperature is Three Bears comfortable: neither too hot nor too cold, only "just right." Then, too, this place lacks any dominant odor, although the plants alone should have provided ample scents: of leaves, of flowers, of earth mold. If there really are animals here, as I suspect, then there should have been odors from them as well, in the case of both the monkeys and the great cats, quite rank.

Clutching Puck tightly lest he bound away with a resumption of his usual exuberance, feeling Muriel's smooth, dry fingers slip into my free hand, I wonder just what new trouble we've gotten ourselves into. I consider reentering the plaza and slipping back in the direction from which we had arrived, but a peek through the keyhole shows me that although most of the fighting has abated, the weird angels still cruise over the plaza. I can't tell whether they seek us or have returned to whatever idle pigeon-play they had interrupted when Puck had bounded into their midst and provided them with a new game.

We must move forward then, into this peculiar jungle, either that or wait here, perhaps for the coming of dark. Surely creatures that look so much like toddlers – albeit toddlers missing legs upon which to toddle – would go to bed with the sun. Then I remember how I was certain the clock had chimed thirteen. What if night didn't fall here anymore than it seemed to come to the tower of seven windows and maybe, just maybe, one door?

If that was the case, we might sit here forever, or at least until one of the jungle denizens takes an interest in us.

The only good thing about our situation is that I am neither tired nor hungry. Now that my terror has subsided, I feel, if not fresh as a daisy, at least willing to take on a new challenge. Venturing directly forward seems to invite becoming lost, but what if we stay closer to the cathedral's interior wall? Might we find a window looking out to where there are no cherubic-faced attackers? Or maybe we could use a window to call for help.

Maybe we could find a flight of stairs that would lead us to the roof or to a belfry. I don't think that cherubs would nest in a belfry, but roofs and belfries both seem like good places to seek gargoyles. Thus far, the gargoyles have shown themselves friendly. At the very least, we could say "thank you" for their timely aid.

The oddity that the very wall which had not so long before been a barrier should now be enlisted as guide does not escape me. Even as I accept that it is the only constant, I fear it will simply vanish when we have left sight of the entryway. Then we will find ourselves stuck in the midst of a trackless jungle. Nonetheless, I refuse to let the possibility paralyze me into inaction.

Puck promises to stay close, so I set him down in order to have both hands free. I need one to push back the abundant verdure, while the other stays firmly pressed to the stone wall. Not as trusting as I, Muriel takes a firm hold on the less injured of Puck's flopping ears, then grabs hold of some of the ample fabric of my nightdress's voluminous skirts. In this fashion, we progress into the jungle.

Close to the lobby or foyer or vestibule or whatever it was that we'd found on the inner side of the cathedral door, the stone of the wall feels smooth and polished, with occasional bits of rough grain. As we move deeper into the jungle, the stone becomes rougher, rasping my fingertips so that I wonder if the prints will be sanded off. Eventually, I become aware of a third texture: swirls, loops, and lines cut into the rock.

I wonder if these are ornamentation, like on the cathedral door. Am I dragging my fingers over a demon's maw or the stiffly tranquil features of a saint? I want to know but, at the same time, I don't. If the image is scary, I might not be able to bring myself to touch it and then what? If I lose contact with the wall, we will surely become lost in the trackless tangle of greenery.

I have no faith that this jungle is contained within the cathedral walls. Lately, I've seen too many things that violate reason and logic to expect that the rules here are like those I, for some inexplicable reason, expect to still apply. Despite my uncertainties, the jungle is not an unkind space. Eventually, the denizens must come to accept that Muriel, Puck, and I more or less belong, because birdsong and insect buzz resume.

I worry that this means that leopard prowl and alligator creep have also resumed, but there isn't much I can do about that. Occasionally, we splash through pools or rivulets, Puck and Muriel clinging to me lest they get soaked. In time, the hem of my nightdress becomes sodden, and slaps around my ankles.

Muriel urges me to gird up my skirts, something I could have managed using some of the long, dangling lianas or vines that the jungle creates so freely. Although the damp fabric is uncomfortable, I refuse. Something in me shrinks from exposing myself to... to me?

I could have voiced excuses, but I don't bother, since my companions are privy to the secrets of my heart.

To distract them – and me – I give more attention to the uneven texture of the wall. More and more I am certain that what I am feeling is not some relief portrait, but rather an inscription in the most usual sense of the word – an "in-writing" – something carved into the wall.

I try "reading" with my fingers, but that proves useless. The words or letter are incomprehensible. I speculate that the script may be in a foreign language or even an alien alphabet – not something as completely different as Egyptian hieroglyphs or Babylonian cuneiform – but closer to the writings I know, like Cyrillic. Cyrillic comes to seem the best possible option, since there are times my fingers almost seem to make sense of what they "read," only to have the meaning vanish into tactile gibberish.

When we come to a rushing stream deep enough to splash over my anklebones, I give in to temptation. Tucking Muriel into my bodice, I squash Puck tight against my side with my left upper arm. This gives me an arm and a half with which to pull the greenery (and pinkery and purply – for there are many flowers here) back from the wall. I'd hoped to be able to make some sense out of what I'd been feeling, even if just to confirm the manner of writing the unknown inscriber had used, but what I see tells me both much more and much, much less.

Although many letters and parts of letters are missing, the alphabet seems to be the one with which I am most familiar, the unusual characters now revealed as the result of erosion or moss filling in crevices. It looks as if the inscriber had used all capital letters, in a blocky script that somehow reminds me of a kid's printing. However, as to meaning? Most of what is written there might as well have been in Chinese ideograms, or the twists and curls of the Arabic alphabet.

Despite the damp that now soaks every inch of me, despite the omnipresence of growing things, for some reason, I had not taken into account the toll both wetness and vegetation would take on anything carved into a stone surface. Yet the passage I examine is as clear as squish, readable as squash. I can make out a few letters, but have no idea if they are part of the same word or fragments of words in a larger phrase. "ES OM ME!" are on one line. Another says, "JE W K P, SE!" And those are the more or less complete ones. A lot of the others are nothing more than curves that could have been the tops of S's or O's or P's or little flat lines that could have been part of almost any other letter in the alphabet.

Only the final exclamation points make any sort of sense, transforming purest nonsense into a shout-out. I wonder if what was – is – written here is even in English. Somehow, deep it my gut, I feel certain that it is, that if there had been even a few more letters, I could have guessed at a meaning, the way you can figure out a text message, even though many of the vowels are missing and punctuation is purely optional. But there's no way I could ever make sense of this.

A hasty inspection of the nearest sections of wall confirms that the condition of the writing is, if anything, worse elsewhere. In some places, it is overgrown with moss. In others, water has caught in the whorls and swirls, dripping down to create a pseudoscript of its own. And who is to say that, even if I figure out what is written there, anything would come from it? This is a cathedral, right? At least the walls are part of a cathedral, or they had been, or something. I'm not ready to vouch for the rest of the place.

Given the cathedral notion, then it is likely that what is scribbled here is a bit of a prayer or perhaps a hymn or Bible passage. It even could be text identifying something depicted higher on the walls over my head, and certainly out of my ability to pull away the plants to get a better look. Stations of the Cross – that "JE" could be part of "Jesus" – or the names of saints and angels. Nothing certainly to do with me.

After I nearly drop Puck, who would *not* have handled a soaking well, who is already looking pretty wilted from the ambient humidity – as well as from being squashed under my forearm – do I allow that this is a waste of time and effort. Certainly the inscriptions will not help us find our way back to the rosy confines of the tower: our base, even if something in me vigorously resists calling it "home."

Home. The word feels strange to me, leaves me feeling very uneasy. Home. Do I have one? I feel certain I did, that I knew much more about it than I can put my mind to. Yet, equally, I feel unwilling to search for the memory. All along, I have felt sure that I don't have amnesia in the classic sense of having my memories taken from me, but now I wonder if the gatekeeper who stands between me and all the myriad things I don't know is none other than myself.

That's a thought not worth dwelling on, or so I tell myself as I move Puck to a more comfortable position and return to my wall-crawl through the jungle. We've just crossed yet another stream – Where *does* all this water come from, and, more worrisome, where does it all go? – when I feel a change in the air. To this point, despite the verdant plant growth and birdsong, I have persisted in thinking of this as some sort of enormous conservatory or greenhouse, all the jungle contained within walls and under a roof.

Now I realize that my conviction has been helped by the feel, or perhaps better stated, the lack of feeling in the air. It moves very little and, when it does, I can usually catch a glimpse of the avian or – more rarely – arboreal creature that has caused the disturbance. This time, what I feel is more like being out-of-doors: a fresh, erratic motion, possessed of shifting currents.

Are we approaching a door out of the cathedral? Have we gone far enough – or been inside long enough – that we will escape the notice of any of the winged toddler heads, should they be back to cruising the air currents? I have long ago lost any sense of direction… as for distance! The only thing to do – as both Muriel and Puck, in rare agreement, urge me – is to go forth and try to catch a glimpse of whatever has caused this alteration in our environs.

Licking my lips nervously, I advance. The plants here possess wide leaves that invite me to take cover behind them, so I do, moving slowly, even though Puck advises me that there is caution and then there is just putting off the inevitable – and don't I want to know what's out there? Reluctantly, I leave the security of the guiding wall. At that point, I nearly give in to nerves and retreat. Only the question of what I will do once I am back by the wall – go all the way back to the cathedral vestibule and sit? – makes me press on.

Step by slightly squishy step, I move along, taking the motion of the air as my new guide. Something small and multi-legged dashes across my foot, but it doesn't pause, so I press my jaw tightly around an "eep" of terror and keep going. A few steps further and what I feel certain is a snake slithers cool and curiously dry across my foot, flicking one ankle with a questioning tongue before moving on. That time I might well have screamed or jumped, but my gaze has caught a differing color through the leaves directly in front of us. Startled as I am by the close encounter with the probable snake, I am more unwilling to alert whatever – if anything – that might be out there where air and light promise a change of venue.

Needless to say, every tentative step we had taken away from the vestibule had been accompanied with speculation. However, even in my wildest imaginings I had not come close to guessing what lay at the jungle's edge. When first I look beyond the screening foliage, I think we have come to the bank of a large pond or small lake. Although I see no waterways feeding into it, almost certainly this is the endpoint of the myriad water drops, the rivulets and creeks, all of which had contributed to making our journey so decidedly soggy.

Or so I think at that first glimpse. That is before my second glance transforms the pond or lake into what it actually is: an enormous tongue stretched flat, slightly undulating over the open clearing that begins just beyond the wide leaves that serve as my cover. Tongues are rarely found without a mouth, nor am I disappointed when I seek such. At the farthest, widest edge of the tongue is an enormous head. It is vaguely human in that it possesses two eyes, a single nose, and a single (enormous) mouth, but in truth it more resembles one of the gargoyles grown huge than anything human.

The eyes are cat-slitted and of a hard, translucent green more usually found in gems than in anything alive. This pair is too yellowish to remind me of emeralds, closer, perhaps, to peridots. These eyes are open and fully aware, moving slightly to track the duck and dodge of dragonflies over the surface of the tongue. I suspect they are aware of me and my two friends, or if not of us specifically, then of the motion we had created in the vegetation during our forward progress.

The fresh breeze that I had detected, and which had given me such hope, proves to be the gigantic creature's breathing. I feel a flash of something like betrayal. Shouldn't breath be warm and wet? This is cool and seems to leach moisture from its surroundings. Then, with a shake – purely mental, for my muscles remain frozen in shock – I adjust my expectations. Why shouldn't a creature made from stone, as the gargoyles seem to be, have cool breath?

The real question is should we try to sneak away or to move closer? True, this thing is enormous and frightening-looking but, to this point, the gargoyles have been friendly to us. Nevertheless, to walk out into the open, to stand full body to only face with a creature so tremendously huge that it could swallow all three of us and probably not even need to belch, that takes courage I suspect I don't have.

Yet I feel certain this creature, this mega-gargoyle, is not something we can avoid. Squeezing Puck against me, I step from cover. I suspect I look quite the sight, my nightdress sodden halfway to my knees, my hair ornamented with leaves and bracken. Doubtless, my face is smeared with mud and slime. It occurs to me that I look like some monstrous denizen of the jungle. Oddly, that makes me laugh aloud.

At the sound, the enormous peridot eyes swivel in my direction, fixing me with a gaze that is intent, yet without any passion that I can define. There is neither anger nor fear nor even amusement. The gaze is clear, analytic, and somehow manages to combine complete indifference and intent focus without contradiction. I feel like a frog must when pinned for dissection: the center of an attention that nonetheless does not care for me one whit.

I try to speak, but find my mouth as dry as cotton. My throat is tight. My heart thumps erratically. I must have squeezed Puck too hard because he gives a thin squeak of protest and kicks out against the air. His motion breaks the spell – if indeed spell it was – and I can swallow again, but my voice when I speak is so thick and tentative that I hardly know it.

"Please... Do you know where we might find a way out of here? A way that won't take us out into the plaza again, that is. I don't think that way is safe for us, and I don't want any more of the gargoyles to get hurt defending us."

This is the longest speech I have made in – how long? The effort drains me so that I nearly collapse onto the damp ground. Yet, for a long moment, it seems as if my effort will be for naught, for no reply comes from the humongous entity in front of us. Then I feel the ground shaking and realize that this is because the titanic head is moving in what must be a nod.

"You do!" I squeak, sounding more like Puck than I would have thought possible.

Again the ground shakes. Then that tongue, large as a lake, ripples along its length, furling like a tremendous slug carpet, then unfurling in wordless yet unmistakable invitation. The huge jaws are open, the mouth forming a tremendous fang-fringed tunnel into darkness.

I have memories of seeing such before, surrounded by amusement park lights and cheesy painted panels advertising a Tunnel of Horror ride, and I had laughed at the clichéd improbability of it. Now faced – quite literally – by the reality, I find it neither improbable nor hokey. I am terrified beyond the ability to accept the offer. Instead I will flee into the jungle. I will find the cathedral door again. I will wait in the vestibule forever and ever, anything but face the moment when I must pass through that horrible, dripping, fang-fringed portal.

At that moment, I hate Puck. If he hadn't been so impulsive, we wouldn't be here. I hate Muriel. Why hadn't she warned me that Puck was about to jump? I hate myself as fool and coward.

Step by step, I back away from that fearsome visage. Leaves brush around me, promising concealment. Bird song caresses my ears with the rhythmic promise of routine. I can be safe here. Yet, as I ease into my escape, I feel the air grow stale, hotter, stifling. Moisture gathers on my skin, not as the promise of growth but as the first stage of rot.

I stop. Fear holds my heart in a long-fingered hand. I can feel each digit, ice and fire mingling without pattern, tightening, tightening… I will not escape here – I would *cease*. Not die. I would cease. As certainly as I know the reality of my terror, I know this. And, for a long, timeless, seductive caress of thought, I welcome that ending. To cease. No more worries. No more choices. Nothing but nothing but nothing but nothing but nothing…

But.

Even as I begin to crumple, to fall, letting my hold on Puck loosen, forgetting what contact with the jungly damp will do to Muriel, I think, "… but." Hardly a word. Barely a thought. Not even a sound.

But. Except. Other than… Nothing but…

"But" is so little, yet it is everything. It is unicorns with horns, now you see them, now you don't. It is mermen with skins of liquid blue-green, cruel spears, and the curiously admirable courage to face the leviathan. It is the leviathan, so huge that it hardly knows how to reconcile the vision of one eye with that of the other. It is tender dog paws on rough concrete, the delight of finding a slice of stale pizza crust, pepperoni and cheese naught but odor yet present nonetheless, giving piquancy to the bready bite.

"But" is so very, very much, and with that realization I realize that no matter how seductive is the lure of nothing and all the relief it promises, I am not ready to make the choice to join nothing. That time might come, but the same impulse that had carried me from the rosy comfort of the soft bed within the tower now makes me shake myself and begin to walk, each step more determined, back to where the gigantic tongue still furls in wet carpet invitation.

The peridot eyes cross to look at me as I approach, watch as I shrink from placing a bare foot on the tongue, envisioning the sensation of slugs or of snails yanked from their shells. Squinching my eyes shut, nose wrinkling in anticipation (or is that dread?), muscles tensed to jump back, I lift one bare foot and set it upon the top of the outspread tongue. All my expectations are destroyed in a single tread.

The surface the sole of my foot meets is certainly damp, it is certainly warm, but it is not in the least unpleasant. I had not expected it to be rough, but it is, rough with the varying bumps caused by taste buds. I am reminded of the feel of a sidewalk after a summer thundershower, the sort that beats down so hard that any caught in it are soaked to the skin in moments, that ends so quickly that after the puddles are warm as wash water and invite splashing.

More boldly, I take my second step, then a third. Almost jump back when the surface yields beneath my foot as no sidewalk ever would, but acceptance of this difference is part of the price for walking this road. Raising my chin in defiance of my own fears, I open my eyes wide and march up to the gargoyle's gaping maw. Those peridot eyes cross even tighter to follow my progress until I climb up and over where the tongue passes up and over teeth and I must take my first step inside.

Any hesitation to do so is hidden in my heart, not revealed in the steadiness of my tread. I had anticipated (dreaded?) walking down a lightless corridor, perhaps climbing through organically detailed internal landscapes: entering the gullet by passing under that dangly thing at the back of the throat, climbing down the esophagus, crossing the acid lakes within the stomach, trudging along the twisting corridors of the intestines (small and large). I'd even speculated that instead of those villi we were taught lined the intestines, a gargoyle might have stalactites.

What I did not expect was that we would get swallowed. When the gulp comes, we are walking down the center of the tongue, and I am trying to convince myself that darkness might be preferable to seeing the interior landscape – the teeth alone, as revealed by the light seeping in from outside, are enough to give me nightmares (if I ever go to sleep again, that is). Then the surface beneath my feet flexes. I hear an audible gulp, and we go – not down – but back and forward.

"Of course," I hear Muriel say, "the gargoyle must have been lying on his stomach."

Then, for only the third time since awakening in the tower of seven windows and maybe (just maybe) one door, I lose consciousness.

Or do I? As I struggle back to the surface of awareness, I realize that I am hoping, trying with all my might to believe that I am back in the tower, back where I will again feel safe. Instead, what meets my gaze when I open my eyes is a skyscape that surely belongs to the Gothic realm of gargoyles and other, even odder, creatures.

Yes. There are spires that must belong to the cathedral. Winged figures that my brain tries to tell me must be pigeons or doves can be seen, but very little concentration is needed to accept them for what they are – gargoyles and those creepy cherubs still involved in their aerial joust. We have gotten away from the cathedral, just as I had requested, but our problem – how to leave this land and return to the tower – is far from solved.

A wriggling and kicking assures me that Puck has survived our trip through the gargoyle's guts. Muriel, too, is well, although her frock is much the worse for wear. Wordlessly, I promise her that I will craft her a new one as soon as we have reached somewhere with appropriate tools. She gives me a smile both sweet and brave, and I press her close to me.

Even as I check on my friends, I sort through our options. When we survey the lands outside of the windows, the tower has always appeared to look directly down over the vista. However, when we enter into the scene, the tower has not been a feature in the landscape. This had not concerned me to this point because we had always entered the scene by becoming an appropriate element in it. This time, thanks to Puck's impulsiveness, we are ourselves and have entered it physically.

Does this then mean that the tower does, in fact, touch each of these places? If so, we need to find it and re-enter. I'm not quite sure how we'll manage that, but first we must locate the tower. After doing that, we can move on to the next part of our plan. After all, if we can't retrace our steps to the tower, any other planning would be useless.

When I share these thoughts with my two friends, Muriel agrees that they seem sound. Puck doesn't disagree but, rotating his ears rather like propellers, he indicates the numerous tall structures surrounding us. Which one – if any – of these is the tower we seek?

I shrug. We won't know unless we look. As I push myself to my feet, I notice that my unremembered journey through the gigantic gargoyle has had an added benefit. My nightdress no longer shows muddy and stained at the hem. It is still rumpled, true, but I am grateful that it is no longer filthy and stiff with mud.

Brushing my skirts down around me, I decide that I will use the cathedral as a point of orientation. We'd come past a fountain, then entered the plaza. The distance hadn't been too great, had it? Reentering the plaza seems unwise, but surely we can work our way back along a parallel course, looking down side streets in the hope of spotting recognizable landmarks.

As we pick our way along the cobbled streets, I am struck by how deserted they are. My initial relief that we are not being attacked by angels – or worse – gives way to apprehension. There are so many buildings. Where are the residents? Where are the builders? Is this place entirely given over to angels and gargoyles?

The few living creatures we see don't provide me with any sense of rhyme or reason. There is an elephant, Indian, I think, though I'm not sure why I would classify it so – something about the size of the ears? In any case, the elephant crosses an intersection in front of us, trundling along in the direction of a large circus tent. When it lifts the flap to pass inside, I hear the crack of a whip. I expect to see a ringmaster then, and even entertain a fleeting thought that maybe I could ask the gentleman (for so I envision him, kindly and mustached, wearing a top hat, slightly the worse for wear) for directions, but then I realize that the elephant had cracked the whip, apparently directing a ballet of ravens and sheep who dance over and around a Japanese torii gate painted a vibrant, eye-searing scarlet.

Another time, I glimpse motion through a high-arched picture window, but when this proves to be a cobra half my height, I flinch back and watch in near hypnotized fascination as it sways back and forth before a cauldron hung from one heavy curved limb of a saguaro cactus. A wheedling tootle of sound comes faintly to my ears, muffled by glass and masonry. Keeping time with this almost unheard music, the cobra is busy dropping sparkling bits of jewelry into the cauldron, flaring its hood with each splash.

Then there is the bespectacled octopus that drives by in some sort of antique automobile, periodically slowing to scan its surroundings through a long spyglass. It holds a treasure map in one tentacle and, as it is clearly comparing it against its surroundings, I don't think it is looking for us. Indeed, after several sputtering halts, one of which completely stalls the car's engine, the octopus drives around a corner and vanishes from sight.

Distracted as I am by these and other even odder encounters, I nearly don't recognize the tower when at last it comes into our line of sight. If it hadn't been irregularly octagonal in shape, and had not each side held an arched and framed band at the top that sparkles when the light touches it, I'm not sure I would have known it.

Perhaps because of the interior, I had always imagined the tower as looking like one from a fairytale: elegant, built from smoothly dressed stone, perhaps overgrown on the lower edges with ivy, honeysuckle, or wild roses. The tower of my imaginings had a peaked conical roof, shingled in intricately patterned slates of the palest blue-grey, shining nearly silver where the sunlight touched it.

This tower is made from mismatched stones, some rough, some smooth. There are chunks of limestone, nearly white and flecked with mica, granite in every shade, boulders slammed into place, even a few courses of brick. It rises high, then peaks in a roof that rises to a sort of point but, instead of the elegant slates of my imagined tower's roof, this is overgrown with some shaggy plant, browned and wiry, like the stems of a vine that has lost leaves and flowers to winter's bite and now reveals the twiggy bones beneath.

Nor were the sparkling areas windows, as I had seen them from the inside. Here they are revealed as eyes, long-lashed and shining. Most of these eyes are partly closed, lids drooping, but one – a rich chocolate brown, not the gleaming red I half-expected – is wide open. This must be the eye – or window – we had passed out through and which now keeps vigil, although whether awaiting our return or alert to prevent it, I can't guess.

It is Muriel who notices – as we make our slow and stealthy inspection of the tower – that one eye is not an eye at all, but is, instead, a door, clearly marked as such by a prosaic knob set right where one would expect it to be. The knob's brass finish gives back the light with a shine like a beacon of welcome. Reaching the door should provide little challenge, for a long staircase curves around the irregular octagon of the tower's form. It will be a long climb, certainly, and whoever makes it will be vulnerable to any airborne menace that chances to notice the climber's progress, but it seems invitingly possible. Laughing in relief, we hasten to find the spiral's beginning.

When we reach it, I half-expect to find some challenger at the base: a sphinx with riddles three or a horn-helmed knight holding sword and shield to block our passage. However, nothing blocks us from beginning our climb. True, seen up close, the winding stair is rather more rickety than it had seemed from a distance, the looping bannister or guard rail full of gaps. Various treads are missing, too, but as best as I can tell, none of the missing segments are too wide for me to get across. If necessary, I can carry the others. Muriel will keep watch for me, providing advanced warning if gargoyle, angel, or other aerial denizen takes undue interest.

I position Muriel where she can take up her watch. Then I extract a promise from Puck that he will not bounce so hard or so fast that he will shake the fragile stairway from its hold on the tower. I also make him promise that he will not push past me, nor do anything so that I will lose sight of him. Still contrite from Muriel's scolding reminder that if he hadn't jumped out the window in the first place, we wouldn't be in this situation, he agrees. With a deep breath, I set my foot on the shaking stair and begin the ascent.

As I move upwards, wherever possible I keep one hand firmly on the handrail, using the other to keep contact with the tower. What good either would do me if the entire staircase comes ripping out of the wall, I don't know, but it makes me feel more confident. I need every scrap I can get, because with each step I feel more exposed. At least Puck keeps true to his promise, restraining his usual exuberant bounces to carefully climb, front paws first, then bringing up each long-pawed rear leg one after the other. Despite his care, I can feel the staircase vibrating with every motion either of us makes.

At least Muriel doesn't see anyone coming after us. The gargoyles and cherubs seem fully occupied with each other, and neither the crows nor the pigeons who occasionally sweep by seem to think we are worth even passing attention. So it goes as we spiral our way up, looping around the tower, once, twice, thrice.

At the conclusion of the third loop, we reach the top. A landing of sorts extends out to meet with a solid stone doorsill. It is wide enough that I can – just barely – stand there, rejoicing in the sensation of something beneath my feet that neither creaks, nor sways. Muriel urges me to try the door, so I lay my hand on the shiny brass knob and turn it – or rather, I attempt to turn it. It moves slightly, so I know it is an actual doorknob, not some ornament intended to deceive. However, it is firmly locked and the key nowhere to be found.

There is a keyhole (which is why we look for a key), but when I look through I see only darkness. Next I knock. My heart jumps when the sharp rapping brings the sound of two voices, one gruff and rumbly, the other higher and somehow slithery: Horatius and Eyebright!

However, from what I can catch from piecing together scattered pieces of their conversation, they aren't about to open the door. The job for which they had been created is the precise opposite – to keep the door from being opened.

Leaning so close that my lips brush the cool metal of the keyhole, I try to project my voice through the narrow opening. "It's me! And Muriel and Puck. Let us in!" But my too, too faithful guardians refuse to be "fooled," as they put it to each other. Indeed, I feel a shudder against the door panel as they move the bed firmly into place, congratulating each other on their cleverness and firmness of purpose.

Clearly, talking to them isn't going to get the door opened. Remembering the unmovable cathedral doors, I ask Muriel if she can slide through the crack between door and frame as she had done there. Together we inspect the crevice and it seems quite possible, for this door does not fit anywhere nearly as snug. Muriel is game, so I maneuver her around. We have a tense time when the winds buffeting these upper reaches seek to tear her slender form from between my fingers, but I shelter her as best I can.

This is harder to do than it might seem, for I don't trust Puck to keep as careful watch as Muriel had done, and protecting Muriel means turning my back on the sky and its fearsome denizens. When she feels stable, Muriel insinuates herself into the narrow space, probing first with a slim arm, then entrusting a leg and her head to the crevice. Puck quivers with excitement, assuring me that soon we'll all be safe inside, asking me what color dress I plan to draw next for Muriel, suggesting color combinations so wild that – even in my tense state – I have to giggle.

But once her head is through the gap, Muriel's progress halts. She grows suspiciously still. At first, I think she must be talking to Horatius and Eyebright, explaining to them all that had happened since we had jumped out the window after Puck. Time passes. More than enough for the explanation and any number of questions to be both asked and answered. Time enough for Puck to grow first restless, then to begin to drowse against my leg, the empty sky holding nothing of sufficient interest to keep him amused.

Licking my lips, I crouch so I can get a better look at where Muriel's remaining bit of torso and the associated arm and leg remain outside the crevice. I am greatly disturbed to find them somewhat faded, their substance brittle. Sudden fear grips me, squeezing the breath from my lungs as I realize that something is drawing the substance from her. First would go the color and then, I felt sure, the surface on which the color had been set. I must draw her back, but how can I manage without doing her further harm?

I lack tools or ink. There is no way I can break down the door or even a segment from it without pitching Puck and myself down. The staircase will separate from the doorsill if we press against it. Yet I must save Muriel! If I don't, I'll never forgive myself.

Desperation becomes inspiration. First I reach over my shoulder and pull my braid forward. The hair, I notice without real interest, is an indifferent brown, bleached at the tip and not unduly clean. I refuse to be distracted. I pull the braid so I can suck the tip into a point. Then I bite into my lower lip – not a worried tug as I have so many times before, but hard enough to make the blood flow. I dip the tip of my braid into this makeshift ink then carefully, so very, very carefully, I begin to repaint the lines of the part of Muriel that I can see.

Adding a bit of spit to my fresh blood gives me a sort of pink. With this, I outline her hand and arm and a bit of leg between her foot and her hem. I make her skirt red and give her matching red shoes. To my delight, when next I touch her, she has lost that terrifying brittleness. Not waiting, I begin to ease her from the crevice, biting my lip again and again so that I can repaint and strengthen each part I expose so as not to risk a tear.

My work demands that I focus with every fiber of nerve I possess. Even impatient Puck holds still, fearful of distracting me from my delicate task. At long last, I draw Muriel free and, holding her close to my chest, I sink down onto my heels on the doorsill, shaking at how close I had come to losing her. It is Puck who – in a voice far softer than his usual squeaks – finally asks her what had happened.

Muriel tells us that she'd been fine at first and had figured she'd slide right through. She'd been concentrating on the exact right words to use to convince Horatius and Eyebright that it was okay to open the door when she realized that the going had become tough. Her initial easy slide had become like moving through sand, then through strawberry jam (the sort with lumps of fruit), then she'd come up against nothing but lumps – lumps she couldn't push through, no matter how hard she tried. She could make a tiny bit of progress forward but, when she tried to retreat, she discovered she couldn't go backwards at all. She'd tried to call out, but that jelly had jammed her voice.

She'd been pretty panicked, even after – maybe even more after – I'd started trying to pull her out. She knew how fragile she was – none better – and how quickly she'd rip in two. She'd just about given up when she realized she was feeling stronger, then, well, here she was, and wearing a spiffy new dress, too! Her brave smile couldn't hide how scared she'd been and once again I pressed her to me.

Puck, ever the impatient one of our trio, wants to know if Muriel thinks we could get Horatius and Eyebright to open the door for us. Muriel replies that she didn't think they would, no matter how we called or even if we pushed a message through the keyhole. (Puck suggests that we go down and pick a leaf on which I could write.) They are too faithful, created as guardians, and so as guardians they would live.

I consider our options. We could stay up here. There are certainly plenty of interesting things to see, and we might eventually convince Horatius and Eyebright that we are us and that they should let us in. But, remembering the broken obsidian surface of what might be the other side of the door, I wonder. On the interior of the tower there is no knob, not even a keyhole, now that I think about it. So, even if we convinced the guardians to let us in, could they?

If we go down to the tower's base, we have a whole city to explore. The gargoyles seem friendly, and the other residents quite interesting. We might even discover a way to get back into the tower someday. Maybe we could find a little airplane or a very long ladder that would let us get back in through the window through which we'd departed. It does seem a positive sign that the eye remains open. Maybe we could find a gargoyle large enough to give us a ride.

Yet, even as I consider these options, something in me shrinks back from asking for aid. I want to solve this myself, not ask for help – at least not until I can ask knowing I'd tried everything I can think of. When a possible plan comes to me, it is so scary that I almost push it away without further consideration. Nonetheless, I force myself to examine it more closely.

I've been thinking only about ways to climb up to the windows – or eyes as they seem to be from this side. What about climbing down? The staircase has taken us nearly to the roof. Can we – or at least I? – get onto the roof from here and then lower myself down to the window? The very idea makes my knees wobble with an acrophobia I didn't know I possessed, but, perversely, the more I consider this plan and the more scared I get, the more I want to try.

After giving Muriel and Puck the briefest of explanations, I push myself to my feet and check out the underside of the roof. Up close, it reminds me of coconut husk, if that husk was thicker, rather like the thick mats of growth that perennial vines like honeysuckle and silverlace form after several years of growth. This means that there are plenty of handholds, although I won't know how strong the stuff is until I trust my weight to it. It seems quite possible that it will break, but I could try to get hold of some of the thicker pieces.

Reaching the underside of the tower's roof from where we crouch on the doorsill would be a stretch, but I think that if I put one foot on the doorknob, I can get high enough to reach. I could even use the staircase as a safety net of sorts. It isn't in the best condition, but I can hope it will slow my fall if I do fall. Certainly that would be better than plummeting down to a smash on the ground below. Or at least that's what I try to convince myself.

For this maneuver, I'll need both hands free. Since I can't risk dropping my friends, I suggest that Puck and Muriel climb down to the base of the tower and wait for me under the open eye. Once I've gotten back inside the tower, I'll lower them a rope. Surely I have enough ribbons left. If I don't, I can tear up and tie together some of the seeming infinitude of sheets and pillowcases.

Muriel and Puck are very reluctant to agree with my suggestion. Only when I point out that if we all fell at the same time there would be no one left to come to the rescue do they agree. My heart sinks as I watch them diminish in size as they descend. I have come to rely on their steadfast companionship more than I realize.

When they are safely down, I begin my attempt to climb. As the roof overhangs both the staircase and the landing, my first goal must be to reach the roof's underside. Bracing my foot on the doorknob, I raise myself to where I can get a grip on the course thatching. I grab hold of two strong-seeming segments and – praying that they will not snap – let them take my weight. They sag but hold.

My nightdress makes the next part more difficult, for I must swing so that I can wedge my bare feet into the matting. Although I lack a monkey's prehensile toes, this awkward posture does enable me to distribute my weight more evenly. Then, head swung back, I choose a new hold for first one hand, then the next. After these are secure and the holds tested, I scrunch up and bring my feet – one at a time – forward as well.

In this clumsy fashion, I make my way to the edge of the roof. Now I need to work my way over the edge and onto the top. This maneuver is one reason I had chosen to tangle my feet in the roof's matting. If all my weight had hung from my hands, I wouldn't have dared let go to reach for a blind hold on the upper surface. Even so, when I do let go with my right hand, I feel myself sag alarmingly.

Quickly, I paw at the upper portion of the roof and find a large, thick cable. Grabbing this with all my strength, I let my other hand loose and, ignoring the snapping and crackling of the matting, reach for a hold on the upper edge. I don't have the luxury to seek anything of matching sturdiness to my first handhold, and am forced to settle for something that feels more like a length of twine than a cable.

Not trusting this to remain unbroken for long, I kick both feet free from their anchor at the same time. For a horrible moment, I hang over the edge of the roof, my lower body trailing and dragging me down with its weight. Panicked, I scrabble with both hands, pulling myself up inch by inch until enough of me rests on the roof's gentle slope that I no longer feel as if gravity has a personal interest in our tug of war.

Only when most of my weight is resting on the roof do I allow myself to choose my handholds with care, rather than in unreasoning desperation. I claw upwards until even my feet are safely on the roof, then pull myself even higher until there are several yards between me and the edge. Then I look around to gauge my situation.

The good news is that the roof's springy thatch or matting or whatever this is, is coarse enough that I don't need to worry about simply slipping off. The bad news is that I am completely disoriented. The roof extends out far enough that I can no longer see the tower's walls and windows. Finding the correct window – or eye – no longer seems the automatically simple task it had when below. True, my rough progress has left marks in the roof's matting, but I had not calculated precisely where the door is in relation to the window I need.

I fight back tears. The idea of climbing down the opposite slope, then poking my head over the edge in the hope that I've arrived at the correct area, is frankly terrifying, as is the suspicion that I might need to do this repeatedly before I locate the precise area. Then I see a small white dot bouncing wildly over the greensward far, far below. Scrubbing my tear-blurred eyes against my sleeve, I gradually realize that the white dot is Puck, and that his wild antics are not merely his usual frantic play, but are meant to attract my attention.

Anchoring my right hand firmly in the roof's matting, I wave my left to show Puck that I have seen him. When he notices my waving hand, he capers for a moment in pure joy, then he bounces purposefully along, halting until he sees that I am following him around the edge of the roof. Eventually, we come to the opposite side of the tower from which I had mounted to my current, far too lofty perch. Once Puck is certain that I am still attending to this game of follow the bouncing bunny, he moves until he comes to a certain point. There he proceeds to bounce up and down in place with the rhythmic devotion of some peculiar dervish or of a basketball beneath the hand of a professional basketball player readying for a game-winning shot.

When I see the minute figure of Muriel in the same place and realize that she is pointing at the tower, I understand. My friends – or more likely Muriel, for she has ever been the thinker – had anticipated my plight. Now she and Puck are showing me where the window/eye is. I wave both my arms crosswise over my head to signal that I understand, then I commence a slow, butt-first crawl down the slope of the roof, glancing periodically over my shoulder to make sure I haven't drifted off target.

When I am almost there I can hardly contemplate going over the edge of the roof whose security I have so recently gained. Taking the first step over, knowing that there is only emptiness… How can I? What if the underside of the roof won't hold me? Before there was at least the staircase landing beneath me, but here there would be nothing.

I freeze for how long? Long enough that I faintly hear the chime of the cathedral clock strike more than once. Long enough that Puck begins to bounce urgently below, his rhythm echoing the patter of my erratically beating heart. Maybe I will stay here forever, but that doesn't seem right. That would condemn Muriel and Puck to remain down there on the green. What if it rains? What if the cherubs – or something worse – find them?

I desperately want someone to show up and help me, but there is no one. Muriel and Puck have done all they can. This final challenge is mine alone – mine to succeed in, mine to fail in, mine to funk completely. But whatever choice I make is mine.

At long last I finish creeping down the slope. There I locate two of the firmest bits of matting I can find in the vicinity of the location where I must make my swing over and down. Grasping these, I peer over the edge. Muriel had been spot on in targeting the location, for when I look over I see the eye still open, still staring in idle curiosity over the land below. Although I am aligned with it, it is many yards back from my current location. As when I had mounted to the roof, I will need to swing over, then climb hand over hand to reach my goal.

Once again, the sheer emptiness of the space beneath me nearly cripples my resolve. Before I had possessed the illusory security of the staircase beneath me. Here there will be nothing but empty air. Even when I draw closer to the tower, I can't count on the staircase to serve as any sort of safety net. It twists far enough below that all it promises is that my fall – should I fall – would be interrupted by bone-cracking strikes against the wood and metal from which it is constructed.

Nonetheless, as soon as I have double-checked my handholds, I force myself out and over the edge. The cables of matting to which I cling creak. The one in my left jerks loose, sliding for several inches before catching once more, but leaving me swinging lower on one side than the other. Hanging by my arms, I pull myself up by force of will fueled by fear until I can get a firm grip on the underside of the overhanging roof. Then, swinging my legs like a kid on the monkey bars, I go forward, releasing my fingers only long enough to hope that there will be another hold when I reach for it.

The distance isn't more than a few yards but, with emptiness beneath me, it seems like miles. Glancing ahead, I feel my breath catch in my throat before I register just what has caused the reaction. For the first time, I realize that the window in front of me is closed. The shining pane of polished eye is perfect and unbroken, giving me back a translucent fish-eye image of myself hanging from my arms, my lips forming a perfect "O" of shock.

I can't believe Muriel would have directed me to the wrong window and, indeed, when I take a quick glance side to side, neither of the other windows are open. They do seem sleepier, though, and from this I take a little hope. Rocking slowly back and forth, pressing my lips together, I fight to remember. We'd been looking out the window, arguing about whether the architecture was properly Gothic, when Puck had seen something and bounced over the sill. Muriel and I had immediately gone in pursuit.

Surely none of us had paused to open the window, but would the same trick work in reverse? Would the tower reject me as an invader, as Horatius and Eyebright had done? My shoulder joints begin to burn, putting an end to my ability to debate. Either I drop or I crash or, I suppose, I could try and make my way back to the edge of the roof and onto the top again. I have a feeling that last would not work out well at all.

The reality is that, even if I choose otherwise, down might be my only destination. There's no guarantee I'll get back in through the window, but at least I'll try. Gritting my teeth so hard that I hear them squeak at the pressure, I swing forward. Motion blurs the disturbing translucent reflection, but even so I feel as if when I raise my legs and kick out that I am somehow trying to break not through a windowpane, but through myself.

I try to protect my bare feet within the trailing hem of my nightdress, but still I flinch from the anticipated impact of my soles against glass. Instead, I feel myself barreling feet first through something that isn't glass, a something that resists as water does the knifing body of a diver. Whatever this is quivers like almost-set gelatin when you stick your finger in it, which is really gross, but at least it isn't the shuddering crash of bare skin cutting against broken shards of plate glass.

All at once, I'm tumbling head over heels, over head over heels, onto the thick pale green carpet within the rosy chamber of the eight-sided tower. Horatius and Eyebright spin around, surprise in every line of their softly rounded bodies. They are crouched near the obsidian panel that I am now fairly certain is indeed a door – although whether a door to anywhere I'd like to go I can't say, a door that I feel I know less about than I had before our expedition.

Seeing me rolling over and over, they hurry to help me. Eyebright cushions me in the soft loops of his pillowed length, while Horatius props me more or less upright. After I have caught my breath, I explain that Muriel and Puck are still out there. Horatius and Eyebright are more than willing to try to lower them a line but, despite that my shoulder joints feel as if they are on fire, I stubbornly insist that I must be the one to effect a rescue.

The ribbons within the nightstand look too flimsy. I suspect that even if I manage to knot together a piece long enough to reach the ground, it would simply blow sideways, like a silken streamer. Instead, I go to the bed and tug off the top sheet. With Horatius' help, I tear this into long strips which I splice into a rope sufficiently long and heavy to reach the bottom. My final touch is knotting a pillowcase onto the lowest section of the line. This way Puck and Muriel can get inside, and won't need to worry about holding onto the rope while I pull it in.

When I go to lower the rope out the window, Horatius insists on holding me around the waist. However, I insist on being the one who thrusts her head out the window and drops the line. A series of rhythmic tugs tell me when Puck and Muriel are safely in the pillowcase. Then I haul them up, carefully lifting the pillowcase over the sill and, even more carefully, letting them out into the safety of our abode.

Once we've recovered and tell Horatius and Eyebright everything that had happened at least five times (once for each of us, then more to clarify points that had still been left out) we all collapse into the pleasure of safe routine.

You'd think that after going to all that trouble to get back in, I would feel no desire to leave the tower. Indeed, for a time, I am – if not content – at least secure. I make Muriel new dresses in a wide variety of styles. She insists that each one have at least some red in it, this now being her favorite color. Using some fresh ribbons, I re-tie Puck's various sections, not removing the previous ties, but covering them with brighter, firmer, joins. He protests that the process tickles, but I can tell that he is pleased. I draw various ornamentations on both Horatius and Eyebright, making the protectors of my tower at once stronger and yet somehow more friendly.

Yet the time comes when I grow restless again. I'd be coloring a new frock for Muriel and find my attention drifting from the tiny little flowers that I was drawing to line the elaborate yoke that frames neck and shoulders, to thoughts of the meadows in the unicorn's fairyland. I don't particularly want to hunt out the unicorn again, but I feel sure there are any number of other wonderful creatures in that place. It had been fun to flutter on a fairy's butterfly wings, but what would it be like to ride on a dragon or on a winged horse? If I still had wings of my own, I wouldn't even need to worry about falling.

I'd barely seen anything of the undersea realms. What are the merpeople like when they're at home? What had happened to the two dogs Puck and I had been back in the city? Had Bob, the antique dealer, indeed adopted them? Are they happy in his care or do they long to go back to roaming the streets?

I'd never entered the realm where we'd seen the moon rabbits. Who was that woman we'd glimpsed? She'd been so beautiful, yet mysterious and even a little sad. Maybe Puck would like to visit the Moon. Would the real moon rabbits accept him? I suspect they would. He is such a cheerful creature.

But wherever we go, we will not go as ourselves as we had during our last visit to the Gothic world. I think that even Puck has learned a little patience, but I decide to withhold from him my plans to go visit the Moon until I've had a chance to consider possible options for Muriel and my own attire. It seems to me that the lady in the Moon had belonged to an Asian tradition. She had certainly seemed Japanese in that beautiful kimono. I wasn't certain I could seem Japanese, but I could certainly wear a kimono. I could make one for Muriel, too.

That sand had seemed slippery, so perhaps taking forms with wings would be a good idea. We could have nearly invisible ones, like a dragonfly's. The idea makes me smile. Turning to a fresh page in my notebook, I start sketching Muriel's costume, knowing that doing this will help me focus on my own.

I know that this careful planning might not be necessary. Hadn't I become part of the whale just by longing to go where it was? Hadn't we become fairies without much conscious planning? This is true, absolutely true, but my helplessness in the Gothic world has made me cautious. I no longer believe that we are automatically safe when we go exploring. Indeed, I now feel certain that we are taking a considerable risk whenever we leave the tower.

When I finish it, Muriel's kimono is very pretty. I've made it pale pink with stylized cherry blossoms in darker pink around the borders and cascading over the back. Muriel insists on some red, so I carefully border the sleeve panels and hem with a ribbon of warm red, and make the obi sash to coordinate. I even draw Muriel a sort of wig, piling her brown hair up high and ornamenting the resulting bun with a red ribbon that matches the kimono's sash. The final touch is pale dragonfly wings, the veins drawn in the absolutely lightest pink pen I can find in the box.

For myself, I envision a similar garment but in pale lilac with sprays of the same flower splashed in windswept abandon over the rich fabric. I make the obi a dark purple, ornamented with lavender, this time light against the dark in a glowing negative relief. I wrap my hair up by touch, and fasten it into place with a dark purple bow from the nightstand. My wings will be transparent, veined in equal parts of misty lavender and palest green.

When I am finished, I feel certain that these gowns or robes – because I can't feel quite sure I managed to get a kimono's design just right – will go very well with the silvery whiteness of the lunar landscape.

Puck bounces up and down, letting me know that he will also need some sort of ornamentation. I agree, for I am beginning to feel as if we are making some sort of formal call. For Puck, I vacillate between blue and green, then decide upon both woven into a collar, complete with a new floppy bow in both colors. The colors are ethereal, but the collar itself is quite strong and, inside my sleeve, I tuck a matching leash. I'm not going to risk Puck bouncing off and getting himself into trouble.

When my preparations are complete, I give Horatius and Eyebright hugs, promising that we won't be gone too long and that when we come back we'll have stories aplenty. They, in turn, wish us well before returning to their current game. I'd made them a chess set and they are immersed in a tournament of some sort. Currently, Horatius is playing white, which I know makes him nervous. Because he is a guardian, he prefers to react, rather than initiate action. Eyebright knows this perfectly well and is quite enjoying himself, sighing like a steam engine whenever Horatius moves a hand toward a piece, as if anticipating the move he himself already plans to make.

Leaving them to their tournament of wits, I gather up Muriel and Puck, then head for the appropriate window. As always, the view directly out is only changeless blue sky, but when we look down we see the world that somehow touches the tower's base. The shining white sands are there as before, but there is no sign of the moon rabbits. Rather than going off blindly, I settle myself in to wait, for if there is anything I have, it is time.

However, as I stare out at the blank white landscape, I let my desire quest out from me, holding all the questions that had filled me as I had laid my plans. Who is the lady? Is she the only person on the Moon? Does she have a house or maybe a palace? What does she do other than stroll about with the rabbits? Are there other creatures on the Moon?

Slowly, as if my questions have created a need for an answer, the perspective shifts so that we are no longer looking down upon the silvery sands, but are looking across the moonscape, as one does a picture – or a TV screen. And there, as if inviting us to step forth, is a path through the shining silvery white sandscape. The path proves to be made from the pearlescent nacreous material found within seashells. It blends into the surrounding sands but, beneath the soft light, glimmers with touches of color that make it easy to follow.

We do so, passing over a series of dunes so gentle that it seems as if we walk over water, rather than land. After we have walked a ways, Puck – who had bounced ahead, although never out of sight – calls back that he can see a vast orchard. As Muriel and I hurry to join him, we catch the orchard's scent well before we see it. The odor is heady and sweet. Within a few deep breaths, I have identified it as the scent of fresh ripe peaches warmed by the sun. The trees themselves look much like their earthly counterparts, possessed of long, slightly curving leaves. The fruit seems as much to have blushed as to have ripened.

Even in a more usual landscape, we would have found this vista beautiful, but here, where all had seemed without color, the contrast is all the more vivid. From the rise, I can see that the path we follow leads through the orchard, beneath the drooping limbs where the dangling fruit offers acute temptation. I reach to brush my fingertips against the velvet surface of one particularly beautiful peach, but I don't see any future in which thievery would be a wise choice, nor any in which we could successfully hide such nefarious behavior.

Muriel agrees with me, but Puck pouts, his long ears growing limp and dragging despondently behind him as he opens his eyes to their widest and most pleading. When I don't relent and Muriel hints that perhaps the leash that resides in the sleeve of my lilac kimono might come out and be added to Puck's own attire, Puck sniffs and points his pink nose to where the lunar rabbits are busy about the same task that we have forbidden him!

I look closely and see that indeed the rabbits are picking peaches, climbing the trees with an ease that recalls monkeys, rather than the more usually ground-dwelling rabbit. After observing for some moments, I point out to Puck that these rabbits may indeed be picking peaches, but they don't seem to be eating their sweet harvest. Instead, they are carefully placing it in shallow carts. When a cart is full – a task quickly achieved, for the delicate fruit is arrayed in a single layer, doubtless so that it will not bruise – two rabbits position themselves behind the long crossbar that extends from the cart's handle and pull the cart out of sight.

Reluctantly, Puck agrees that perhaps it would be best to await an invitation. Then he hints that we should hurry directly after the peach-laden carts so that we will hopefully be invited to dine. To Puck's disgust, Muriel and I veto this suggestion as well. Instead, we continue to follow the mother-of-pearl pathway. After several twists and turns, seemingly for the convenience of the trees, the path leads us out of the peach orchard and into a series of flower gardens. These are both ornate and delicate, much as fine lace embodies those often contradictory qualities. White or silvery flowers are much in evidence, but their ethereal hues are enhanced by lavish sprays of vividly colored azaleas, old roses, and heavy-headed peonies or dahlias.

A crescent curve of the path reorients us so that now the gardens are placed into context as the trailing skirts about a palace of crystal and pearl, the whole chased with light tracings of silver and sparkling with moon dust. As a stream flows into a river, so our path spills into a grand avenue, and we become just a few of those processing toward the palace, nor, for all that I thought our appearance rather outlandish, are we the most extraordinary among the throng.

We see many creatures with the heads of animals and the bodies of humans – or at least human-like, for some possess tails and paws. Many of the guests, for guests I feel we are, are attired after the fashion of the exotic Orient, but many are not. I see a great-bellied bear bursting the seams of a Renaissance tunic and doublet; an elegant, long-faced doe in a gown that would have made a Victorian debutant proud; a golden-eyed barn owl in a slinky beaded cocktail dress right out of the most roaring moments of the Roaring Twenties.

Not all the travelers along the road of mother of pearl are theriomorphic. Many are humans and show skin tones and features from all the nations of the globe. An ebony-skinned courtier in samurai garb escorts a pale-haired damsel who proudly wears an eagle-feathered war bonnet. A man with skin the color of burnished sandalwood and hair of shining jet sports the ruffled shirt and nicely tailored trousers of a Regency dandy with a flare that Beau Brummel himself would have awarded an approving nod.

Muriel and I are not the only humans with wings, nor are wings the most exotic additions sported by the company that now processes toward the shining palace. Indeed, we blend into this exotic procession as if we are responding to an invitation upon which the dress code had been indicated by neat letters that read "Come as you are not," or perhaps, "Come as you would be."

From the whispered comments of our fellow guests, I learn that we are all going to witness a grand occasion. This is the day when the Lady of the Moon welcomes the Lord of the Sun to her palace. Events set in motion long, long ago have forced them to dwell apart, but they have never ceased to love each other. Those days when he comes to her – for the sun always shines on the moon, never the reverse – are days of wonderful, joyous celebration. Everyone is delighted to share in their pleasure.

Or rather, almost everyone, for as we chat with a fox-headed lady in a gold-tissue sarong and a tuxedo-clad Indian brave – a peculiar carriage passes by. It is as round as Cinderella's pumpkin coach, but painted an uncomfortable shade of pale green. Intricate and irregular carvings over its surface create the impression that it has been incut with numerous holes of various depths. This strange vehicle is drawn by numerous toads, haughty as the finest turnout ever boasted by some rich bravo. As it passes me, I glimpse the profile of an old man whose face, though etched with lines of jollity, is drawn into a fearsomely brooding expression.

"The Man in the Moon," the kitsune explains in her sweet, if husky, voice. "He claims to love the Lady of the Moon and says he would be a far better spouse for her than some infrequent visitor."

"She'll never have him," says a new arrival to our little group, a sleek dragon lady clad in scarlet and gold, who drapes herself over the brave's shoulder, leaving a trail of shimmering opalescent scales on the black fabric of his tux. "For all her isolation and that they see each other so infrequently, she truly loves the Sun and – more importantly, given their situation – he loves her."

As we drift along toward the palace, engaged in idle converse and gentle gossip, I wonder why the Moon's Lady would choose to entertain so many at this time. Surely if she only is able to visit with her husband infrequently, then she would prefer to have time alone with him. Then we arrive at the palace and all thought vanishes as I gape at the splendor before us. The ornamentation is incredible. No brilliant color is used, but intricate patterns that celebrate variety and texture are enough to make one forget. Part of me longs to wander from mosaic to frieze to inlaid gemstones, but another part of me is distracted by the lavish banquet that has been laid out around us.

Now we understand why the moon rabbits had been so busy down in the orchards. The air is alive with the odor of ripe peaches. The scent fills our lungs, perfumes our hair and skins. Bothering to eat any of the many elegant dishes created around the fruit, or drinking the nectar, brandy, and wine that are being offered on all sides seems redundant. We are infused with the essence of peach. Yet, perversely, for the first time since I had awakened in the rosy tower, I feel a real desire to eat, to taste.

I hesitate, afraid that I will lose the curious immunity to hunger and thirst with which I have been blessed, but surely I am safe from contamination. I have been whale, fairy, dog, and none of the yearnings felt by these creatures has stayed with me. So I accept a fluted goblet of chilled nectar and take a tentative sip. The flavor is so intense that I seem to experience it with each and every individual taste bud, yet it does not overwhelm. Instead it makes me aware of the act of tasting in a fashion I have never before known.

I am still trembling from the impact of the nectar when I become aware that Muriel is tugging at my sleeve. Puck, impatient as ever, is hopping toward one of the tables where creative canapes are spread on lace doilies set upon trays of burnished silver. It takes not even a glance to realize that he does not intend to nibble and sample as the other guests are doing, but to dive in – in the most literal sense of the word.

Thrusting my goblet of nectar into Muriel's hands and beating my wings so fast that they blur into invisibility, I take off after my errant ersatz rabbit. Luck is with me. By going over some guests, skimming low over the ground (actually, the polished alabaster tiles), and darting between other obstacles, I reach Puck as he is gathering himself to leap onto the buffet table. I had tugged the ribbon leash from my sleeve pocket as I flew, and now I loop it through Puck's collar, stopping him in mid-leap. Then I fly up, so that he dangles like a plump moon amid the starry chandeliers that illuminate the high ceilings.

I am so intent on keeping him out of everyone's hair – for the hairstyles worn by many of the women and not too few of the men rival those popular in France during the reign of a man arrogant enough to call himself the Sun King – that I don't realize that we are the cynosure of every eye – human, animal, spirit, up to and including an elegantly dressed couple who could be none other than the Sun Lord and the Lady of the Moon.

Him I recognize by the brilliance that comes from him, a brilliance deliberately damped within the flowing robes he wears, but that peeks out whenever he shifts, as light peeps around the closed blinds over a bedroom window. I hardly know the Lady of the Moon, for all that I have seen her before. Like her spouse, she glows. Although her light is silvery and pale, while his is golden and vivid, hers seems brighter to me, for I can see the contrast between the pale lady of sorrow and this gleaming creature whose fire is fed by pure joy.

Still smiling, indeed, smiling more broadly, the Lady of the Moon beckons for Puck and me to join them. I nod and begin a careful progress across the crowded room. Around us the conversation rises again, for all can tell that crisis is averted. What amazes me is that none there seem to think it would be amusing to create dissention. As I carefully fly over the party – dodging chandeliers above and groups of guests below – I hear none of the catty comments about Puck's bad behavior that I had fully expected.

Puck is quite heavy and seemingly unaware of how close he had come to creating if not a disaster, then at least a tremendous mess. He does little to help me, seeming most interested in straining downward whenever we come close to some dainty – both those resting on trays and those held between the fingers of various guests as they lift the treats to their lips. Puck might have indeed succeeded in his aerial poaching, but that Muriel comes flittering over to help me. She grabs hold of the leash and helps me lift. With both of our wings beating to naught but crystalline rainbow glimmer, we make our way to where the Sun and the Moon stand chatting with a few of the guests.

As we lower a suddenly meek Puck to the dais and then come to rest watchfully on either side of him, these guests take their leave, their expressions holding grins, not of mockery, but of genuine amusement. In this mood of friendship all of us – except possibly for Puck, who is now embarrassed as he registers the gravity of the occasion – we begin our audience.

The Moon Queen is holding hands with the Sun, but this does not hamper her movements in the least. Rather, the pair are like dancers inventing perfectly harmonious choreography with their least motion.

"Come, sit with us," the Lady says when introductions are completed. "There might even be a slice of peach pie for your impulsive friend."

The Sun grins, boyish despite his incredible glow. "Or even an entire pie! He seems to have appetite enough to do one credit."

When Muriel sniffs disapproval, the Lady laughs and pats Muriel's hand reassuringly. "Don't worry. These peaches are cullings from the orchard, not yet grown enough to be the fruit from which the elixir of immortality will be distilled. There are more than enough for all. Would you also like a slice of pie or perhaps a tart or a dish of sorbet?"

Muriel allows that a sorbet or perhaps one of the many-layered parfaits that a waiter is carrying by on a silver platter would be nice. I also accept a parfait, but only toy with it, too nervous to eat, no matter how heady the aroma.

The Moon Lady asks us a few polite questions and I do my best to answer, but I find myself distracted by half-remembered stories. Finally, I blurt out, "How did you two come to be separated? You clearly love each other very much."

A look of deep sorrow flits across the Lady's lovely face. "I suppose you could say that we are separated because, although I was amply supplied with curiosity, I found myself lacking in courage."

And she goes on to relate how once, long ago, both she and the Sun had lived on Earth. She had been the daughter of a water spirit. Her father was an evil creature who had done so much harm that a semi-divine hero – here she smiles upon her husband, so that I am certain of whom she speaks – had been sent to destroy the monster. After the battle, when the daughter had been fleeing from the ruins of her father's palace, she had been seen by the hero, who had been immediately smitten.

She had returned his feelings, and they had been wed. They had lived happily for many years. Then, in reward for yet another great deed, the hero had been awarded a pill that would grant him immortality. Uncertain what he wished to do with it – for immortality is more than simply living forever – he had hidden it away.

"But I could tell he had a secret," the Moon Lady says, "and I snooped. When I saw light glimmering from where there should have been no light, I guessed that the source was what my husband had hidden away. I took it out, only meaning to look at it, but then he returned unexpectedly. In a panic – for I did not want him to know that I preferred snooping to asking him to tell me what had him so distracted – my only thought was to hide the pill. On impulse, I swallowed it.

"Perhaps because of my already non-human nature, perhaps because of some capricious spirit's action, I suddenly grew lighter. I could no longer stay on Earth, but rose higher and higher until at last I came to rest upon the Moon. There I could finally cease to rise and so, perforce, I made my home there."

She smiles, raising slender shoulders in a very human shrug. "So curiosity seduced me, but cowardice condemned me. My dear husband didn't blame me – he wasn't even angry. We might have tried to live on the Moon together, but the Moon already had residents. The rabbits would have welcomed him, but the Old Man in the Moon is a jealous sort. He knew that dear Yu would quickly outshine him and so forbad him to live here. Since the Old Man had prior claim, there was no gainsaying him.

"In time, as yet another reward for his heroism, my dear husband was given rulership of the Sun. Since the Moon is under the administration of the Sun, Yu could now visit me, no matter how much the Old Man in the Moon might complain. So Yu comes to me but, since these are considered visits of state, we must also hold court."

Muriel had been listening wide-eyed, not even noticing that Puck had stolen her half-eaten parfait. "Do you mind too horribly?"

The Queen of the Moon shakes her head. "We have actually come to enjoy these events. They are the appetizers before the banquet and, as many a good cook knows, a little bitterness can emphasize the sweet."

I nod. Hadn't I appreciated the tower more when I had feared it would be lost to me? Didn't I, even now, appreciate my inability to feel either hunger or thirst now that I was being tempted by those nearly forgotten impulses? Deliberately, I set the parfait aside, wondering whether this is cowardice or prudence. I don't know, but I'm not ready to find out. Puck had been wallowing chest-deep in his promised pie. Now he is finishing my parfait as he had Muriel's. Surely he is indulging enough for both of us.

When Muriel asks the Moon Lady if she ever feels afraid of the Old Man in the Moon, the Lady laughs. "He, too, is under the rulership of the Sun. He may have opinions that differ from ours, but he can't forbid Yu to live here, based on his seniority within the established hierarchy, and then violate the rights of the Sun - not without consequences, and there are always consequences."

I feel that the time has come to permit the Sun and Moon to visit with others of their court, and so we begin to make our excuses. Under the guise of helping me gather up Puck (who is certain that there will be more pie if he just searches hard enough), the Lady kneels next to me and whispers softly: "Although your tower is ever beneath the blue sky of day, your ventures are not unknown to me. Feel free to visit again – even to bring your voracious friend."

I stammer thanks, then we give our place on the royal dais to others who have been waiting. We rejoin the party for a while. Then, worn out from the chatter, Muriel and I escape to the gardens. We need to drag Puck away from the buffet, but soon he is romping with some of the real moon rabbits, vying in a contest to prove who can bounce highest.

Even as I revel in the beauty of the gardens and discuss with Muriel how we might adapt this vine or that flower into a new ornament for her, I feel a curious melancholy stealing over me. I tell myself that this is born from sympathy for the Lady, who must eternally pay in the coin of loneliness for one moment of impulse but, even as I justify my feelings to myself in this fashion, I suspect that the root of my sorrow comes from elsewhere. Where that might be, I don't know, nor do I care to examine my feelings more deeply.

After our return to the tower and some time spent amusing Horatius and Eyebright with tales of our adventures, I suggest to Muriel that a trip beneath the waves might be enjoyable. Our previous venture had been purest chance, and we – or I, for I am not certain how much Muriel had experienced of that journey – had been caught within the perspective of the whale.

I long to know more about the merfolk. Surely, they could not be as cruel as the whale had seen them. Yet, what if they are? What if they come after us as had the creepy cherubs in the land of Goth and Gargoyle? Should we represent ourselves as mermaids? Might we be safer as mere observers? From our venture into the cityscape, I know we can choose to be watchers only, but that passivity seems all wrong now, not nearly as fulfilling as being part of the story.

Eventually, we decide to accept the most daring option and go as mermaids. We take great care in designing our costumes and, for added safety, let Puck come along as an enormous spiny sea urchin, large enough that we could take refuge within his mouth if the need arises.

Whether we had been unduly worried or whether the merfolk are impressed to good manners by Puck's size and apparent ferocity – for he does bounce and show off his prickles – we are well-met and given every kindness. We take part in a race, riding on the backs of hippocampi. (Mine is pearlescent teal, Muriel's a vibrant pink.) We frolic in the spouts of undersea geysers, and go tobogganing on the backs of penguins. Puck so wants to partake in this last that we transform him into a fat white penguin – an act that gains us the reputation of being powerful sorceresses.

This then leads to an appeal that we help rescue some of their small fry who have been captured by a terrible kraken who is devouring them as particularly choice appetizers. We are successful in our quest, although only just. The gala held to celebrate the return of the adorable little merbabies is of boundless beauty, held beneath a dome of coral encrusted with phosphorescent pearls and decorated with drifting sea nettles whose sting has no ability to cause pain, but instead tickles delightfully.

The undersea trip is such a success that I suggest we return to the fairy realms. This time I don't want to seek the unicorn. Indeed, although I don't confide this to Muriel, I more wish to avoid it. I still feel I would not care for whatever it had tried to relate to me. Instead, I suggest that a place that hosts unicorns and fairies with butterfly wings must have flying horses as well. I've always thought that these were among the most lovely of magical creatures. To see them up close – to perhaps take part in their aerial dance – would be wonderful.

We venture into the fairy realm as we had before, Muriel and I as fairies, Puck as a woodland rabbit. This time, Puck insists on wings of his own and, with some trepidation, we give in. We streamline his form into something less rotund, but we might as well not have bothered. Puck immediately takes advantage of his new wings to fly to the top of a cherry tree. There he eats himself pink – and round. But we don't mind. At least this slows him down.

While Puck gorges, Muriel and I scout for signs of winged horses. In a remarkably short time, we sight some flitting over and among distant mountains capped in what looks more like sorbet than snow. Indeed, when we fly closer (towing a mildly protesting Puck between us) we realize we've found a land where the trees have candy stick trunks, candy floss foliage, and are fruited with hard candies. The flowers look as if they are cut from fondant – but they turn out to have petals of a living sugar that looks like fondant, but is neither heavy nor cloying. The rivers sparkle with an effervescent liquid like soda pop, but which proves to be neither sticky nor tacky. You could even swim in it – as we discover when Puck "falls" in, and comes out fluffy as ever, though smelling of ginger and oranges.

In this landscape, the winged horses could have been insufferably cute, but they are instead noble and elegant. To say they are sweet-tempered would be unfair. The landscape might be sugar, but they are spice – fierce and wild, filled with power and grace.

The manner in which Muriel and I fly is a fluttery sort, as befits our wings, but these winged horses can soar and dive like eagles, yet twist and hover like hummingbirds. When, after we'd exchanged increasingly hyperbolic compliments, milk and dark chocolate twins deign most regally to give the two of us rides (Puck is offered a steed, but he chooses instead to eat candy carrots that taste like citrus and candy peas sharp with spearmint) I realize that our fairy wings may be charming, but that flying with them is as much like the flight of the winged horses as paddling in a plastic wading pool is like swimming with the merfolk.

We enjoy ourselves so much that the next time we visit, we decide to return as winged horses ourselves. My coat is cinnamon with wing feathers, mane, and tail of amber honey. Muriel chooses a coat of scarlet with wings the orange and yellow of flame, a vivid contrast to her mane and tail which are a brilliant blue-white.

Puck likes the idea of fast and dangerous flight even more than he does that of eating himself sick. He selects peppermint swirls for coat and wings *and* mane and tail, a combination that is dizzying even before he starts flying in tornado spirals that grow tighter and tighter with each twist and turn.

Another time, we return to the Gothic realm, this time as gargoyles ourselves. On that journey, we go to cobwebby manses wherein we learn something of the secrets that underlie the ancient rivalry between the angels and gargoyles. A crumbling ancient, who claims to have been born upon Notre Dame itself, tells us haunting tales that touch upon deep complexities and mythic lore.

On another occasion, we go back to the city. Checking in at the antiques store, we are pleased to see that the two dogs who had helped us foil the robbery are comfortably situated into their new lives as resident guard dogs. Bob, the old shop owner, has further expressed his gratitude for their fortuitous intervention by becoming part of an animal rescue association.

From a poster on the wall of his shop, we learn that a big fundraising concert is being held that very night. Of course, we decide to attend. While snooping backstage before the concert, we learn that the entire fundraiser is threatened because the star – a major pop idol – has caught the flu and is too ill to perform.

I have the brilliant idea of transforming myself into her double – a small-time but extremely talented performer who has been doing covers of the idol's act. Muriel and Puck are, of course, my band. Muriel shows an unexpected talent for playing the drums, while Puck rocks out, trading licks with the lead guitarist of the idol's own band.

Later, back in the rosy tower, we play an impromptu encore for Horatius and Eyebright. It's great. So are a bunch of other adventures we have, travelling out through various windows in a wide variety of forms.

But, of the six window realms we know – for we still have not yet investigated the seventh – there is one in which neither Muriel nor Puck have any interest. That is the one in which I had seen the two girls in the kitchen, washing dishes and sweeping the floor.

Although I'm not ready to look out the seventh window – I guess I don't want to close off all the potentials – what Puck and Muriel see only as dull domesticity holds for me some of the charm of "playing house." Watching the comings and goings of the daily routine can hold my attention for hours.

I never try to insert myself into the action, just watch the daily dramas unfold. Someone forgetting their math book. The last-minute preparation of three dozen cupcakes for a class birthday party. The anguish over a failed test. The day the dog eats the African violets.

I gather that the two sisters are not related by blood, but are part of a blended family that consists of the son and daughter of the father and the daughter of the mother. There is a baby, too, a little boy at the age of staggering about making unintelligible comments and breaking things, mostly by grabbing hold and trying to pull himself up.

This tendency to break things (or spill things or tear things) causes a lot of drama, especially since the three half-siblings can remember perfectly well how much easier life had been without a baby around. In addition to the two parents and the four children, there is a great mop-like shepherd dog, an elderly grey cat, and a calico kitten.

Don't ask me why, but I find their various adventures – report cards, occasional visits from friends, birthday parties, and small intrigues – completely fascinating.

After a while, I realize that there is an undercurrent to the family dynamic that I can't quite figure out. Something that has upset everyone except the baby (whose name is Matthew or Matt, but is most often called "Rug," which is either a pun on "mat" or short for "rug rat" or maybe both).

Since whatever this upset may be is one of those things that everyone knows but no one will talk about, I can't figure it out. After a while, the mystery starts driving me crazy. I think about inserting myself into the household somehow – maybe as a kindly housekeeper or the kid next door – but I have this weird feeling that this won't work. This window realm is too solidly grounded in a here and now logic for the family to suddenly accept a housekeeper they didn't have the day before. And I notice that while the kids definitely have friends, they don't have buddies.

At first, I think that this is because they are still working on the whole blended family thing, as well as adjusting to a new house. (They'd moved into this one shortly before the Rug was born because they'd needed more room.) However, that doesn't fit either.

Up to this point, I've kept my watching – you could call it "snooping" (at least Muriel does) – to the public areas of the house: the kitchen; the dining area, which adjoins the family room and which is where most of the interactions occur; the back yard, and the garage, which doubles as a workshop.

I've stayed out of the bedrooms and bathrooms. Each of the kids has his or her own room, and I gather that finding a house with so many rooms had been a serious strain on the family budget. That's why, when I make my first tentative venture into the bedroom areas of the house, I'm surprised to find one room with the door firmly shut. A little sign on it says, "Jessie's Room." Under this, written in blue marker on orange construction paper are the additional words: "Seriously! This Means You! Yes. You!"

I stare blankly at the words, wondering who this Jessie is. That isn't the name of either of the girls. They are… Well, I'll remember their names the next time I see them. The boy is Adam? Alan? Arnold? The Rug is Matthew or Matt. At least I'm sure of that. Mom is Mom. Dad is Dad.

As I struggle to place Jessie, I feel seriously creeped out, worse than I'd felt when we'd been chased by those baby-heads with wings. Worse than when we'd met the Swamp Slime Monster. Worse than when the alligators in the sewers had come up and tried to eat everyone on the subway platform. In fact, I'm so creeped out that I'm not even tempted to ease through the door, even though the sign couldn't have been meant for me.

I'm glad when Puck – who'd been playing ball (with himself as ball) with Horatius and Eyebright – crashes into me, breaking my concentration and bringing me back to reality. To celebrate my relief – or maybe to distract myself from thinking about why I can't remember the names of any of the people who live in the play house – I set myself to work drawing an entire deck of cards for Horatius and Eyebright to use when Puck, Muriel, and I go out. I reassure Puck that he can play with the cards too, as long as he plays properly, not Fifty-Two Pick-up or any of those wild games that would risk the cards being torn up.

Do you have any idea how long it takes to draw fifty-two cards? Face cards aren't bad, but the numbers!! I start with hearts and, after I've drawn ten carefully spaced hearts on the final number card, I'm nearly ready to scream. Sighing, I consider what suit to do next. Spades are sort of like upside-down hearts, except that you need to draw a stem, too. Clubs are all lumpy. As for Diamonds! Getting all four lines just right so that the image looks like a diamond, not like a kite!!!

As I am considering, Puck comes bounding through and I get a great idea. Tucking him under one arm, I carefully unscrew one of the pens, then drip ink on his right front paw. Getting the impression right takes a little experimenting – especially since Puck insists that it tickles – but before long we have a suit of bunny-paw cards. These are in a vivid violet, not black, but I think they're a lot more fun than clubs. What should I substitute for diamonds and spades?

Tentatively, Muriel offers one of her tiny shoes. I'd already used red – her favorite color – for the hearts, so I suggest sunburst orange. Muriel likes that and sets to work printing the newly-created suit of Shoe Prints. Meanwhile, I draw the face cards for both Shoes and Rabbits. I give the Rabbit royal family bunny noses, round eyes, whiskers, and long ears. The King and Jack wear their ears up and perky, but for the Queen I draw them lop-ear style, trailing out from under her crown.

On Muriel's suggestion, I model the royal family of the Shoe suit after birds. The King is a robin, the queen a wren, and the Jack a bright-feathered cardinal. We're all seriously jazzed now, and have a cheerful discussion as to what the fourth suit should be. In the end, I decide on a five-pointed star. These are pretty easy to draw and, by now, I'm not nearly as worried about symmetry.

We select a super vivid green for the stars and arrange the numbers five through ten in fanciful constellations. After that, figuring out the face cards is easy. The King is the Sun, smiling and regal. The Queen is our beloved Moon Lady, and the Jack is the Old Man in the Moon. I draw him smiling, though, not scowling and sour. After all, who wants to be unhappy?

The cards prove to be a terrific hit. I teach everyone Old Maid, Go Fish, and Rummy. Because there might be times when only one person would want to play, I also teach them a variety of forms of solitaire, including a really intricate one that involves a pyramid of cards.

This last gets us talking about Egypt and how cool it would be to go exploring there, back in the olden days, when there was still magic. What I mean is that we all agreed that there had to have been magic there once. It's obvious from their art and amulets and everything. Even the Bible backs this up, what with Joseph's prophetic dreams and Aaron's rod blooming and stuff like that.

The more we talk about it, the more it seems as if there must have been a time when magic was a lot more common than it is nowadays, because it's mentioned so often in older stories. Even if you leave out miracles, like those Jesus did, because he was the son of God and so had an advantage, there is just too much evidence to ignore. This whole conversation starts making me feel weird, like I'd had it before and at a time when it made more sense than it did in my current situation.

After all, if I look at the situation logically, clearly there is magic and to spare, not just out the windows, but here in the rosy tower where I sit on a plush carpet teaching card games to a giant, a dragon, a moon rabbit, and an extraordinarily versatile little girl. I admit, I'm relieved when Muriel and Puck start arguing about just which window we should try if we want to find olden days Egypt.

The city might be a good bet. Muriel feels certain a museum would have some artifact or talisman we could use. Maybe we could even enter a reconstructed temple or tomb, then imagine ourselves back to when it was fresh and new. Puck is all for trying the seventh window. After all, we haven't yet, but it might go to Egypt and didn't we want to check? I'm against that for the same reason I've resisted all along. I hate the idea of having no new windows to explore. I'm also not sure about Muriel's idea. Museums are super cool, no doubt of that, but did we have any indication that we could use them for time travel?

Then Eyebright suggests that maybe the Gothic realm would have a connection to Egypt. Instantly, we all agree that he's probably right. There's something in that mishmash of buildings that seems perfect. To make even more certain, rather than just roaming around looking, we'll start by consulting the gargoyles.

Following some heated discussion as to options, we decide we'll go as sphinxes. They're sort of like gargoyles, by which I mean they mix up animal and human in ways that just don't happen. They also have been made into statues. A lot. I try to think if I've ever seen a painting or read a story of either that isn't based on that whole statue thing. I can't. Well, except for the bit with Oedipus and the riddle, and for all I know that could have been based on that statue. Sphinxes aren't like the Pegasus or the unicorn that started with stories and went from there into art. They're statues that became stories, because people had to make up more about them. I like that.

When we start planning and designing, Muriel reminds me that there are lots of different types of sphinxes: ones with ram's heads and ones with hawk's heads, and ones like women, as well as the one everyone knows about, who was supposed to be modeled after a particular pharaoh. Puck immediately decides he wants to be a ram-headed sphinx, which is just right for him, because he's always butting heads with things. Muriel and I both opt for a variation on the human one, but decide we'd like to be girls. We also decide we want wings, because those have proven really useful.

We pretty much drive Puck to bouncing off the walls as we work out the details, including how we could work some Egyptian jewelry into our newest selves. Once we're all sphinxed-out, we take off for the Gothic realm. I do check, both by flying back to our exit window and by unthinking myself, that we can get back to the rosy tower. I do not, absolutely *not*, want a repeat of our first visit. Sure, we'd ventured out since, but I always check. If I ever slept, I'd probably have nightmares about that time we nearly didn't make it back.

Our first stop is the fountain near the plaza, because that's always a good place to find gargoyles. The cathedral is contested ground, but the angels rarely come this direction unless they're chasing someone. Bubbles, the gargoyle who more or less lives in the fountain, is pleased to see us. She doesn't know much about how we might find a way to Egypt, though. She suggests we talk with Razorwing, a very warlike gargoyle who knows a lot about pyramids.

We've already met Razorwing. In fact, he'd been among the gargoyles who'd covered our escape during our first visit. We knew he was likely cruising near the cathedral, looking for a fight. Trusting in our new forms to offer us some protection, we pad off in the direction of the sharp-pointed spires. I glimpse some of the creepy cherubs, but they either don't see us or they don't register us as either their hated rivals, the gargoyles, or as potential playthings.

We don't find Razorwing right off, but we do find Drizzlespitler, a frog-faced, snail-horned, would-be mighty warrior. He directs us to where Razorwing lurks in convincingly stony stillness among a cluster of purely ornamental statues in the cathedral's graveyard. Razorwing isn't much of a talker, but his big bat ears stretch wide as he listens to our request. Turns out, he knows of a very nice pyramid, sleeps there from time to time, when he needs to sharpen the edges of his wings.

The pyramid belongs to… Well, honestly, I can't quite make out who or what, but Razorwing seems confident that if anyone knows how we could get to an older Egypt, it would be this fellow – or maybe his mother. Gargoyles are great people, rock solid, salt of the earth, and all that, but they have a completely weird way of seeing things, and they do tend to mutter.

Seems that Razorwing has been getting bored – the angels haven't recovered from the last battle, or so he brags, and the battlefield is slow these days. After he admires our new shapes, he tussles with Puck as we follow him to the pyramid. He flies just fast enough that Puck – head bent so he can keep his curling ram's horns ready to butt – chases after, certain he can catch up and launch Razorwing into the upper clouds. Razorwing stays just out of reach so, by the time we reach our destination, I feel certain that the extremely exhausted Puck won't be going anywhere fast.

The pyramid that is our destination is no great pyramid in size, but it is very impressive nonetheless. Unlike the ones I've seen in pictures, this pyramid is built from blocks of malachite, the green stone varying from nearly black to a pure leaf-green, and many shades in between. Razorwing indicates a dark-shadowed rectangular portal set on the east-facing side. This entry is flanked by a tidy colonnade of columns capped with carved lotus flowers. The colonnade stretches between the pyramid and a long pool that reflects part of the pyramid to the sky.

Muriel and I exchange nervous glances, then pad on our lion paws down the avenue between the columns. We stop a few paces from the shadowed door. It is open and, indeed, does not seem to be created to be closed. I'd expected the interior to smell dusty or musky, but instead the powerful odor of various gums, resins, spices, and herbs eddies forth. Sniffing, Muriel gives a politely catlike sneeze and rubs the back of her nose with one paw. I manage to keep from sneezing, but it isn't easy.

Since there isn't a door, we can't knock but, equally, it seems impolite to simply barge in. Clearing my throat, I call softly, "Hello? We're friends of Razorwing. He thought you might be able to tell us how to get to Egypt. We'd like to see it as it was in days of old, when magic still worked."

For a long moment, there is no reply, not even a sound to indicate that someone is moving within. Then, as Muriel is glancing back over one shoulder, clearly considering asking Razorwing if he can help, there is a loud thump that would have startled us out of our shoes if we'd been wearing any. Then the odor of spices, gums, and resins grows even stronger – if that could be possible. This time I do sneeze and so does Muriel, so we're both scrubbing at our noses when a pale figure appears in the rectangular doorway. She moves in small hops that remind me a little of Puck, but that is where any resemblance ends.

I freeze in surprise, otherwise I might have run away in pure reaction. The pyramid's doorkeeper – and resident, as we learn a moment later – is a living mummy. I'd read stories in which the resurrected god Osiris is described as such, but I'd never thought how very strange it would be to meet one. My panic fades as quickly as it had flashed into being, for this is no monster from a creaky horror film, nor does it resemble a modern CGI animation. This is a mummy in all her burial glory, complete with gilded and gem-encrusted mask, numerous talismans and amulets swinging free. Her linen bandages are painted to resemble the clothing she might have worn when she was still alive.

When she speaks, I see I had been mistaken. She does not wear a mask – or if she does, it's nearly as mobile as a natural face would be. Still, whether gilded and enameled face or mobile mask does not really matter. The effect is weird and unsettling.

"You are friends of Razorwing?" comes a sweet voice, touched with the notes of an exotic accent. "Welcome, then. I can sense your purpose. You wish to travel to Heka Egypt – the Egypt of ancient magic? I may be able to help you, but only if you can find the doorway yourselves."

"Is it here, ma'am?" Muriel asks, gesturing to indicate the pyramid and surrounding gardens with one paw.

"It is." The golden lips curve in an enigmatic smile. "You may search freely. No door is locked against you. I will even give you a small clue to guide you in your search. You will know the location of the portal you desire because it will be concealed within the most valuable thing displayed in either this pyramid or the associated grounds."

Muriel and I trade flashing smiles. Surely that clue will make our search easy. We stretch our leonine bodies in a long bow to the golden lady, then pounce off on our search.

The interior of the pyramid owes more to the fancies of modern architecture than to the actual pyramids of ancient Egypt. Those had been nearly solid stone – or at least masonry – into which tunnels led (or failed to lead, in the case of routes meant to confuse thieves) to burial and treasure chambers – or to dead-ends meant to frustrate and entrap. This pyramid's interior is structured around a vast multi-storied atrium.

"It's like a hotel," I say to Muriel.

She nods, adding, "A whole lot more elaborately decorated, though."

She's right. Even the ground floor contains enough gilded statuary, be-gemmed vases, intricately carved and painted screens, and furniture rich with gold leaf to make the combined collections of the British Museum and the Metropolitan Museum in New York seem to contain little more than a few tawdry baubles. Each floor contains more and greater variety, for most of the rooms prove to be temples to the various gods and goddesses worshipped throughout Egypt's many millennia of recorded history.

We start our search with enthusiasm, certain we'll recognize the portal as soon as we see it. After searching the ground floor and at least glancing into all the rooms on the next two floors, we're no longer so sure. We sink down beside a statue of some god or pharaoh – the separation is not at all distinct – and trade sighs. My head swirls with all the beautiful things we have seen. My eyes are weary from the flash of gold, silver, and electrum polished mirror bright – not to mention copper, brass, and bronze, as well as gemstones with improbable flash. There is the more muted richness of faience, alabaster, and carved wood, this last oiled so that it holds a sheen like the coat of a prize racehorse.

"Most valuable," Muriel says, not for the first time. "*Most* valuable."

I consider the words and find myself remembering a rotund snowman singing about the worth of silver and gold, while a confused squirrel rubs his mouth – having nearly broken his impressive incisors on a walnut-sized metal nugget. I tell Muriel about the scene, singing a few lines for emphasis.

"You think we may be going about this all wrong?" she asks excitedly. "You could be right. What else could be considered 'most' valuable? How about knowledge? There are a lot of written texts here. But, no, that can't be it. Golden Lady said we'd know it – or at least she implied that we would be looking for something that we would recognize. That wouldn't apply to texts we can't read."

I use one hind foot to scratch between my shoulder blades. The lion form of a sphinx's lower body is certainly more useful than a human's for things like this, although, when it comes to opening doors, I'd take hands over dexterous paws any day. I chew my lower lip, trying to think of other options. If material wealth is not indicated, nor knowledge, then what?

The Egyptians had valued ma'at – a sort of spiritual state wherein the individual is in harmony with others, with nature, with society. Ma'at is a complicated ideal but maybe, just maybe, we'd find our portal within the temple to Ma'at, the goddess who had personified that ideal. She'd been depicted as a goddess with wings along her arms and a feather balanced improbably straight on the top of her head.

I suggest this to Muriel and she's game, so we set out on our quest once more. I'll admit, as we walk along the corridors, looking for the right temple, I entertain a hope that the mummy lady will come hopping up to congratulate us on our brilliant insight, then offer us a shortcut to success. No such thing happens and, indeed, it's probably a good thing that I don't seem to get tired or hungry or thirsty, because checking room after room, even if it's just to say, "Nope. This one has to be for Anubis," or "Here's Ra! Wow! He has most of this side of the corridor all to himself!" or whatever, the search takes a long time.

Muriel is limping slightly when we finally locate Ma'at's temple on the topmost floor. It's a wonderful temple, but we don't find the hoped-for portal there. I'm wishing that I did get tired or hungry or thirsty – anything that would give me an excuse to take a break. We pause next to a huge window on the pyramid's front – probably the same one Razorwing uses for his comings and goings, if the scrapes on the floor are any indication.

I look out. Puck is rolling lazily back and forth on the grass, playing some game with a flower stem and his toes. Razorwing is nowhere to be seen. He's probably gone back to hunting angels or whatever. Other than Puck and a few birds, the only thing moving in the tranquil garden is the water flowing from the fountain that feeds the reflecting pool. The water trickles slowly from the mouth of an urn held by an elegant, if barely clad, female figure, a goddess, I guess, although she could have been a dancing girl for all I know.

The flow barely distorts the tranquil waters of the pool, the ripples fading a few feet out, so that the pool gives back the pillars, the pyramid, and the sky as would the most perfectly polished mirror. And, staring down into that pool, I suddenly have the answer. I understand what is the most valuable thing of all. I pull Muriel to her paws by the scruff of her neck, then whisper the answer to her. She breathes, "Of course!" and together we fly – quite literally, for when we come to stand before the mummy lady, I don't remember finding or using stairs.

"It's water!" I say, motioning toward the tranquil pool. "That's the most valuable thing. I'm sure of it."

"And you are quite right to be so sure," comes the dulcet reply, the words laced with a hint of laughter, "for water is life, as all desert people are constantly reminded, and what could be more important than life?"

I feel funny when she says this, like the words are saying more than what's obvious, but I bury the feeling under my pleasure and relief.

"Then the gateway is there?" I ask, indicating the pool with a twitch of my ears.

"It is," she replies with a graceful gesture of one slender (if bandaged) hand, "and if you wish, I will send you through it to Heka Egypt."

"And let us come back again," Muriel checks, doubtless remembering, as I do, being shut out.

"And back again," the lady promises.

Confident that she is being honest, we gather up Puck and go over to the edge of the reflecting pool. I keep expecting the lady to tell us to dive in or something. I lean so that I can look more closely, trying to discover where the portal will appear. Would it be something already there? A crevice between one edge and another? Or perhaps a whirlpool, its concentric swirls sucking us in and carrying us as Dorothy had been carried by a tornado into Oz.

Yet none of these options occur. I am about to turn and ask the lady when we are going to get started when I realize that there is something peculiar about the image in the reflecting pool. It is *not* a precise reflection of the scene behind us. Surely there had not been goats grazing in the distance? Nor had there been vultures circling in the cloudless sky. For that matter, how can we see so far in a reflection? And if we can see that far, then where are the towers and spires of the Gothic city?

Are we then meant to enter the reflection, much as we entered the images seen from the tower windows? How can we do this without breaking up the reflection we need? I am considering possible options when I hear the bleating of goats interspersed with the flat, metallic clang of a small bell, such as a goatherd might put around the neck of a particularly adventurous charge. I spin about, stumbling over my own legs, for I have completely forgotten that I am in the guise of sphinx.

When I regain my balance, I see that we are no longer in the Gothic city. The only structure that remains from our previous location is the pyramid, and even that is subtly changed. The door through which Muriel and I had entered is gone, as is the high window through which we had gazed out. This is a proper pyramid, set in the midst of a vast mortuary complex. Shaven-headed priests quietly make their way about mysterious rituals. A few glance our way, but do not seem alarmed.

This reaction – or lack of reaction – would not have surprised me in the Gothic realm, for there the odder the shape, the more usual it seems, but I do wonder at this. Then I realize that not all the inhabitants of this mortuary complex are human. Over to one side, a slender priestess moves with cat-like grace because it is her birthright. She is more than cat-headed. Her body is lightly furred and a tail peeks from beneath her robes. Sand-colored cats with eyes of sun gold or peridot green parade with her, although I sense that the solemn progress of their stately procession might degenerate into a romp at any moment.

Above, a winged man circles down in wide arcs, accompanied by a flight of hawks. Down a long avenue lighted with pillars, I see a group of jackal-headed men carrying a bier on their broad shoulders, their muscular – and completely human – legs moving in perfect step, the ripple of corded calves and thighs barely concealed by their short, many-pleated kilts.

And this is the least of the spectacle. There is so much that even Puck quells his usual impulsive desire to bounce off and explore. Truly the gilded lady has kept her promise and we are in an Egypt where magic works and where magical creatures abound – or do I mean abide?

If I had possessed hands at that moment, I would have rubbed them vigorously over my eyes in an effort to assure myself that I am not hallucinating. As it is, I settle for shaking my head violently. I hear the jingling of the many rings I wear in my oversized, more feline than human ears, and the flap of the linen folds of my headdress. The unlikely scene remains and I smile.

We might have stood longer watching the scene, but a voice addresses us from the waters of the reflecting pool.

"Sssoo," it says in a long hiss that contains a chuckle beneath the sibilance. "You are impressssed? You ssshould be sso, for thisss iss a playssse of wonder. It iss the playssse firssst built by the Missstresss of Magic, Ississs herssself. It iss where sshe resssurrected her sspousse, Ossirisss."

I gasped (I almost feel I should have "gassssped" after all the sibilance in the speaker's words, but I don't.) I look into the pool and find that we are being addressed by a very large crocodile. As it pulls its massive armored body from the water, I see it wears bracelets on its forelegs, as well as earrings of cut crystal that sparkle like dewdrops. Earrings seem odd on a creature that doesn't really have ears, but I can't doubt the evidence of my eyes.

"Are you here for the contessst?" the crocodile asks. "Ssso am I, though I haven't desssided if I will compete or merely watch."

"Us either," I reply, fighting not to hiss out the "s" in "us." The crocodile's speech patterns are more than a little addictive.

Muriel clears her throat. "We aren't sure about joining in because we haven't figured out exactly what the rules are." I'm impressed with how she manages to phrase things so that it sounds as if we know far more than we do. "Would you mind telling us?"

The crocodile thumps his tail and I fear he thinks Muriel's question is peculiar. Then I realize that this is his equivalent of a nod, a gesture that would be hard to manage for a creature built so close to the ground.

"Sssertainly," he says. "There'sss been sso much gosssip that it'sss not ssurprissing that you don't know which ssstory iss true."

He – I realize I have no idea if the crocodile is male or female – but he is definitely not an "it," eases himself into a sunny patch of sand and wriggles until he is comfortable. Watching his gaze rest with deceptive sleepiness on a little bird that is hopping close by, rooting in a tuft of grass for seeds, I feel relieved that Puck wears his ram sphinx guise, rather than his usual appetizingly plump form. The crocodile seems pleasant enough, but asking it to give no attention to Puck's usual round, fat exuberance would have been too much to ask.

Muriel and I rest comfortably in the sand, she so upright and proud that she might have been mistaken for the sister or the original Great Sphinx, me a bit more relaxed, a lioness anticipating a hunt, idly watching the herds of wildebeest and zebra graze, unaware that to me they are naught but lunch on the hoof.

"The contessst," the crocodile begins, "iss after the fasshion of a treasssure hunt or perhapsss a ssscavenger hunt. Do you recall how after Osssiriss was murdered by hisss brother god Ssset, Ississss located hisss body but, before ssshe could bring it to life again, Ssset located the corpssse and cut it into fourteen piesssesss which he then flung into the Nile?"

"Yesss," I reply, only realizing that I am imitating that seductive hiss when Muriel glares at me and Puck snorts out a laugh. Happily, the crocodile does not appear to notice or, if he does, he takes the sibilance as a compliment. I hasten to continue. "Yes. Isis sought the parts of Osiris's dismembered body and found all of them except his, uh, male part."

"Hisss phallusss," the crocodile agrees, drawing out the "s" sounds in satisfaction. "That wasss eaten by a fisssh – an oxyrhyncusssss. I hear it was delisssiousss. The ssscavenger hunt isss a recreation of her sssearch. Thirteen portionsss to be found and a bonusss for finding the fisssh with the phallusss. Of coursse, it won't be asss easssy as that. Ssset claimsss a right to opposssse the finding of the portionsss. That ssshould add consssiderable ssspice – and danger – to the competition."

Puck bounces, butting his head at the air, clearly ready to start as soon as I give the word. Muriel is more cautious.

"From what you have said, this is a new competition – indeed, I don't remember anything like it before. Why is it being held?"

The crocodile can't help but seem to be smiling, so I'm probably imagining that his smile grows rather sly. "Ississs iss called the Missstresss of Magic. Yet magic is losssing itsss hold on the ssspiritsss of the human world. Jusst as Ssset'ss murder of hisss brother, Ossiriss, wasss meant to change the paradigm of the world, ssso thisss contesst iss meant to dessside which paradigm will dominate the mindsss of thosse great dreamersss, the humansss."

"So," I say, winning my struggle not to hiss, although just barely, "is it something like science against magic?"

"Nothing ssso sssimple," the crocodile chides. "Sssciensse requiresss imagination. The greatesst discoveriesss come from making the imposssible posssible – if thisss iss not magic, what elssse isss it?"

"Then," Muriel says, her tone excited, "what is being challenged is the ability to dream big and to make dreams come true."

"That'sss about it," the crocodile agrees. "How each and every persson ussses the ability is up to that persson. Red-haired Ssset isss the desssert's drynessss, the focusss of fear of heat, of the beating ssssunlight. Ssset demandsss practicality to the point of sstagnation, ssurvival mosst ssertainly, but ssstability and sssecurity firsst. All very good thingsss and bessst achieved without the foolisssh disstractionsss of dreaming about thingssss that, in most casssesss, will lead only to disssapointment. Ssset doesss have a good cassse to make. Progresss doesss not end under hisss domination. Indeed, it may happen with more sssertainty when pursssued one sssstep at a time, absssolutely ssstable."

I think about this, enjoying the caress of sunlight on my flanks, the certainty of… of what? Surely, if stability is what I value, I would never have left the rosy tower and its soft comforts. I might never have gotten out of that comfortable bed or, at the very least, after leaving it and making my first explorations, I would have climbed back in and enjoyed the enfolding warmth, the calm surroundings, the peace of near silence, the brilliant blue of the sky, the unwavering light through the windows.

But I had left the bed and, although many times I'd been scared and confused, I had enjoyed myself, too. If I hadn't ventured out, I never would have met Muriel or Puck, Horatius and Eyebright, not to mention everyone in the wonderful (if often weird and frightening) realms through the windows.

"What happens if no one enters the contest?" I ask, for it occurs to me that with Set and his minons as adversaries, many who might enjoy a scavenger hunt would instead choose inaction.

"Then Ssset winsss by default," the crocodile replies, "for he advocatesss the cautiousss approach."

"Is there a prize for winning?" Muriel askes shyly. "I mean, besides helping to define the universal paradigm?"

The crocodile shrugs, something I would have though impossible given his lack of shoulders. "I sssusssspect ssso, sssince Isssiss isss generousss, but the sssort of prizesss that godsss and goddesssesss grant are often the ssssort that mortalsss later wisssh they had not been given."

"Still," I say with such firmness that I'm not even tempted to hiss. " I want to play. Muriel? Puck?"

My friends nod agreement but, when I glance at the crocodile in tacit invitation, he waggles his huge, toothy head in a decisive shake. "I believe that, after all, I ssshall watch. Good luck to you sssphinxesss. You sssign up to partisssipate over there, where the line isss forming by that offeringsss temple."

So, after thanking the crocodile for everything he had told us, we leave him drowsing in the sun. Somehow, I know he will watch our progress in the waters of the reflecting pool, but whether he will root for us or against us, I really can't be sure.

"Do you think that was just a crocodile?" Muriel asks *soto voce* as we join the line.

"What else?" I ask, my attention split as I try to assess the competition.

"I thought he might have been Sobek, the crocodile god, or one of his avatars," she replies. "He was certainly very conveniently at hand – or paw or claw…"

"He certainly was," I agree, thinking of the gold and crystal ornaments the crocodile had worn. "Do you know whose side Sobek was on? I mean, did he ally himself with Isis or with Set?"

Muriel shakes her head. "I don't, but our crocodile sure sounded wistful when he talked about how Osiris's you-know-what tasted."

I admit, Muriel does have a point. How reliable was the crocodile's description of the contest? Seeing the number of teams that are lining up, I can't help but feel that – chatty as the big reptile had been – something had been left out. Are we all one big team, trying to assemble the thirteen pieces (fourteen, if you find the bonus fish and phallus) or is there something else going on?

If so, I'm not sure I want to be part of such a game. We aren't badly equipped for a tussle. Sphinxes have the lower bodies of lions, after all. A surreptitious check confirms that I do have claws – even if they are nicely gilded. Puck has horns as well, and looks as if he's eager to have a chance to use them. Still, by nature, we're not really fighters. Most of the time, in fact, we've been the ones running from a confrontation.

I hope we'll be given all the rules when we get to the sign-up table. No need to quit before we know what we'll be up against. If we don't like how the game is to be played, we don't need to sign up.

When we reach the front of the line, we do indeed learn more details about the game. The first thing we learn creeps me out quite a bit because it's something I hadn't even thought about asking. I'd assumed that if Set is the opposition, then all the teams are "for" Isis and Osiris. Instead, I learn that whoever wins the scavenger hunt will have the choice of awarding the completed Osiris either to Isis or to Set. After all, or so it is explained by a smarmy fellow with reddish hair and – by now I hardly noticed – ass's ears, why shouldn't those who favor Set's position have an opportunity to act in a proactive manner, rather than only being permitted to react? Proactivity should not be restricted to one philosophical position or the other.

I consider this weasel-thinking since, as far as I can tell, Isis has no intention of preventing anyone from participating. After learning that we're going to be up against Set's forces on both sides of the game, the rest of my questions hardly seem to matter. However, we do get answers.

It seems we don't need to worry about another participant coming after us to steal what we've found. The scavenger hunters will not actually "find" Osiris' body parts – since currently Osiris is alive and well. Okay, "well" as a living mummy without a you-know-what can be said to be. What we'll be looking for are amulets representing each of his body parts. Collect the whole set. Make the tactical decision whether or not you choose to go for the bonus by seeking that problematic fourteenth. Return to base and deliver the collection of amulets to the god or goddess of your choice. Now that we know the rules, do we still want to sign up?

I glance at Muriel who nods, her brow furrowing as she tries to figure out where we should start our search. Puck bounces, managing to be both kittenish and romping lamb all in one silly contortion. I'm moving to sign our names on the ledger – hoping I can manage a reed pen in my paws – when a girl , her eyes wide-set and liquid brown says, "Let me help you. Step over here so the next team can be interviewed."

We do so. I'm starting to give our names when the girl shakes her head slightly. Only then do I notice that she has floppy ears like a cow's and the most enviable, amazing eyelashes. Her voice is gently melodious, like a cow's lowing.

"I don't need your names. Indeed, here you should not give them, for in Heka Egypt we know that names have power. I shall record you as the Three Sphinxes, two ladies and a ram. I brought you over here so I could remind you that you know this is not the search on which you should be focused. Please participate if you wish, in hopes that searching for Osiris will lead you to the search you are avoiding."

"Avoiding?" I have no idea what the cow-girl could mean and my expression must show it.

"Seek, then, after Osiris. Just remember, hide your names."

97

She motions for me to rejoin Muriel and Puck. As I pad over to them, I find myself caught in sudden cold shock. I realize that I have no idea what name I would have given the cow-girl, for I can't remember what my name is. Suddenly, I wish she had let me finish giving her our names, so I could have learned what I might have said. Whatever had been at the tip of my tongue, it is gone now.

Among the gathered teams, we are far from the strangest. There are shaven-headed priests who consult papyri, presumable in hope that the sacred texts will offer some clue. There are numerous odd creatures, all or partially monstrous, including one made up of really buff guys with wings and the heads of hawks. There are family groups, teams of warriors, and even what looks to be a cluster of dust devils, defined only by the detritus they have picked up from their surroundings and a slight sparkling of sand.

When the word is given to begin, we set off at random. I let Muriel take the lead in making suggestions, saying (truthfully) that she is better than me at this sort of thing, but also because (less truthfully) what the cow-girl had said had really unsettled me. Am I avoiding anything? Immediately, I recall the unicorn. It had wanted to tell me something and I've gone out of my way to keep from learning whatever that might have been.

The sky above is perfectly blue. The area in which we search is as ideal a segment of the Nile Valley as any could desire: golden sands, stark rock, distant purple cliffs, scattered ruins, palm-tree shaded oases. Our competition is fearsome and focused. The opposition (which is completely different from the competition in that they have, like us, agreed to follow the rules of the search) is terrifying, being servants of a god who had not only murdered his brother but had dismembered said brother – and who later had sought to poison his brother's posthumously born son, but that is a whole 'nother issue.

Yet I am so distracted that had Puck and Muriel not looked out for me, I would have fallen into the first trap we encounter. This is a pit filled with venomous serpents, amateurishly covered with palm leaves over which sand has been unconvincingly spread as concealment. After that mishap, I force myself to be more alert.

We hadn't been given any clues as to where to begin our search, but Muriel has a brainstorm. She suggests that the landscape itself might provide clues as to hiding places. Following her suggestion, we seek the "head" at the "headwater" of one of the Niles. There we are attacked by some curious monsters that look like a hybridization of a donkey, a jackal, and something snake-like. They have teeth that remind me very much of our acquaintance the crocodile, as well as a green poisonous gas attack right out of a nightmare.

It's a good thing I'm alert and ready to help, because otherwise we probably would have gotten seriously hurt. As it is, we only manage because we can fly and our opponents can't. This lets us get above the green gas. From there, we drop rocks and sand until the monsters are defeated.

As we're collecting the amulet, we see ample evidence – scuffed rocks, broken vegetation, even some splashes of blood – that we aren't the first to follow this train of thought. That means someone is ahead of us in the race. This doesn't dampen my companions' enthusiasm in the least. Muriel strings the head amulet on a piece of cord and hangs it around her neck. (She's much better with her paws than I am.) Puck does a crazy victory dance. I'm less confident.

"We've gotten the head," I quip, trying to sound more cheerful than I feel, "but the evidence shows we haven't gotten a-head. Where next?"

Muriel considers options. "Foothills seems like an obvious choice. We might as well start with the obvious. No need to lead anyone else to a clue – and maybe we'll have some inspiration along the way."

So we progress to the wrinkly foothills of the distant mountains. There – sealed in a boulder that bears a passing resemblance to a canopic jar – we find an amulet representing both feet.

"I'd been hoping they'd be missing their toes," I say as Muriel adds the feet to her necklace. "because I thought 'toehold' might be a possibility."

Muriel considers. "Handhold is still possible, though. The problem with either of those is figuring out just where to look."

"Do you have any other suggestions?" I ask, trying not to sound miffed. "We have 'head' and 'foot.' That covers extreme directions. What else is there?"

"Heart is possible," Muriel says almost immediately. "There's 'heartland.' 'Heartwood' is a possibility, too. Wasn't Osiris's body first discovered in a tree trunk or something like that?"

We sit there, considering options, all too aware that sitting around isn't getting us any closer to our goal, that even as we dither someone else might be finding some key part. I'm about to suggest we go look for that fish, since at least that's likely to be in the river, when a thought hits me with almost physical force.

I don't want to finish this search.

The cow-girl had told me that there is something more important that I need to find, and I realize she's right. In any case, I don't doubt that some other team – like the Hawks, who I strongly suspect are being led by none other than Isis and Osiris's own son, Horus – will be far more suited than my two ersatz sphinx companions and me to finding the parts. They'd certainly be better at dealing with Set's agents.

I feel odd about giving up before we finish. At the same time, I feel equally certain that I'm not giving up at all.

Muriel and Puck are rather shocked when I tell them that I want to quit. I encourage them to finish off the scavenger hunt without me, reminding them that they've been doing the lion's share anyhow. They try to convince me to keep going, but give in without too much arguing. I suspect that Puck – whose nature is essentially that of a moon rabbit – might be finding the hot climate less fun than he had imagined it would be. Muriel seems to be finding the puzzle offered by my sudden change of mood an ample replacement for the scavenger hunt we are abandoning.

They're a little surprised when we don't just depart for the rosy tower from where we are, but that I insist on returning to the pyramid. I promise I'll explain when we get back, so they come willingly enough.

We're spiraling in for a landing when I see the cow-girl coming to meet us. I know her now, though I hadn't when she had spoken with me at the sign-up table. Her cow ears had made me think she might be Hathor, but now I remember that Isis herself sometimes uses that guise. I realize, too, that the golden mummy lady who we'd met when Razorwing first took us to the pyramid had also been Isis.

Why she'd shown herself then as a sort of living mummy –a role belonging to her husband, not herself – had to do more with our expectations than with her own desire. Ask anyone about what they associate with pyramids, and they'll likely say "mummies." And by mummies they don't mean the quiet sort, lounging in sarcophagi, serving as the link between the burial offerings and the spirit for whom those gifts were meant to benefit. No. They mean a mummy who is up and about.

"You're leaving us," Isis says, not asking, already knowing.

I nod. "There's something I should be looking for. Can you tell me what it is?"

She shakes her head, the gesture wafting over us the heady perfumes with which she has been anointed. "Knowing what you seek is a crucial part of finding it in the end. If I would tell you, you would waste energy telling me that I must be wrong. Return to your tower and consider your next actions carefully."

"I will," I reply. "Thank you. Good luck. I hope you win the scavenger hunt."

She smiles. "I think we will. Even those who gainsay the value of dreams and imagination can't, in the end, do without both. Now, farewell and fare wisely."

Upon this dismissal, we bow and take our leave.

Once back in the rosy tower, I consider what Isis had told us when she'd been the cow-girl. Another search? What might there be for me and my friends to seek? And why had Isis acted as if I should already know what I should be looking for? Even if the unicorn is the key, I have no idea what it might tell me – only that I still was nervous about learning whatever it is.

While Muriel settles in to play chess with Horatius, and Puck romps with Eyebright, I sit down at the little table and open the notebook, determined to list anything that might help me sort through this. I decide to begin with the tower, then work outwards, considering each window and its associated realms in turn. I'd leave out the seventh window for now. Isis had represented my search as for something I already knew needed searching for. (Does that make any sense?)

Since I haven't looked out the seventh window yet—saving it for a rainy day that has not yet come (and might never come, since neither the weather nor even the lighting outside the tower ever seems to change). The seventh window can't be the answer. I know Puck will be disappointed, because he never stops agitating for us to try that view, but I can handle his disappointment. Very well, the first window… Wait! Maybe I should start with the tower itself.

I consider. The only thing left unsolved is the ladybug box. I've tried a few times (and so has Muriel) but it still proves impossible to open. I'm not sure that opening a box that is right here counts as a search, although maybe it does – the search for the solution to the puzzle. Muriel does like that sort of thing, so maybe I should ask her to give the box another try. Maybe she can go flat and slip inside, unlatching it that way.

Anything else about the tower? The shoes and socks are odd, since I can't figure out how to open the door. I don't need shoes when I go out through the windows – at least when I go out properly and make myself a form suited to the area. They wouldn't have been at all useful that time Muriel and I dove out after Puck. Honestly, most of the time, bare feet are better. I give up on the shoes and move to a closer consideration of each of the windows.

The first window I had looked out of had been the one with the unicorn in the glade. Then there had been the one where I'd seen the monster and the water. That had turned out to be the Gothic realm. Based on what I know now, I figure that the monster must have been one of the gargoyles. Briefly, I wonder why the view had been so different between that first glimpse and those thereafter, but since I really have no idea how the windows work I need to dismiss that, too. Clearly, given how the perspective pivots from above so that one can look out as if on the same plane, the windows aren't bound by normal restrictions at all.

Well, what of it? I already know these aren't usual windows looking out into usual places. Why should I try to fool myself that any normal logic applies? Then I remember the third window, and my theories go, well, out the window, so to speak.

My third look had been into the relatively normal household. Well, normal except for Jessie's empty room, and even that is more or less normal. Maybe she is off at college or has joined the Peace Corps or something. Anyhow, aren't I jumping to conclusions when I think of her room as empty? I haven't gone through the door, crossed the forbidden threshold, or anything like that.

There had just been a closed door, a keep out sign, and that was it. How can I even be sure that the room doesn't belong to one of the girls I've watched, since I can't remember their names? There is that undercurrent of tension I'd sensed, but Muriel insists that that is just my imagination, that we'd encountered so much weird stuff in other places that I need to put weird into a place that exists to be normal.

"Undercurrent" reminds me of the undersea realm and its associated lands. The undersea areas were apparently widely varied – as is the Gothic realm. Surely if there is something for me to search for, I should be looking there or, maybe, in the Gothic realm. In fact, the Gothic realm has an edge, since we'd encountered Isis there.

She wouldn't tell me anything about my particular search, but maybe she knows more about the areas or realms or whatever you call them that we reach through the other windows. Part of me argues that she won't, since the various realms seem to operate on distinctly different paradigms (is that the right word?). Part of me argues that if Isis really is a goddess, then she should have a much greater awareness of things. Shouldn't the Mistress of Magic be able to go anywhere?

I stop to tick locations off on my fingers, suddenly aware that my orderly progression had fallen apart some time ago. Okay: unicorn, Gothic, normal family, undersea, city, and Moon. That covers six. Seven is unknown. Eight doesn't exist except that it just might be a door and probably is a door since Horatius and Eyebright report hearing something on the other side when we'd been trying to get back in. Whether a door that doesn't open on either side counts as a door or really is just an ornamented bit of wall is a question I'll leave to philosophers.

Logically, I've narrowed the area for our search down to the Gothic realm, because of its extensive reach and proximity to Isis, who might advise us. Thing is, I feel vaguely that I'm missing something, but what that might be remains as elusive as the almost remembered words of a song, the part where you sing "la-la," confident that the rest will come back if you only keep singing loud enough.

Muriel finishes her game with Horatius and wanders over to inspect my notes. "Aren't you ignoring the obvious?" she asks. "You even dodge it here, early in your list. When we met the unicorn it told you that it had something important to tell you, something that you need to be free. You refused to listen." Her expression becomes sad, but bravely she keeps on talking. "Maybe what you need to search for is related to what the unicorn knows, something important to you..."

I stare at her, realizing that I'm blinking back tears, even though I have no idea why. "Me? I'm here. What would I need to search for?" But my voice breaks and I sound unconvincing even to my own ears. I realize that I'd thought of the unicorn back when I'd been talking to Isis. That hadn't been that long ago. Why do I keep forgetting it?

Muriel reaches out and strokes my cheek, my tears soaking into her hand and making it darker. "You don't believe that. You are the greatest mystery in this place. When you first told us what Isis had said, I didn't even consider you yourself because – well, you've always been here. You've been the center around which we all spin, but now that I consider it more carefully, we know so little about you, not even your name. We haven't needed a name because you're just *you* but it's strange."

My heart is thumping so hard that I honestly think it will burst out through my breastbone like in one of those cheesy romantic cartoons. I wish I could forget again or do whatever I'd done those other times, but there is no such relief. Muriel looks scared now, scared but determined, too.

"As long as you didn't think about it, it didn't matter," she says. "We could go from window to window. But now? Can you just push the mystery aside?"

I remember the Lady of the Moon, how she'd talked about lacking courage and all that had happened because she wouldn't admit to her husband – a man she sincerely loved and admired and should have trusted – that she'd been snooping. She'd swallowed the pill and ruined any chance for them to be together.

"Muriel," I manage in a voice so thick that it doesn't even sound like my own, "I'm scared. I don't want to look because what if I don't like what I find?"

Muriel nods. "I'm scared, too. I'm scared we'll lose you forever, but I think that if you don't at least try we'll lose you anyhow, in a different way."

I press my lips together so tightly I can feel my blood humming in protest when I finally open them to speak. "You're right. I can feel it even now, a desire to crawl back into the bed and pull the covers over my head. I'm afraid to go out a window because I'm afraid that some chance encounter will tell me what I'm afraid to learn. You're right. Either way I risk being lost. If I at least try, maybe I'll also learn something to make it possible to… Oh! I don't know anymore!"

Muriel pats me again. I feel a solid bump and realize that Puck is bouncing against my legs, both seeking and giving reassurance. Horatius and Eyebright are looking over, worry in all their gazes.

From some well of courage I hadn't known I had, I draw out the brightest smile I can find. "All right! It's decided then. We'll start searching and worry about the consequences when we've found whatever it is we're searching for."

Puck gives a bounce to indicate the seventh window, but I shake my head, Isis's words still shaping my plans.

"Not yet. First we'll find the unicorn. It's time I did some listening."

Muriel and I spend some time debating whether we should wear the same forms as last time we went searching for the unicorn. I'm all in favor of novelty – after all, isn't the ability to be anything we want part of the pleasure of going out into the window worlds? Muriel thinks that we should wear the same fairy forms as last time, arguing that this will make it easier for the unicorn to recognize us. When I continue to balk, she flat-out accuses me of trying to impede our search!

This sobers me up. Am I? Just in case she's right, I give in. So, when we leave the tower again, Muriel and I flutter off in our butterfly-winged fairy forms. We do permit ourselves some stylistic changes. She adapts her reddish orange dress so that it has a many-pointed handkerchief hem, and dusts a little gold onto her monarch butterfly wings. I, in turn, decide on a multi-layered skirt that is blue (to go with my wings) on top, but that reveals a rich purply-pink underneath, so that when I pirouette, the whole resembles a flower coming into bloom.

Puck is happy as a woodland rabbit, happier as one with knife-edged wings like those of a hawk, and antlers like those of a jackalope. We make him promise not to poke anyone with the tines, and he promises. Frankly, I think he's a greater danger to himself. Most likely he'll end up hanging himself up in some low-hanging tree limbs. He does look quite dashing though. He may set a new style for the moon rabbits the next time we visit.

Promising Horatius and Eyebright that we'd be back before long, we go to the appropriate window. The view is as tranquil as ever but, unsurprisingly, now that I am so firmly resolved, the unicorn is nowhere to be seen. We'll need to go a-hunting again, but this time we have some idea how we might attract its attention if it should decide to be coy.

As usual, Puck is the one who chooses our direction, if one can call dashing over to look at an interesting flower, sample it, spit it out (too peppery), then eat a little clover, run after a dragonfly, dive under a bush for no apparent reason, then lope down a hillside, "choosing."

Muriel and I have no real idea where to go anyhow, so we're content to follow Puck's lead. I wonder if unicorns are browsers or grazers or both. If I knew that, and I knew what sort of plants they prefer, then maybe I could pick a direction. All I know for certain is that "our" unicorn likes flowers. Thus, almost without meaning to do so, Muriel and I start gathering the prettiest of the flowers we see and weaving another wreath.

I am contemplating adding something brightly orange that I *think* might be a variant of a ranunculus when Puck comes bounding up the same hillside he'd only recently pelted down. At first, I think he is simply involved in one of his rabbit games of chase, then I realize that his ears are back and his warm brown eyes show white all around. The reason for his panic buzzes past us a moment later: an arrow fletched in blue-jay blue, incongruously cheerful for such a deadly thing.

A cold wash of fear courses through me. Looking downslope, I can see this is not the only arrow that had been fired after Puck. Three, no four, others are embedded in the turf, their feathers colored in hues borrowed from tropical parrots: brilliant scarlet, sunshine yellow, violent green, and a brilliant blue that matches the first arrow. Is this the work of one (thankfully incompetent) archer with a taste for strong colors or evidence of a troop? Puck is in no position to answer – not that he is talkative at the best of times.

Muriel in her bright dress and brilliant wings would make a terrible scout. I'm not much better off, but at least my frock and wings will have a chance of blending into the foliage, especially in the shadows. Motioning for Puck and Muriel to retreat into cover, I get behind the thickest tree trunk I can find in the nearby grove. Then, using it for what concealment it offers, I drift up and into the branches. Folding my wings flat, I slide through the network of tree limbs, alert for any sign of the archer(s). What I discover is enough to cause me to gasp aloud. Happily for my safety, the sound puts me in no danger, for my quarry is retreating.

The archers prove to be a brightly colored company of four, tunics matching the colors of their arrows, their hair woven with ribbons to match. Since I am seeing them from the back, I am unsure whether they are male or female. I am still trying to resolve this solidly unimportant question when I glimpse their destination and all more minor considerations vanish.

When Puck had been leading our aimless exploration, he had gone down a hill. If he had not been prompted to come bounding up again by the archers' arrows, he would have discovered a streamlet, hardly more than a sparkling line of crystal over polished rock. Had he mounted the opposite slope, doubtless he would have been pleased to find the grade less steep, though he would have been puzzled by the somewhat trampled nature of the turf. From my treetop vantage, I don't need to guess, for over the next hill is the beginnings of a vast military encampment.

The camp is actually very beautiful in a knight and damsels of yore sort of way. The tents and pavilions are as colorful as one could wish. I am reminded of a flight of hot air balloons rather than a war camp. Pennants and flags with elaborate heraldic devices snap in a breeze that seems to exist solely to show them off at their best. Beautiful steeds – some richly caparisoned, some showing only the sleek and shining coats they'd been born with – prance and curvet on a brilliant greensward. The colors on tabards and tunics worn by the knights, retainers, pages, fair damsels, and other such folk as one would expect to see in such a place are equally brilliant and fanciful.

Nonetheless, despite the beauty and luxury, I feel certain that this is a true war camp and not merely some enormous band gone a-Maying. For one, once my gaze recovers from the confusing dazzle, patterns begin to resolve as do the bits in a kaleidoscope when you stop turning the barrel and settle to appreciate the image. For another, there are far, far too many weapons, their edges glinting in a fashion that leaves no doubt as to their sharpness. Then, too, the shields may be gaudily painted but, even at this distance, I can see evidence that the blazons have been freshened and repaired.

So here before us is a real war camp, and one guarded by such heartless fiends as would shoot without a second thought at a creature like Puck who – despite his new wings and antlers – is still a wholly delightful and adorable creature, not a threat. I suppose that they might have desired his plumpness for the stewpot, but something in the set of the archers' shoulders as they retreat toward the camp speaks of satisfaction in a job well done, rather than the frustration or disappointment I would have expected if they'd just missed a chance to augment their supper.

What is going on here? We three had ventured into this window realm repeatedly, and never encountered even a single questing knight, much less an army so vast. What has brought them here and – worse – is there a matching army they expect to fight? Surely we will not find the unicorn in these environs. Wisdom says that we should retreat and seek elsewhere or, perhaps, even give up the search altogether.

When I rejoin my companions, explain what I had seen, then conclude with this suggestion, Puck is eager enough to agree. Muriel just gives me a long, thoughtful look. Anger momentarily flashes through me. Surely she doesn't think the army is somehow *my* fault! I'm not suggesting we give up entirely, just that we wait until the army has moved on or fought its battles or whatever it is going to do. Yet, even as I begin to argue, the mute rebuke in Muriel's gaze cows me.

"Well, perhaps it *is* too soon to give up. Maybe we should look in the other direction, the one farthest from where the army is gathered. One rule if we do, though. No splitting up! No more of Puck romping off after whatever looks yummiest. Understood?"

Puck's nod is enthusiastic, while Muriel's smile is warm with approval. We take wing, flying close to the ground until we feel fairly sure that we are out of range of the army's archers and their deadly rainbow of arrows. Even when we permit ourselves to fly higher, we make sure we are within cover until we have assured ourselves that the surrounding area is clear of danger.

When Puck had scampered up to rejoin us, pursued by arrows, we'd dropped our floral tribute. Now we debate the wisdom of beginning the collection anew. After weighing pros and cons, we decide against doing so until there is some sign of the unicorn. That way the flowers will not become wilted and bedraggled.

Now that we feel safe from attack, we drop closer to earth once more, flying close to the turf, looking for indications of fresh cloven hoofprints in the greensward. A few times we do find some, but they always prove to have been made by the graceful red-coated, liquid-eyed deer – except for the one time they turn out to belong to a flock of completely adorable goats with rounded flanks and floppy ears.

Eventually, we land in a natural bower of honeysuckle to rest our wings, which ache from all the flying. I've just shown Muriel and Puck how to nip off the end of a flower and suck out a tiny bead of sweet nectar when I am struck with an inspiration so acute that I have no doubt in the least that it is correct.

"The unicorn is with the army," I say. "We may even have seen it all unknowing. Remember the horses? Some wore barding and were ready for battle. However, there were plenty without any tack at all. I think the unicorn is among them, though whether for refuge or as a prisoner, I can't say."

Puck squeaks, perhaps requesting clarification, but perhaps because he's just gotten some nectar up his nose. I decide to take the sound as the former.

"Why do I think this? Well, the first time I saw the unicorn – this is before I'd met either of you – I remember thinking, or being told, or something like that, how the unicorn's horn can become invisible or unnoticeable or something of the sort. I'm not sure why, but I'd bet all the dust on both my wings that it's using that trick to seem a mere horse."

Muriel considers, then nods. Puck shifts, flattening his ears – these are less floppy than his natural ones – in a vivid pantomime of dodging a near strike from an arrow.

"We'll all be careful," I promise. "Maybe the best thing would be to sneak into the camp after dark."

Muriel frowns. "We won't be able to closely inspect the horses in the dark. If the unicorn is able to hide its horn in broad daylight, I can't see how darkness will be of any help."

"Well," I say, rather miffed, "you're doing a great job of shooting down my suggestions. How about something helpful?"

Muriel shrugs. "I'm all out of helpful."

Not for the first time, I find myself considering how odd her moods have become. On the one hand, she chides me for avoiding figuring out whatever it is Isis wants me to figure out. On the other, she's not being the helpful, thoughtful person I've come to rely upon. That last thought irks me. Have I become so dependent on Muriel that I've forgotten how to think for myself? This makes me think harder than ever and eventually I feel myself grinning as an idea comes to me.

"We'll take a page from the unicorn's book and change our shapes. I bet we won't even need to go back to the tower to do so. Shifting shapes seems like a perfectly natural thing for a fairy to do. We just need to figure out what shapes would be best."

"How about horses?" Muriel suggests. "That way we can move among the herd without being noticed – sort of like hiding a leaf on the forest floor."

Puck suggests that we should be soldiers. No doubt inspired by his recent close call, he fancies himself as an archer. When Muriel points out that Puck wouldn't have the least idea how to use a bow, Puck protests that he hadn't know how to fly until he had wings. Why should this be any different?

There's such a twisted logic to this that I nearly give in. After all, isn't the moon associated with an archer goddess? Maybe moon rabbits came with the ability to do archery hardwired in. In the end, though, I veto Puck's suggestion. Even if we do miraculously know how to use a soldier's gear, I can't believe that new shapes would come equipped with knowledge of passwords or the military hierarchy or of which troops were posted where.

"Dogs?" Puck suggests next, reminding me how much fun we'd had chasing those jewel thieves when we'd been in canine form. That option is tempting, but I wonder if strange dogs would make the horses nervous.

"Cats?" Puck is free associating by now, but this time his suggestion brings matching smiles to Muriel and my lips. Perfect! Who ever notices a cat, especially in the dark? They have good night vision, too, solving the difficulty of how we might see through the unicorn's disguise. Cats we will be.

Enthusiastic now, I suggest a few adaptations. Our jaunt as sphinxes had taught me how completely inconvenient it is to only have paws, so I suggest that we opt for sort of paw-hands. Nothing too obvious, but enough to untie a knot if the unicorn is tethered against its will.

I also want us to have wings, since that would make us more mobile – and maybe make it easier for us to escape if necessary. Muriel vetoes this, saying that even small wings would alter our silhouettes, and that might make the guards suspicious. I give in, though I promise myself I will try a winged cat shape one of these days.

Color is next. I suggest that we all pick colors that won't stand out in the dark. Ben Franklin might have said that all cats are grey in the dark, but a lot of white will certainly show up more than not. Muriel chooses to be the closest thing she can to red – a dark marmalade tabby with just a touch of white on the paws to be elegant. Puck selects a wildly colored calico, heavy on the black and orange, but with little lightning bolts of white snaking through, making the darker colors more exciting. He tries to keep the antlers, but Muriel glowers him out of it.

Me? I decide that old Ben Franklin had a point and opt for a shimmery blue-grey ticked with black. As the sun begins to set and twilight to gather, I am just about invisible – more than I would have been if I'd chosen solid black. That knowledge comforts me some since, as the time to seek the unicorn draws closer, I find myself increasingly on edge – and I know that what I'm afraid of isn't the knights with their swords and spears, but whatever knowledge it is that the unicorn has kept behind those deceptively placid eyes.

We'd sneaked close to the field in which the horses were turned out before effecting our transformations. When sunset brings the concealment we desire, it is a simple matter to venture out into the pasture. This area must have been freshly put to use, for the grass is still thick and the piles of horse apples scattered. Even as I take care not to startle any of the drowsy equines,

I can't help but think that horse manure is a whole lot different when viewed from a head that is only six or eight inches above the ground.

Oddly enough, though, it is poop, not any more ethereal clue – no scent of flowers nor dainty cloven hoof print – that puts me on the unicorn's trail. When I first notice the somewhat ovoid droppings, compact as those of a rabbit or guinea pig, I think they might belong to a deer who had browsed or grazed here before the erection of the knights' encampment had made it flee to some safer, shadowed forest demesne. Then I notice that the shape and size aren't quite right. I don't claim expertise, but I know I'm correct. Maybe it is something inherent in the fastidious cat whose shape I have taken, but I know these are unicorn droppings.

I alert Muriel and Puck to my discovery. In a relatively short time, we find the glimmering pearlescent white "horse," who, upon inspection through eyes unbiased by expectation, proves to be, in fact, a unicorn.

As when Muriel and I had seen it before, the unicorn seems a shy beast, skittish even at the approach of three house cats. Had I been human, I would have held out a hand for it to sniff. As a feline I can only sit, wrapping my tail around my toes, curling my whiskers forward in what I hope is a friendly fashion.

Muriel follows my lead and so, for a miracle, does Puck. We sit there motionless as statues of Bast in her temples, although the wind does stir our fur in a fashion that gives lie to our imitation. Around us, the horses stir uneasily, aware of intruders among them but not really afraid. We sit and wait as only cats can wait while the unicorn watches us, its horn now visible as a pale sliver of moonlight where no moon can shine.

At last, on dainty hooves, it picks its way closer. Now that I can catch its scent, I realize that it is nothing like that of any of the creatures it resembles, but closer to that of a bouquet of early spring flowers if that bouquet – all narcissus and crocus, tulip and jonquil, forget-me-not and honeysuckle – were given blood rather than sap, flesh and bones and silken hair rather than petals, stems, and tiny rootlets.

As it draws closer, the unicorn flares its nostrils, pink within the pearl. I guess that just as the cat that is me can tell this is neither horse nor goat, so the unicorn can smell something about me, and about Muriel, and about Puck, that makes it draw in its breath sharply. Those enormous, long-lashed indigo eyes blink in astonishment, then widen in recognition.

"You were fairies last time, fairies who bore floral wreathes, freely gifted, so freely accepted. I scent expectation on your breath, see apprehension in the curl of your whiskers. Have you come at last for what I offered when last we met?"

I lick my nose with nervousness, but manage a soft mew that means, "Yes. You said then that you had what I would need if ever I was to be free."

The unicorn nods, the silken mane fluttering as delicate as spider webs. "Indeed I did and indeed I do. I have it and would still give it to you, for it is yours, always yours, never mine, except as caretaker."

Puck bounces, kittenish, the motion asking as clearly as any words, "What is it?"

The unicorn spares him a flicker of an ear, but those deep indigo eyes remain so fixed on me that I feel I could drown in their depths. At last it speaks the words I both long for and dread. "I can tell you your name. Would you have it?"

As soon as the unicorn says this, I know what the answer will be but, nevertheless, I know I need to hear it spoken or I can continue in denial.

"Tell me," I say, and I am not certain if what comes from my mouth are words or a meow, but it is loud enough to make the nearest horses stomp in displeasure.

The unicorn pays them less heed than it had Puck, instead breathing out a single word:

"Jessie."

And with the word I remember so much that the memories break not only my hold on my cat form but my connection to the unicorn's world. I am back in the rosy tower, huddled on the floor, my legs bent under me, my torso forward, my hands holding my face inches from the plush green carpet.

Muriel and Horatius are calling out to me but, although I can feel their nearness, their voices sound as if from a great distance. Although my eyes are open and I glimpse Eyebright undulating around the tower room in an agitated wave of motion, on some deeper level, I am blind – seeing nothing other than the wash of memories that I had buried to this point.

Jessie. Short for "Jasmine" by way of "Jass," not for "Jessica," as other kids and teachers and co-workers usually assumed. I'd been named for the flower, not the Disney princess, as I also had to keep explaining. My mother has a Masters in botany, and another in horticulture. She married my father – who's a Classics professor with a wide interest in mythology, folklore, and fairy tales – when she was only twenty.

They had another child, my sister Glory, short for Gloriana, who was the poet Spenser's Faerie Queene. Guess who picked her name? Yeah. Dad. Glory spent less time explaining her name than I did, not really minding, maybe even relieved, that people assumed either it was her full name or short for Gloria. We're different in a lot of ways, but that doesn't matter. She's my little sister and I love her. I also realize she's one of the two girls I'd seen doing the dishes that first time and had watched so many times since.

The other girl is named Nancy and she is my/our stepsister. And, no, Dad hadn't died tragically or anything like that. If you listen to our mother, they'd just grown apart, like a couple of trees that stretched different ways to find the sun. They're even sort of friends still, which is something I can't quite get my head wrapped around, but maybe it's because of me and Glory. Or maybe not.

They had shared custody, or that was what was on the divorce papers but, in reality, we lived more with Mom because once Dad and Mom split, he started taking jobs far from home. Lately, he'd been doing overseas tours, being the guide to all sorts of places, especially in Greece, Italy, and Egypt, places where his Classics expertise is really appreciated and where – whether coincidentally or not – two girls, even now that they are almost grown-up, really aren't all that welcome or something.

So we live with Mom and she does her best to be a good mom and run her business and teach courses at the local community college, too. She actually met Creighton – or Creigh or "Craig," as he's more often called (something both Glory and I sympathize with, a lot) through us, or more through Glory because she and Nancy were in the same grade school and both were on the soccer team and Mom and Creighton and a couple of other single parents formed what they called the "Cheering Squad," which combined sharing carpooling jobs and making sure that the kids in the group have at least one parent-type to cheer at games.

Except what ended up happening was that Creighton and Mom found they cheered each other up so much that they decided to get married. This was a few years ago, when I was in high school, and Gloria and Nancy were in junior high, and Nancy's younger brother, Henry, was still in middle school.

Try as hard as I might, I can't fit Matthew the Rug Rat into the picture, and that seriously scares me. The others treat him like a little brother. Could I have completely forgotten an actual brother, especially when I remember so much other stuff, like how Nancy's and Henry's mom had decided she was actually gay and now lives in California, where she is still "finding herself," but from where she sends all of us really fantastic gifts. I don't think these are guilt-gifts or anything, just that Dizzy Izzy, as Nancy and Henry call her, though never where Creighton can hear, really isn't cut out for motherhood. When I'd gotten old enough to think about it, I started putting together a fact here and an anecdote there, and I'm pretty sure that Nancy isn't a honeymoon baby, but the reason for the honeymoon, if you follow me.

I think I've been thinking of all of this stuff about family history and all, rocking back and forth so hard that my nightgown is in danger of ripping out over my back and butt, all to keep from thinking about Jessie, Jasmine – that is to say, me. Now, exhausted enough that I'm not panicking anymore – but no more able to fall asleep than I've ever been (except those two times, early on) – I make myself think harder, or more focused, really, because I've actually been thinking pretty damn hard.

I am Jessie and Jessie is who? Age twenty and almost done with college. Decidedly undecided as to what she/I wants to do with my life, so like lots of kids, I'd basically taken up the family business. Majoring in Biology and Minoring in Classics. What I am going to do after graduation, I don't know, but I have all of senior year to figure that out. Probably grad school, if I can get a scholarship, since Dad doesn't need to pay support after I've finished four years of college. (Not until after I've *graduated*, as I'd been dryly reminded during one of his custodial visits.)

Unlike Nancy, who is actually a very good athlete, I'm not into that sort of team thing. I read a lot, do a little drama, and, basically, hang out with some friends I'd made in college. No great love affairs, although a couple of devastating crushes. In fact, I lack the focus of either my mom or my dad or even of Creighton, who is some sort of wizard accountant. In fact (again), if I take after any of my "parents," I sometimes fear it is the absent, rarely seen, Dizzy Izzy.

Hard as I try, I can't remember anything beyond that point. I can't remember what had happened to put me here in the rosy tower. I try tracing back step by step, but there's a disconnect I can't cross. Eventually, I swim out of the swirl of memories and face the friends who are all looking at me in deepest concern. In a few words, I tell them what I've learned, how much I still don't know. I end up by saying, "Jessie's room. My room. It's still there. Maybe I can find something more in there. It's the most logical place to look, right?"

No one says anything. I can tell I'm making them nervous, or maybe "sad" is a better way to put it. I don't push them. I know Muriel and Puck don't really like going to the House. I think, or I had thought, or something like that, that they didn't because they find the whole setting boring, which it really is compared to the other windows. Now that I know it is an opening to the me who had been me before the tower, an opening to "Jessie," I wonder if this is why. Jessie is me before the tower, a me before them, a past rather than the ever-now of the other worlds beyond the windows.

Still, whatever the reason for their reluctance, I'm not going to make the mistake of being so considerate of their feelings that I come across as shutting them out.

"Coming?" I ask, hoping I don't sound too desperate.

Puck and Muriel share long looks, then Muriel says, "What shapes shall we wear?"

I'm so relieved I grin, feeling my cheeks just about split. "Let's go as us, only invisible. We'll wait until it's mid-morning there, when everyone is off to work or school, and we can sneak around."

Puck bounces. "Spies!" that bounce says, clearer than words and after that nothing will do but for me to make all three of us masks and rings that are also two-way radio links to the tower, so Horatius and Eyebright can be Base Command.

I finish these up just as Muriel (who is already wearing her red mask) announces that the last resident of the House – Mom, taking the Rug with her – has left. I check, too, more because I'm insanely nervous than because I don't think Muriel is right. Giving Horatius and Eyebright hugs that are meant to reassure me more than them, we go to the window and send ourselves out and over.

We land in the kitchen, which is completely empty (if you don't count the housefly that Puck insists on sneaking up on, completely delighted by his triumph over the multi-faceted vision of his opponent). From my prior visits, I'd learned that the cats usually sleep on an east-facing porch in the morning. The dogs would be out in their super-roomy kennel run outside. I'm still bothered that despite my renewed connection to Jessie, I don't remember this place better. It bothers me as much as that the one inhabitant whose name I have no trouble remembering – Matthew the Rug Rat – doesn't feature in my memories at all.

Pushing this aside, I lead the way from the kitchen through the house until we reach the Jessie room. The door is still closed but, this time, getting in offers no problem at all. Maybe my learning my name is the necessary key, maybe (whispered in a nasty voice in the back of my brain) I hadn't really wanted to get in before. Turning the doorknob, I slip inside, followed by my friends. Then, carefully, I close the door behind us.

I don't know what I'd expected, but it wasn't this. The room is full and completely empty as well. There is a single twin bed (mate to one Glory has, I know) unmade except for a shabby blanket drawn over it to keep dust off the mattress. There is a student desk with a hutch, the sort you get from office supply stores. It looks pretty new, and I remember that I'd been given it at the start of my junior year in high school, a hand-me-down from a friend who had moved the summer before. I'd used it some but mostly it I'd used it as it is being used now – as a place to stack things.

And stacked it is, with boxes, still sealed with packing tape and bearing labels like "Books," or "Winter Shirts," or "Toys." There are more boxes on the floor, in front of the seven foot high bookcase that lays on its side, still swathed in that quilted blanket stuff movers use. What's weird is that I remember the boxes, remember packing them, remember knowing they'd be coming to this room, but I don't know why they'd never been unpacked.

One heap is different from the others, a smaller group of boxes and duffles that I recognize as my college stuff. I examine this, trying to fit it into the puzzle. I have no idea why it's here, still packed, even though, based on what I've seen the other kids doing, it's during the school term and I should be living in the dorm.

I'm just about to see if I can pry some of the tape loose in a fashion that won't show, when I hear a loud thump from the direction of the kitchen. Well, not a thump precisely, rather a door slamming, more specifically, the door that opens from the garage to the hall that connects to the kitchen.

All three of us freeze. Muriel raises her spy ring to her lips and gives Base a *soto voce* update. Then I hear Glory's voice, clear and yet somehow scratchy, say, "Gosh, I'm sorry to make you come from work, Dad, but the nurse really didn't want me to stay at school. She said I'm probably infectious."

"Dad"? I don't need to puzzle long because Creighton's voice comes right after.

"No problem. Mom's teaching lab this afternoon. She can't telecommute that, but I can work on the incorporation agreement I'm doing right here. You go get in your jams and into bed. Can I get you soup or something?"

"Later, maybe," Glory answers. "My stomach really doesn't like the idea of anything in it that much."

"Okay. I'll go with that for now, but we can't have you getting dehydrated."

Their voices have been getting closer and closer, probably as they cross the kitchen toward the hall that goes back toward the bedrooms. When Glory speaks next, her voice comes from right on the other side of the door.

"Dad, today is my turn to go see Jessie. I guess I can't now, can I?"

Silence that I envision as Creighton shaking his head, then the sound of ice cubes dropping into a glass.

"No way. Not feeling sick and maybe about to infect the whole family. Don't worry. Someone will go in your place."

Glory's voice, softer, though I can tell somehow that she hasn't moved. "Dad, will Jessie ever come home? It's been so long and what they said…"

Quick steps, a man's dress shoes on linoleum, then Creighton's voice, closer but, paradoxically, softer than it had been when he'd been in the kitchen. "Honey, I know what they said, but I still have hope. So does your mom. So do you or you wouldn't be so upset. Now, off to bed. I'm going to bring you some iced water and tuck you in. Then I'll go into my office. Don't get out of bed if you can help it. If you need something, just call."

"Okay." A long pause, followed by what is certainly a sniffle. "Sorry. I guess I do hope. It's just hard."

"Especially when you're coming down with the 'flu. Go!"

She does. I turn and stare at Muriel and Puck. What's going on here? Visiting Jessie? Wondering if she'll come back? Was I in prison or something? I keep my questions inside. We're invisible, but that doesn't mean we're inaudible. Now that there are people in the house, I worry that someone will come in if they hear anything. Maybe someone will come in before they go to visit Jessie, whatever that means. Quickly, I sweep a part of my nightdress skirt over where Puck's big feet left prints as he hopped from dusty box to dusty box. Then I mouth "Back to the tower."

The time has come to look out the seventh window. I know I'll find the rest of the answer there. What I am a lot less certain about is whether I'm going to like what I learn. Fear makes me drag my heels. Only the fact that I'm even more scared that if I delay I'll completely funk it keeps me going.

"Let's start by looking through the window," I suggest. "Then we'll have a better idea what sort of shapes we'll need."

The others agree. Puck bounces forward in his usual reckless fashion. Muriel and I are slower to follow. Nonetheless, we do so and, before long, we're staring down at a room that manages to simultaneously be both very white and formulaic, and full of color and personal touches. At first, I think it's a hotel room – one of those long-term ones where people live for weeks, even months at a time. Then the images fall into perspective, and I know it for what it is – a hospital room.

What had fooled me was the relatively small amount of medical gear visible, but there is no mistaking the style of the bed, nor the racks (or whatever you call them) from which bags of various liquids are suspended. The room's furnishings have that peculiar character found in hospital rooms. Although there are several chairs – at least one of which looks as if it could be adapted to be slept in – there aren't any dressers or bookcases or suchlike that indicate that anyone is really *living* here.

This is a room in which one exists, but doesn't really live. Nonetheless, an effort has been made to humanize it. Plants crowd the windowsills. Cheerful stuffed animals - mostly rabbits - are set about. A cobalt blue balloon emblazoned with butterflies is tied to the bed's upper rail. Currently, one of the chairs is occupied by a woman with a little kid, not quite a baby, but not much more, in her lap. Although some part of me resists, I know them at once: Mom and Matthew the Rug Rat.

Mom is talking steadily, but not to the Rug. She's talking to the figure in the bed, a figure with eyes neither open nor shut, with features slack, unmoving, still except for steady breathing. A young woman, still showing traces of the girl she'd been not long before, balanced on the cusp of adulthood as the Rug is between baby and boy. A young woman who I know is Jessie – who is me.

Back in the tower, I drop to my knees, ignoring Puck's delighted squeaks at seeing so many rabbits. Muriel comes over and pats my hand but, other than this, she shows me no pity. Her voice level, she asks me what shapes we should use to continue our investigation. I don't answer, so she keeps offering suggestions. Puck would be easy. Another rabbit would go unnoticed in all that - as long as he holds still.

Muriel sounds doubtful as she says this last, which makes Puck indignant. Oddly enough, that mild insult is probably the best way to get him to make the effort. Muriel sniffs disbelief as he squeaks his protestations, but there is a tiny smile at the corner of her mouth, so she knows exactly what she has done.

Next, enlisting Horatius and Eyebright, since I'm still not talking, Muriel explores options for herself and me. We could try snooping around invisibly. Maybe we could learn something from records and charts. Unhappily, most of the details are likely to be in electronic format, so viewing them might not be as easy as we could hope. We could disguise ourselves as visitors or nurses, but such would likely already have the answer to the most basic question we need to ask: "What happened to put Jessie in that hospital bed?"

Horatius suggests that we might manage to pass ourselves off as visiting clergy or the like. Friendly strangers, the sort who are expected to ask questions so they can offer comfort. That makes sense. I bestir myself enough to help Muriel consider details. We settle on a kind-eyed woman somewhere in her early thirties. She wears her hair in a neat bun. Her dress is simple in cut, ornamented with a tiny print of stylized hearts and flowers – both red, of course.

Muriel insists that I shape myself as her companion or assistant. I opt to look younger, mousier, less conspicuous: the trainee shadowing to find out how one behaves during a hospital visit. That way Muriel can ask most of the questions, but I can cut in if needed.

Our forms are perfect except for one thing: when we orient ourselves to make the crossing, I can't go. At first Muriel accuses me of trying to wuss out but, as I look into the scene, where Mom is now massaging one of Jessie's slack hands, working her way up the forearm, her motions showing that she's done this many, many times before, I know the answer. I can't go through as someone else because I'm already there. My choice is to be Jessie or to end my search here.

I'm scared all over again. What if I go and can't get back? But if I don't try, won't I be stuck in another way? Stuck with my search almost but not completed? I think of how Isis had sought the parts of Osiris' body, only to have to admit that his phallus had been eaten by a fish. She hadn't given up. She'd made him a new one, and that one must have worked because otherwise there wouldn't have been a Horus, right?

So even the fact that this should be impossible, or that I might get stuck aren't excuses to quit, much as I might wish this could be so. I pull at my lips until they throb, but no matter how hard I think, I can't see a way around it. I'm going to have to take the risk – but that doesn't mean I need to be stupid about it. Except for that time we had gone after Puck, we'd been able to get back, and that was because we hadn't gone out body and soul.

Turning, I look at Horatius and Eyebright. "I'm going to risk it, but I have a job for you." Two-faced giant and many-eyed dragon straighten to indicate I have their full attention. "If I start to go out like I did that one time, I want you to grab hold and pull me back."

They nod. If Muriel looks relieved that I'm not diving Puck-like into the unknown, she tries to hide her feelings. In turn, I pretend not to notice that though she'd been the one pushing me to keep going, she's nervous, too.

Now that I've resolved to be Jessie, the next time we begin our transition, I'm no longer prevented from going along. When I slide into the body on the bed, I find that my connection to it is different from what I'd expected – or dreaded. I'm there and yet I'm not or at least I'm not there in the same way I'd been a fairy or a sphinx or even a whale. I can feel the sheet under me, that the pillow on which my neck rests isn't quite comfortable. I can feel Mom's hands rubbing my feet, moving up and pulling on each toe, then flexing the tendons before progressing to the Achilles tendon, then up the calf. I can even feel the tube through which I pee and the ones that touch my arms. I know there are aches and pains, but I feel them distantly. I wonder if one of those tubes is giving me – Jessie – some sensation stealing drug.

All the time her hands are busy with the massage, Mom is talking, both to me and to the Rug, who is doing something with toys that ring like soft bells down on the floor. Mom is talking about work, about a new class she's teaching on herbal remedies and how interesting the student's reactions are. I understand that the nice-smelling ointment she's using right now is one she'd made up herself: "All the ingredients approved by your doctors, of course, even the couple of drops of jasmine oil."

And I can smell jasmine, a scent as familiar to me as my own name. That bothers me just a little, but I don't have a chance to follow the thought because there's a tap at the door and then it swings open. Muriel comes in, cheerful but not abrasively so. She holds a toy stuffed white rabbit with pink satin lining ears and shaping nose, as well as overly large, really, really cute brown eyes – Puck at his most impossibly angelic.

Mom looks up and over, her fingers automatically continuing her massage. "Yes?"

Muriel smiles, friendly, just a little shy. "I came up to this floor to see a friend who is off at P.T. I thought I'd look for someone who might welcome company while I wait for my friend to come back."

Mom smiles and gestures to an unoccupied chair with a toss of her head. "Please do. I'm Ella. This is Matt and this," gesture with her head again, "is Jessie. My youngest and my oldest."

Matt spots Puck. Crowing in delight, he scoots over, arms lifted. Muriel hands Puck down, causing Mom to protest, "Oh! You don't want to do that. Matt's at the put-everything-in-his-mouth stage. He'll ruin it!"

Muriel laughs. "Oh, that rabbit's tougher than you might think. It'll be okay. Besides," she gestures around the room, "it seems to fit in here with all the other rabbits."

I see Mom's sad smile. "Jessie always liked rabbits, so her sisters and brother each got her one for company. That started a trend."

Muriel shuffles her feet, then asks. "What happened? To Jessie, I mean?"

Mom sighs, moves to where she can reach my – Jessie's – other foot, glances down, presumably to check on Matt, make certain he hasn't eaten Puck or anything. Puck must be doing a good job at keeping Matt entertained though, because she doesn't stop her massage. She doesn't say anything either, not for a long while and I've just about figured she won't when, between one toe tug and the next, she starts up.

"It was an accident. Jessie is – was – in college. She'd finished her junior year and would have already been home except she stayed to work graduation. A friend was graduating, so she was particularly eager to be there."

Tony, I think. *Not so much a friend as one of those impossible crushes.*

Funny, though. I remember how important it had seemed to be there, to have a couple more days basking in Tony's aura, but I don't remember anything about the ceremony.

Mom's still talking. "The night before graduation, Jessie went out with some friends. They were crossing a street and she was hit by a car."

Muriel gasps, her hand flying to cover her mouth. Mom mistakes her shock for something else. "No, she wasn't drunk or anything. Neither was the driver of the car. She – the driver was a graduating senior – was high on nothing more than anticipation. She ran a yellow light. Clearly at fault and all that – which has certainly helped with the medical bills, but I think the cost to… Oh, never mind. I'm wandering."

Muriel makes a sympathetic murmur. "No. Please, go on. An accident. You said you aren't angry at the other girl, but that doesn't change that Jessie was badly hurt. How severely? She doesn't look too bad now."

Through my half-closed eyes I can see Mom's weak smile. "Not compared to then, no. She never looked as terrible as you think someone who'd been hit by a car should, because most of the injuries were internal – that and a few broken bones," she adds, as if this is an afterthought. "She probably would have died except that the university hospital was only a few blocks away and some people who'd just gotten off-shift at the E.R. were walking to their cars. They ran over. Someone called 911. Jessie was being treated practically before the poor girl who'd been driving the car fully realized what she'd done."

Muriel frowns. "This was in the spring?"

Mom nods. "I was three months pregnant with Matt. We were waiting to make the announcement until Jessie was home from college. We'd just moved into a larger house, though we didn't let on why. And then, there we were, putting away the champagne we'd gotten for the toast and wondering if Jessie would make the week."

"She did though," Muriel says encouragingly.

"She did," Mom agrees, gently squeezing my still fingers. "She's been in a coma since. At first the doctors told us that the coma was actually a good thing, the body's way of healing, that they might even have suggested a medically induced coma if Jessie had come around. The readings – all those EKGs and other things – didn't show any severe brain damage. Basically, Jessie was just deeply asleep."

Muriel nods. "And her healing from the other damage – all the broken bones and internal injuries and all?"

"One by one, each has healed. I won't bore you," Mom says in a tone of voice that actually pleads, *"Don't make me go through it all again,"* "with the details, but everything that can has healed. There have been problems, of course, but not all that long ago the doctors admitted that they don't know why Jessie hasn't come around. There doesn't seem to be any medical reason. We've been visiting her all along – the other kids were actually more than fantastic when Matt was born and I wasn't up to much, but we're all stretched thin. I was here yesterday. I'm back because Glory – that's my middle daughter – is down with the flu."

Muriel nods to where Mom has just finished massaging my other arm. "Do you all do that – massage and other physical therapy?"

"I do and so does Creighton. The kids try, but I've told them that I don't think the PT is as important as talking to Jessie. When we can't be here, we've set it up so that Jessie has other stimulation. We play music, soundtracks from her favorite movies and television shows, recorded books, basically, anything we can think of to give that sleeping mind a reason to wake up."

Muriel makes an encouraging noise. Mom laughs, a dry, not entirely humorous sound. "Jessie's dad – Matt's father is my second husband – recently suggested we find a prince to kiss Jessie. That sounds crude, but he didn't mean it that way. It's just how crazy we're all getting."

I'd told Muriel a bit about my – Jessie's – dad right after I'd remembered who I was. Now she asks the question I want to ask. "Does Jessie's father help with her care?"

Mom laughs again, but this time the sound is warmer. "Actually, he does. He used to travel all the time, but when Jessie was hurt, he got a job teaching at the university. He has a Ph.D. in Classics. He's been a huge help, not only with his share of the caregiving – which he should be doing anyhow – but with helping with the other kids, both our own Glory and my steppies, Nancy and Henry. Weirdly, I think this has been a maturing experience for him. Before this, he never could focus beyond himself, which was one of our problems. We'd been divorced for years before Jessie's accident."

Muriel and Mom keep talking, but I am only half-listening now, trying to soak in everything I've learned. I wonder if I'd woken in the tower when my body had finally healed. It makes me shiver when I realize that I'd been nineteen and, if I've figured everything right, a year or so had passed. I have a little brother I've never really met. Nancy and Glory would be thinking about college. Henry's voice would be changing.

I now understand why I hadn't recognized the house. I'd never seen it furnished, just once when Mom and Creighton had come and gotten me from school – the college was a good hour or more away – so I could see it and join in the bedroom lottery. I'd taken the room nearest to the kitchen on purpose, because it would be the noisiest and I figured I wouldn't be there as much, so I wouldn't be bothered.

Lost in thought, I don't so much choose to leave the world behind that mysterious seventh window as I just fade out. I'm not aware of the transition at first but, eventually, I became aware of the warm ever-present sunlight in the tower. The regular sounds provided by the medical monitors have been replaced by that unique quiet that comes when everyone is trying hard not to make a sound. I don't think I realize that I'm fully back until Puck, who can't ever hold still – moves and "accidentally" tugs at the hem of my nightdress.

I'm still standing at the window, but no longer seeing anything in it but my own distorted reflection. Turning away, I walk over to the bed and climb in, surrounding myself with pillows and pulling the poofy comforter up to my chin. Puck bounces up and I wrap my arms around him. Muriel is more hesitant, but she joins me too, along with Horatius and Eyebright. They bring their chessboard, so they can pretend not to be paying attention, even as they keep a watchful guard.

Muriel climbs to where my knees make a peak and settles herself into the folds as if they are an armchair. I remember playing games with her soon after she'd joined me, how simple it had been to lose myself in fancies. I remember how the Lady of the Moon had condemned herself to permanent exile because she lacked courage. Do I lack courage?

Do I say this aloud? I must have, because Muriel asks, "But what do you have to be afraid of? Your mom is wonderful. Your whole family loves you, has never stopped loving you. Look how worried Glory was. They aren't going to be angry with you."

"I'm afraid of pain!" I snap. Sensation had been muffled during our window journey, but I'd become aware of it: the pain in waiting. The pain of muscles that – no matter how massaged and electrically stimulated – have atrophied. Pain from bones broken but never fully rehabbed. Pain, too, from having to rebuild *me*, to rebuild Jessie, whose friends would have moved along, who would have lost a year and more than a year, because waking up won't magically take me back to who I was before.

Pain from trying to figure out how I fit into a family I've never really belonged to, not this new blended family where Matthew the Rug makes seven. Don't get me wrong. I genuinely like Creighton's kids, Nancy and Henry. I had been thrilled when Mom and Creighton had gotten married but, by the time they did, I'd already been partway out of the nest. That had been an element in how I felt about the marriage. The new blended family would be more about all of them, than about me. Or so I'd tried to tell myself.

Now I find out that all of them – not just Mom and Glory and Dad, but Creighton, Henry, and Nancy, even little Matt in whose infant memories there would be hospitals – had been reshaping their lives around me being mortally injured. Even when I'd watched them through the window, I'd sensed that the whole family (who I didn't know then were my family) were haunted by something, something that had come between them and the lives they should have been living. I'd just found out that I was the ghost at the wedding banquet. Could I face coming back, knowing I'd ruined their lives?

I look around the tower, at the six windows that take me to places full of wonder and adventure. I can go through them into places where I can be anything I imagine: play with sea serpents, frolic with gargoyles, dance with fairies. What will I get if I give this up? Pain. Isolation. A new role as the crippled girl, body forever marked by someone who impulsively ran a "pink" light. That isn't even tragic. It's just plain dumb.

I wonder what happened to that girl. Muriel answers, "Don't you remember? Your mother told us. She had a horrible time for a while. She never did go to graduation and, until she moved, she came to see you every day once you were out of ICU."

"Moved?" I ask, grabbing one word from a flow I can't seem to let touch me.

"Yes. She'd majored in something like psychology but, after everything, after talking to counselors, she decided to start over. She's working to become an EMT, because she feels that maybe someday she can save someone, the way the EMTs saved you – and, when they did so, saved her from being a killer."

"Oh." Weirdly, the more I learn, the more angry I get. Dad has reformed and is now more or less a model parent. My siblings, even baby Rug, are models of familial support. The whole new clan has bonded over my beat-up carcass.

For the first time, I wonder if Osiris had been grateful when Isis had patched him (minus penis) back together. Had he been happy or had he resented being a living mummy, hopping along, given the new job of judging the Dead because, well, after all, he'd been one of them for a while. Maybe he'd been pissed off. Maybe he'd wanted to yell at Isis and Horus and their good dog, Anubis, "Why didn't you just let me die and get on with your lives?"

Because that's what I want to yell. If I wake up, their vigil will be over. They'll be free, because it will just be me and Pain.

I can stay here. Muriel would like that, I feel pretty sure. She'd never thought the house window was so great. Puck would like if I stayed, too, and who would Horatius and Eyebright watch if I go away? I could just stay away from the house window and the seventh window. Maybe, even better, I could serve as a sort of glorious guardian angel to my family. We'd proven we could go over there invisibly.

We could visit every so often, flitting by, scenting the air with jasmine, providing encouragement for tests or Big Dates, or other of life's challenges. I can just hear them, "I feel as if Jessie's watching over us."

But could they feel that way if they were still hobbled by that fading, sleeping body, and the ever ebbing hope it represents? To make this work, I'd need to go through the seventh window again, unhook me from that bit of meat in the hospital bed. It shouldn't be too hard. I already know for sure that what is *me* isn't limited to that. It would be a good action. I wouldn't just be setting myself free, I'd be setting them free, too.

Perfect. I'll be doing the best for my family, for me, and for my new friends here in the rose tower – these four who are my dearest heart-friends. I smile, feeling as if a huge weight has left me. For the first time, I dare look at myself, realizing that my reluctance to this point had been from a subconscious awareness of the pain-haunted wreck my body had become. Here, though, my body would be fine.

Completely free of apprehension, I peek under the lavender nightdress and see that everything is there and better even than I'd remembered: perfectly round breasts; a flat belly with a really cute "innie" navel; long, shapely legs and arms. I pull my braid around and happily inspect my hair. It's honey-brown, thick and strong, with just a little wave.

Perfect. It is all going to be perfect.

Muriel is looking at me, a funny expression on her face. Quickly, I tell her what I've decided. Rather, I start to, but I find that my mouth has turned sour, not lemon sour, but bitter sour, like sucking on an aspirin. I pucker up, wishing for some water to rinse away the taste. I rinse it with truth instead.

"I've got to go back," I say. "I'm scared stiff but, now that I know the full story, I can't fool myself. I had a beautiful dream, but there's no denying that there's a difference between dreams and nightmares. This has been a dream, the best sort of dream, right through the gate of horn, not of ivory, as Dad used to say, but, afraid as I am of what going back will be like, I know that staying here would transform what has been a sort of truth into a lie."

Puck meeps, a sound both sweet and sad. He snuggles closer, like he's getting in all the cuddles he can before there are no more.

Muriel manages a smile. "I knew as soon as I spoke with that lady your mother what you'd decide in the end. I knew you'd realize that you had to go back and leave us behind."

I shake my head. "Go back. Yes. But I'm not leaving you. I'll take you with me, I promise."

Swinging my legs over the side of the bed, I lean down to open the cabinet under the nightstand and draw out those ridiculous socks and neat little shoes. Then I lift up the ladybug box. This time it's easy to find the hidden clasp that opens it.

"Get in," I say, and all of them do. Even Eyebright with his many bumps and coils manages to fit. For good measure, I add the notebook and pens, all of Muriel's dresses, and Horatius and Eyebright's cards and game board.

Then I climb in with them and say "Ladybug, ladybug, fly away home!" And we do.

Or so we try, but it turns out that it's not that easy to come back from the dead and that's where I've been "living," if you want to call it that: Asphodel, the Fields of the Dead.

The ladybug box is big enough to hold us all, the wings stretching out to the sides buzzing so fast that they vanish into spotted blurs of almost but not quite invisibility. But, despite all her effort, we aren't going anywhere and we are doing that fast.

Puck, of course, loves the speed, but Horatius and Eyebright don't look well. Muriel, one hand on Puck's collar, the other firmly gripping onto the side of the box looks over at me.

"What do we do? Do we go back?"

"No!" I say firmly, although, if I am the least bit honest with myself that's exactly what I want to do. The rosy tower with its windows offering a safe view on marvels seems more than ever a haven. My mind flies back along the stories my dad had told me and Glory, stories we'd loved even when we'd only half understood them because they were bridges between us and the world in which Dad lived, a world we felt was more important to him than we ever could be. After all, hadn't he left us for those stories?

Older now, I realize that Dad hadn't left us for those stories. He'd left because he'd never really been there, for our mom, for us. But he'd given us those stories and in my heart and dreams – in Jessie's heart and dreams and soul – the stories reverberated powerfully. Bridges. And tales that reassured, reminded, that even death is not inescapable, not if you were willing to try hard enough.

I remember how shocked a college friend of mine had been when I'd told her the Jesus coming back from the dead bit wasn't that big a deal, that Jesus was just one in an extensive lineup of dying and resurrecting gods. Heck, I'd added, even heroes could do it.

Now I wish I hadn't been so flip. It looks as if coming back from the dead or the almost died or whatever I am going to be trying is a lot harder than it seemed to be in stories. Harder, even, because I realize that I'm not just interested in getting myself stuffed back into that sorry excuse for a body that I'd re-tenanted for a short time. I want to make things right or better or something, and that's going to take a miracle.

Here's the problem. I really don't believe in miracles. They're right up there with love at first sight on my personal list of completely impossible and basically super-destructive things. The crippled don't just get up and walk. The halt don't start hopping. The lame don't start legging it – at least not without a whole lot of PT and braces and surgery and medication and all of that.

Belief that a "positive attitude" makes a difference is one of those horrible punishing things because when you lose the battle (and the battle always gets lost, right? Sure it does, because everyone dies in the end) well then, it's your fault because your lack of positivity is what did you in.

So I'm thinking all of this and Lady Bug is buzzing in loops and circles, closer and closer to the rosy tower. Eyebright has about seventy-five percent of all his eyes squashed shut and the rest are barely open. Horatius' faces are losing all his familiar guardian-at-the-bridge look and instead are peering around as if wondering where he can throw up without doing it on Lady Bug's wings and so showering vomit over all of us. And I'm thinking "bridge."

Bridge. That's something between here and there, or there and there. Maybe once "bridge" was between outside the tower and inside but now – because I realize that I'm *not* going back – now that I'm out here and so is Horatius, then there's got to be another "there."

So I yell to Horatius, "Throw up over the back if you have to!" and then to Lady Bug I yell, "Straight ahead, fast as you can. We're leaving the tower behind!"

Muriel gives me one of those looks that mean "Are you sure you know what you're doing," but Puck moves to the prow of our peculiar vessel, floppy ears streaming behind him, eyes enormous with wonder and joy. I want to reassure Muriel that I know where we're going, that I know exactly what I'm doing but I don't because I can't do so – at least not and stay honest with her and with myself. What's honest is that I have ideas, but I'm not sure if they're any good.

We could try to find paths blazed by those others who managed to escape the underworld in the past. Maybe I could look for the Boat of a Thousand Years on which Osiris sails. I mean, we know his wife, right? And have met his son. Maybe he'd give us a lift.

Or maybe we could seek a tunnel guarded by three-headed Cerberus. That's got to be pretty much a highway, given the number of heroes, demi-gods, and flat-out gods who have used it in various stories. Volcanoes are considered a good bet in several traditions, as are bodies of water. Hel, ruler of one version of the Norse underworld, had a ship crewed by drowned mariners, so we could probably sail that between Death and Life.

But even as I shift through possibilities, I know that this is not the way to do it. I realize that these are *their* ways, not mine. I certainly don't want to follow – look how much good that did poor Eurydice and even more to be pitied Orpheus. When Jesus joined the ranks of those who had managed the dance from Life to Death and back again, he might have spent time in Hell, but he got out his own way, even though he would have had lots of traditions to choose from if he wanted to copy.

So finding my own way is what I need to do. After all, I'm not looking for the same answers as all those others. I'm looking for my own. And along the way, I'd like to find a miracle. (Other than coming back from the dead, I mean.)

Once the rosy tower isn't even a possible shadow on the horizon behind us, I call out to Lady Bug that she can slow down. She does, though I sense she isn't in the least tired. I pat her flank by way of thanks, then move up behind Puck in the prow, getting where I can see the landscape over which we're now passing. Thing is, there *is* no landscape, there's seascape instead, wind tossed water wherever the eye – at least my eyes—can see.

Eyebright, who is over his motion sickness now that we're no longer going in loops and twists around the tower, helped because we've slowed down so that our surroundings are no longer a Monet-blur, indicates that he can see something off where the sun is beginning to sink below the waves. At my request, Lady Bug carries us in that direction. Before long even those of us with only two eyes can see an archipelago painted in oranges and pinks by the setting sun.

There are shapes scattered over the islands, even as the islands are scattered over the sea: dark figures, vaguely humanoid in that they each have a torso, two arms, and what may be a head. Some of these figures seem to be waving or maybe they're dancing, for there seems to be something full-body about the motion. Puck starts waving back, bouncing up and down and squeaking excitedly, as if the sound might actually carry over the crash of surf along the stony shore.

Then, somehow, somewhy, my perspective shifts and snaps into place and I see the figures as what they are: saguaro cacti, most shaped after the classic "two-armed" style popularized by cartoon and yard art, so that it's almost become an icon for "desert," even though, as my mom explained to us one time when we were driving through Arizona, saguaro cacti live only in Arizona, California, and northern Mexico, and in a relatively narrow zone even in those places.

If what Mom told us is true – and she is a botanist, so I figure it must be – than I guess that what's below us must be a part of America, at least an honorary one – because there are a *lot* of saguaros down there. The motion that Puck (and I) had taken for waving or dancing proves to be stark black shadows cast by the setting sun over rippling waves.

The islands aren't exactly inviting, but they're the only land I can see – or that Eyebright can see, either. Lady Bug could probably keep on flying, even in the dark. She doesn't seem to get tired and she can fly very fast. For all I know, maybe she could even catch up with the sun. Nonetheless, it seems wiser to land and await daylight.

For three of our company – Horatius, Eyebright, and Lady Bug – this is their first time outside of the tower. It seems wisest to give them a chance to get used to the idea of a world that is not bordered by walls, floored with carpets, and lacking a ceiling overhead.

Someone has tossed a bunch of pillows into Lady Bug, so we'll be comfortable enough when we make our camp. Well, we would be except that I have a problem I've never faced on any other of our expeditions. I'm hungry. I'm thirsty, too. I'd like to take these new sensations as good signs, the tug of life or something like that but, to be absolutely honest, I'm annoyed.

Sure, I'd eaten plenty of times when we'd been out and about, but there's a big difference between *wanting* and *needing,* and the rumbling in my tummy feels a lot more like needing. Puck says he's hungry, too, but I don't believe him. Puck's like a tummy on big feet with long ears as much as he's like a rabbit. But, when he indicates with wiggling pink nose and enormous pleading brown eyes that he smells something delicious, I set Lady Bug's course by the intensity of his excitement.

In two shakes of a cottontail, we come to an island bigger than most of the rest in the archipelago. It's shaped like the moon midway between crescent and half. It's surface is rocky and prickled with saguaros, but Lady Bug finds a pebbly stretch where she can set down. She's barely stopped fluttering her wings when Puck's out and over the prow or bow or nose or whatever you call the front of a traveling ladybug.

Then, before Muriel can yell (and she's had lots of practice at this) for Puck to stop, he's vanished down a dark pit at the base of the largest saguaro. The hole's decent-sized, but there's no way that Horatius or Eyebright, or Lady Bug, unless she learns how to go small again (and that might cause problems of its own, so I do my best not to think about that), can go down there. I look at Muriel.

"Well, shall we go after him?"

"Do you even need to ask?"

When we get close enough to inspect it, the hole is sort of scary interesting. For one, it's quite obviously not just a hole. For two, the four sides are too regular. For three, two of those four side slope into steep steps. The remaining two are finished in shining tiles the westering sun shows as a rich maroon. Or, I think, though I don't say it lest I scare Muriel, the color of dried blood a couple days old.

Horatius and Eyebright settle to guard our backs, their chess board balanced on the curved carapace of a completely content Lady Bug. I'd wondered what we'd do for light but, as we descend, each stair tread glows softly underfoot, not enough to really provide light to see by, but enough to keep Muriel and me from falling all over each other or our own feet.

Puck's big bunny feet have left faint elongated oval prints on the floor. They change colors with every step – lavender, pink, green, yellow, blue, orange – each color soft and simultaneously intense. The colors don't repeat in any pattern I can figure out. When I look behind us, I see the marks of my cute little shoes and Muriel's dainty slippers added to the slowly fading mosaic of movement's memory.

By the time we reach the bottom of the stairs, Puck's prints are nearly faded. Muriel and I find that our cautious pursuit has led us into a vast subterranean space interrupted with pillars of irregular shape, height, and girth. We can see this and nonetheless lose Puck's trail because the area is defined not by light but by the fluttering phosphorescence of thousands – maybe millions or billions – of gossamer-fine wings. They don't so much light the place as outline the solid spaces they don't occupy.

It's like seeing by the light reflected by stars on a storm-tossed sea, but it works. Well, almost works. We can see the pillars because they're where the glow isn't, but we can't see Puck or his tracks and, creepiest, we can't see what is flapping those wings. Sometimes I almost think I've caught a glimpse. One time I think it's some sort of bee, complete with a long, curving stinger dripping with something viscous that gleams brighter than anything should in this not-light. Other times I think what I'm seeing is a bird, long-tailed like a mockingbird or some of the warblers, that the glowbright isn't liquid at all, except in the way an eye is liquid.

My brain is struggling to put all of this together and not doing a great job when Muriel gives a soft gasp and points. Following the shadow of her arm against the backdrop of fluttering phosphorescence I see there's a light, a real light, as solid as an electric flashlight. Even though it's moving, by comparison with the paler glow, it gives the impression of solidity. It also gives a perspective we'd lacked before.

For the first time, I realize that a certain amount of the floaty disorientation I've had since we followed Puck's prints to this place is because we're not on the floor of the pillared cavern. We're on an outcropping or ridge or something about halfway, well, partway, at least, between the floor and ceiling. By contrast, the lightbearer is down at floor level and moving with a great deal of purpose.

With one mind, Muriel and I race around our elevated walkway until we're more or less above this more or less solid light. I guess I've been hoping that Puck is going to be the one holding the light but, as we get closer, I realize that whoever is holding the light – while smaller than me – is nowhere near small enough to be Puck.

The overlook perspective doesn't make it particularly easy for us to figure out what – I guess "who" might be better, given that lots of my recent acquaintances have blended both "who" and "what" – anyhow, what (or who) the lightbearer might be. It's wearing a floppy stocking cap, the sort that the dwarfs in illustrations for *Snow White* are always shown wearing. That, combined with the height – or rather the lack thereof – and that it's carrying an old-fashioned lantern and we're underground makes me wonder. Could this be a dwarf? Given some of the creatures I've met lately, a dwarf wouldn't surprise me one bit.

Muriel must be thinking the same way because she whispers, "No beard."

I'm about to whisper back that – at least in *Snow White* – not all the dwarfs had beards when the path along which the lightbearer is pattering twists enough that I can see its face from another angle.

"What a big nose you have," I'm thinking in an irreverent Little Red Riding Hood mode when I realize that while what I've seeing would be a really big nose for a human, and a pretty sharply-pointed one for a dwarf in most of the artistic depictions I've seen, it's a perfectly good nose, even a dashing and handsome nose, for a rat. That this rat is bipedal, wearing not only a hat but baggy trousers (complete with a neatly stitched tail opening) and a loose shirt doesn't make me doubt my identification one bit. By now a rat wearing clothing and carrying a lantern is positively normal.

So, a rat with a lantern in a cavern otherwise lit by the soft glow of some sort of flying things and Puck – a hungry Puck – missing. Would the rat be able to help us? Muriel thinks it might, but suggests we follow and see where this Rat in the Hat is going first.

I'm only momentarily tempted. Sure I'm a bit scared about talking to it. Rats can be fierce, but those are usually cornered rats. If anyone is cornered here that's us – me and Muriel – not literally but by the predicament our bouncing bunny buddy has gotten us into (again).

Why I discard Muriel's sensible suggestion that we follow the Rat is this. I know how I'd feel if I realized that someone was sneaking along after me in a dark cavern. First I'd be scared, then I'd be upset, maybe even angry. Sure, calling down to the Rat is risky, but we *are* above it. Maybe, since the Rat is bogged down by a bulky lantern, it won't be particularly swift if it decides to come after us.

Do I think all of this? Not in any sort of linear fashion. That's not how thinking works. Instead, I'm giving Muriel a reassuring squeeze on the shoulder, then I'm kneeling on the edge of the ridge or outcropping or whatever we're on and leaning down, calling as softly as I can while making my voice carry, "Excuse me, Mr. Rat? Sir, could you spare a moment?"

The rat stops in mid-step, his tail stiffening behind him like some sort of organic exclamation point. Lifting the lantern high, he turns slowly, beady eyes bright as he tries to sort us out from the shadows.

"Who's there?"

"Uh, me. I mean us, uh, Jessie…

"… and Muriel."

"We're up here."

The rat reorients on our voices, but we're still out of the range of the lantern's light.

"We could jump down," I suggest. "I mean, if we wouldn't be trespassing."

"Isn't *my* cavern," the rat replies, lowering his lantern so that he can adjust his floppy cap. "Why don't you come over this way? There're steps, easier, safer, than jumping."

He must figure we're going to take his suggestion – it *is* sensible, after all – so he walks in the direction indicated, stopping where the light illuminates a roughly cut set of stone stairs. We go down, me first, Muriel close behind.

"Salt and sour-sweet sap," says the rat, "blood and ink, flesh and pulp. What brings two such here?"

I wonder how to respond to that. Do I explain about being dead or as good as dead? Do I mention miracles? In the end, I settle on the simplest explanation.

"We have a friend, a sort of rabbit, I guess you'd say. He went down the hole back there and hasn't come back. We're looking for him."

The Rat in the Hat – who now that we're on the same level, I can tell is about four feet tall, the top of his cap coming to just below my breasts –

pushes back the edge of his cap so he can scratch above one eyebrow – well, where an eyebrow would be on a human – with a narrow paw-hand.

"A rabbit of sorts? I can't say I've seen one, nor sniffed, nor heard, not even a sort of rabbit as your friend is a sort of girl and you are…" He pauses as if considering, "… a sort of Jessie."

Muriel speaks up, heartened, I think, at being known as a girl. "Puck's a greedy sort. From how his nose was wriggling, we guessed he was going after something good to eat."

As if on cue, my stomach rumbles. The Rat in the Hat's whiskers twitch, but he remains the soul of good manners. "Well, that helps matters a touch, leastwise for finding this Puck of yours, although maybe not for him. Doubtless he caught scent of the hummingbirds' nectar."

"Hummingbirds?" I repeat incredulously. "Puck wouldn't get much satisfaction out of eating those – even if he would. He's not much for eating other than rabbits' sort of food."

"And sweets," Muriel adds. "Don't forget. He's a demon for sweets."

The Rat in the Hat chuckles then, a deep, throaty sound, completely at odds with the sort of noise one would expect from a rat, even one with a hat. "Not 'hummingbird,'" he says carefully pronouncing the word, "'*honey*bird.' That's what's flying all around us – well, leastwise over there. They harvest salt and limestone, then use these to make both their nests and a nectar so delicious that it makes honey taste like dust and dead dreams. "

My stomach growls again. "I bet that's what Puck scented. How do the honeybirds feel about sharing their nectar?"

"Depends," the rat says. "Definitely depends. Mostly they save it to nurture their young, but sometimes they make more than they can use right away."

"I don't suppose…" I begin, then firm up my resolve. "Could you tell us how to find the honeybirds' nectar store?

The Rat in the Hat gives me and Muriel a curious once-over. "I might. I might. But maybe first you could introduce yourselves. I understand your concern for your friend, but manners is manners."

I flush, embarrassed, but even so my mind's questing after some detail. Then I have it. The Rat in the Hat already knows my name, doesn't he? Hadn't he called Muriel some sort of girl and me some sort of Jessie? Had I misheard him, the way I'd heard "hummingbird" when he said "honeybird"? What had he called me then? I want to ask, but this isn't the time for that.

Muriel apparently doesn't find this request at all odd and is already introducing herself. "I'm Muriel, good sir. Very pleased to make your acquaintance." She dips a little curtsey, catching the hem of her dress with both hands.

The rat's beady bright eyes turn to me.

"I'm Jessie," I say, still finding my name and all the history that goes with it heavy on my tongue. My nightdress – or rather the nightdress in which I'd awakened in the rosy tower, for I don't remember ever owning such a fussy bit of attire – invites a curtsey, so I lift the floor-length hem and manage not to make too great of botch of it.

The Rat in the Hat offers a smile that shows his long front teeth. "And I am Cooter Dandelion." He dips a bow, deep enough that the top of his cap brushes the floor. "Pleased to meet 'cha."

"Pleased to meet you, Mr. Dandelion," Muriel and I say, pretty much together.

He gives us another of those long incisor grins. "My friends call me Dandycoot."

I've never quite known what to do when someone says something like that. Is he inviting us to call him "Dandycoot"? We're not exactly friends, after all. Or is it an invitation to consider ourselves friends – at least until proven otherwise? I decide I'll just avoid names as much as possible. That should work. After all, I hadn't known mine for what seems like just about forever.

Muriel, by contrast, is positively perky. "Mr. Dandelion…"

"Dandycoot."

Muriel blushes, which surprises me. Then I get it. Proper little etiquette mistress she is, she's embarrassed by his forthrightness.

"Uh, Dandycoot," she continues, "you said you might be able to help us find the honeybird's nectar store."

"That is so," he replies, "but the question is, do you want the nectar store or do you want to find your friend – this Puck?"

"Why, Puck, of course," she replies, while I nod vigorous agreement. "We told you he's a complete glutton. If he smelled this nectar he'd go right for it."

"True enough," Dandycoot accedes, "but that doesn't mean the honeybirds would let him help himself. They're fierce creatures, makes bees seem as mild as a fall of apple blossoms."

"They can't have killed Puck!" I protest.

"Whether they did or didn't, depends on if they felt they had a use for him," Dandycoot replies with a certain amount of callousness. "You say he's a glutton. Is he plump then?"

Muriel sketches roundness in the air. "Very plump. Just about all plumpness except for ears and whiskers."

"Well, that's good or might be. Likely they'll be saving him as a host for their babies."

We'd begun walking along the tunnel after introductions had been completed, but at those words I freeze in mid-step. Muriel, by contrast, dashes ahead a few steps, as if off to the rescue, before realizing that she has no idea where to run. Instead she spins around and grabs Dandycoot's paw-hands in her own hand-hands and gives him a shake.

"How can you be so nonchalant! Puck needs our help – and from what you say, he needs it *now!*"

Dandycoot gives her a shake back, then drops her hands. "You're right, Miss Muriel. I've been a bit slow on the uptake, but can you blame me? The honeybirds are rare dangerous critters, and if you were seeking their nectar, rather than…"

Muriel cuts him off. "We want Puck! Please, if you don't want to risk yourself, that's well and good. Just point us in the right direction and we'll be off."

"Might not be wise," Dandycoot replies. "I've heard Jessie's tummy rumbling like the coming of a storm and that's no condition in which to go into a honeybird's lair."

I want to agree. After feeling no hunger for so long, I'm half-crazy with this. But Muriel has expectations of me – come to think of it, *I* have expectations of me. That's going to need to do in place of the meal I crave.

"Point the way," I manage, hoping Dandycoot doesn't notice how I've pushed the heel of my hand into my gut in an effort to mute the rumbles of my rebel tummy.

"Point the way?" Dandycoot muses, beginning to trot down one of the branching tunnels, setting quite a nice pace, "and abandon two brave visitors to these underground reaches? I couldn't sleep if I were such a coward."

With those words, he breaks into a real all-out run, going so fast that I must gather up the hem of my nightdress in both hands and hurry after, feet in those fancy shoes tapping and slapping on the stone. As we race along, Dandycoot provides us with a gasped briefing about honeybirds, their ways and habits, especially when protecting their nests and nurseries.

Honeybirds attack in two ways. The first is sort of like a bee-sting, except that unlike bees they can shoot their stingers, nor does doing this hurt them, except for robbing them of one means of attack until another stinger takes form. But this disarming is only an inconvenience, for the honeybirds still have their beaks. If their stingers might be likened to envenomed darts or daggers, their beaks are sharp swords, twinned blades sharp as fencing foils but stronger, meant for more than "touché."

"You speak of swords and daggers," Muriel manages when we needs must slow to make our way along a treacherous passage, salt water slick over stone underfoot.

Tingly cold drops fall from above. Each time one hits me, I remember what Dandycoot had said about these tunnels being underground. I can't forget – no matter how hard I try – the vast ocean over which Lady Bug had carried us the day before. My awareness of the crushing weight of water overhead is so great that I nearly forget the nagging hollow of hunger inside me. Given how very hungry I am, then that's a good measure of how scared I am.

Both fear and hunger diminish not the least for all that I'm now adding sodden and tired to the myriad sensations coursing through me as I slip and slide my unsteady way along ways barely lit by Dandycoot's bobbing lantern. As when we'd gone out the windows of the rosy tower into the gargoyles' realm, I wonder at my wish to leave that safe and comfortable place. Now that I think about it, that excursion had been Puck's fault, too, but that time I'd followed him out of impulse and ignorance. What excuse do I have this time?

And, thinking of Puck, I know I need no excuse. Puck is somehow incredibly reason enough. So it is that I find it possible to listen intently as Muriel completes her question.

"When you talk of daggers and swords, you're being metaphorical, right? The honeybirds we saw back in the cavern, they're far too small to be said to wield more than pins. I admit, being poked by enough pins would hurt quite a lot, but…"

Dandycoot is shaking his head so hard that the tip of his floppy cap goes back and forth with the motion. "Ah, Miss Muriel, I can understand why you'd be thinking that, hoping that, but when I spoke of swords and daggers, swords and daggers were what I meant. What you saw were not so much honeybirds as one sort of honeybird. The nectar collectors are small and dainty, for their business is with the gathering of tiny things, a task where great size would be a disadvantage. But the guardian honeybirds are much larger, so it is true swords and true daggers – and even true teeth – that we must dread."

"Have they any other sizes and shapes we should be prepared to meet?" I ask.

"One more at least, other than the infant forms," Dandycoot replies promptly. "The nursemaids, or so I may as well call those that are the caretakers of the eggs and the young."

"Do these have swords and daggers?" Muriel asks, sounding to her credit, more curious than scared.

"Not swords, perhaps, but their bills or beaks make a fair enough weapons if needed, but they rarely have the need."

"Why not?" I ask when he falls quiet. At first I think it's because he's forgotten how much we don't know. Then I realize that he's holding up a paw-hand for us to slow, gesturing for us to come slowly forward to where we can see whatever it is that has made him halt.

We do, moving quietly, although there is sound enough - buzzing, humming, cheeping, twittering - that I suppose we could talk in soft voices and not be overheard. If the sound is the first thing I notice, the second is the light. Thus far, we'd made our way by the erratic glow of Dandycoot's lantern, but now I realize that he has turned the wick down, for the honeybirds' own light is ample for us to see by.

It's a peculiar shifting glow in a hue that reminds me – after a long moment of careful cogitation – of the sort of light opals would give off if opals did such a thing. A whitish, pale blueish glow, flecked with shouting sparks in darker hues – orange, indigo, a silver white that is somehow both harder and firmer and yet more ephemeral than the pale background white. But neither sound nor the light can hold my attention for long, for when the smell touches my nostrils, I go down onto my knees as the storm of hunger cleaves me in two.

I feel Muriel's hands on my shoulders, though but distantly, for all sensation has been drowned by the powerful craving. Even more faintly, I hear Dandycoot's voice, though it takes me time to get the sense of the words.

"…why I worried about her coming along while unfed. The scent of the honeybirds' nectar is enticing even for one just stuffed from a banquet. For one already in need of sustenance…"

Neither Muriel or I ask why he hadn't insisted on warning us in greater detail or insisting that we stop and find food. Once we'd known of Puck's danger, we hadn't been of a mind to listen even to good sense.

"Is the nectar poisonous then?" Muriel asks.

"Worse," Dandycoot says solemnly. "One taste of it can rob the imbiber of any desire for any other food or drink. Since the honeybirds are not inclined to share, this can be a sentence of death."

To my surprise, Muriel laughs, genuine laughter, not the sound that so often accompanies false courage. "Then Jessie will be okay. She's stronger than you'd guess. And if there's any taste that could rob Puck of his appetite – well, I just don't believe any such exists."

Dandycoot apparently doesn't like his warning being shrugged off so lightly, for his reply is tart. "Well, you'll need to save this paragon of gluttony before you can figure out if you're right. As for Jessie, she is…"

But he stops in mid-phrase, for I've struggled to my feet. Sure the hunger is still there and my thoughts are pretty muddy, the way they can get when you need a good meal, but I'm not going to fail Muriel – or Puck. I push in front of the other two, getting to where I can look down and see what the opalescent light may reveal. Muriel's right beside me, leaving Dandycoot, perforce, a poor third.

The opal light is strange, but no stranger than a lot of things I've seen lately. Strangest, perhaps, is the omnipresence of it, a directionless glow that leaves no room for shadows, not even under what I take for oddly-shaped furniture cast from amber. I'm still trying to figure this "furniture" out when Muriel hisses in shock and points.

Creatures that must be the nursemaid honeybirds are busy tending something pearl white and pearl round set on a table of a translucent greenish-black substance that I now realize is a darker variation of the amber. The white roundness is, of course, Puck. It takes me a moment to figure out why he hasn't hopped down off that dark amber pedestal and bopped out of there. They've got him in a cage – a cage they're still weaving around him by drawing a delicate tracery of a gleaming pale golden syrup with their sharply pointed beaks.

How to describe the nursemaid honeybirds? If the nectar gatherers had seemed a cross between a hummingbird and a honeybee, these nursemaid birds owe something to long-legged walkers like storks. Their sharp beaks are akin to the frog-stabbers of the stork, but their billowing pouches under the lower bill are pendulous enough to make a pelican green with envy. The nursemaids' plumage is the eye-searing blue and red of an emergency vehicle's warning light. Their round eyes also flash with changing colors. Right now, those eyes are predominantly a vivid scarlet but, as the nursemaids begin extruding a line of syrup, the color fades to white, then shifts to an equally violent blue.

To this point, they've succeeded in encasing Puck in a sort of domed birdcage. The bars top to bottom are tightly enough placed that His Rotundity can't possibly squeeze between. The nursemaids have also put several wider horizontal bands in place. These prove admirable for stabilizing the whole contraption, as we witness firsthand when Puck braces his upper body against the bars and kicks out with his large bunny feet. I know how solidly those feet can kick, but the bars only bend a little – maybe.

"How did they even get him to hold still while they built that around him?" Muriel asks.

As if in answer, Puck scoops a large, deep soup bowl from the floor of the cage, puts it on his head helmet-wise, and tries to head-butt his way out of the enclosure.

"Oh," Muriel continues with a sigh. "I get it. They fed him and while he was otherwise occupied..."

I nod. "I don't like how that cage doesn't seem to have been designed with a door. Take a closer look at those other 'tables.' See the bulky things on them? I think they're cages just like Puck's except finished."

Muriel and I had just about forgotten Dandycoot, so we both jump when his voice comes from above us, where he'd climbed onto a sort of shelf on the wall of the dripping tunnel.

"You're right to be worried, Jessie. They'll weave the bottom of the cage tight enough to hold a thickened nectar syrup, then they'll pour in enough to glue the prisoner into place. When that's done – and usually the prisoner helps by being more interested in drinking the syrup than in getting free – then they implant the eggs."

"In the prisoner?" I ask, thinking of parasitic wasps and certain types of spider.

"Nope, in the nectar," Dandycoot replies. "The nursemaids keep weaving and filling and planting until the level of the syrup reaches the top of the cage. The prisoner is candied, filled with sweetness inside and out. This way he – or she – is ready to provide the nutrients necessary for the honeybird young when they hatch and need more than just nectar."

"That's disgusting!" Muriel says, but Dandycoot only shrugs.

"I agree with you, but there're some who think drowning in honeybird nectar is a fine way to go."

Muriel shudders. I try to look horrified, but the really terrible thing is that I can almost – no, not almost, let me be completely honest, and it's not just the hunger gnawing in my gut – I understand why someone might make that choice. Living is tough. Dying though, that can be so easy, such a relief, even.

"But," I say, choosing not to upset Muriel by sharing these thoughts, "here's the thing. Puck is most definitely *not* a volunteer. So, as I see it, it's up to us to help him get out."

I lean forward, scouting out a way down to the nursery cavern floor. I've been so preoccupied with watching the nursemaids and Puck that I'd forgotten that Dandycoot had mentioned a third type of honeybird: the guardians. Now I see them ranked along the chamber's walls, brilliantly feathered in the vibrant colors that opals only contain in minute flecks: green, orange, sapphire. They're so violently shaded that they're hard to focus on. Let's just put it this way – they make the nursemaids look dull.

When Muriel sees the guardians, she breathes a single word: "T-Rex."

"Roadrunners," I disagree, but I don't really. These guardians remind me of both creatures. They're big for roadrunners, small for most dinosaurs, at least I think so. But whether these are roadrunners with lots of teeth or drastically reduced T-Rex with wings (instead of those stupid little fore-claws) and a long feathered tail, one thing is perfectly clear. They're dangerous.

And Puck is running out of time. It's taken three of the nursemaid honeybirds, but they have him effectively immobilized. The first has him pushed against one side of the bird cage. The second pokes its bill at his feet whenever he kicks. A third is madly weaving strips to raise the level of the base. It won't be long before the cage is solid enough that they'll be able to pour nectar in and glue Puck's feet into place.

My stomach growls again, but instead of hunger making me crumple up, I just get mad. Stupid body! Shut up and let me think! My stomach doesn't stop grumbling, but I guess the rest of my body must agree with my mouth because my feet are working (legs, too; I mean it's all connected, right?) and with some help from hands and arms and fingers, I'm climbing sidewise and down angling right over one of the biggest, meanest, nastiest looking of the guardian honeybirds.

My target is primarily an eye-searing violet – a violent violet – flecked with sparks of sapphire and emerald. Real sparks, as I learn when I plop myself squarely down onto its back and a stinging cloud rises. I swing my legs so they go over the wing joints. When the shocked and startled honeybird swivels its head and all those teeth around to find out what's going on, I wrap my fingers (and hands) around the beak and smash it shut.

As I'd hoped, most of its muscle is meant for biting and holding. Letting go isn't really something it needs much muscle for, because whatever ends up in those jaws usually isn't up to doing much once the shutting happens. I'm in the process of ripping a strip from my nightgown when I hear an enthusiastic whoop from Dandycoot. A moment later, a leather belt lands in my lap. I don't stop to say "thanks," so I've got my shocked steed's mouth cinched tight shut before T-runner knows what's going on.

And what are the rest of the honeybirds doing while I try out a new form of rodeo? The answer is "not much." It was seeing how many nursemaids it had taken to deal with one idiot moon rabbit – a caged one at that – that had clued me in to how these honeybirds might have stingers big as daggers, but they weren't exactly the sharpest knives in the drawer.

Why should they be when just the scent of their nectar was enough to transform the majority of nose-gifted folk into quivering tummies? Muriel is an odd one and so am I. As for Dandycoot... Well, I suspect we hadn't encountered him loitering in that tunnel by chance. The question is, a chance at what? But speculating about that is going to have to wait until I'm not bouncing up and down on an increasingly annoyed runner-rex.

Muriel has scrambled down to join me, and now she's trussing the legs of my reluctant steed together. I feel when it starts tottering over and spring free. Good thing because, while honeybirds may not be top-drawer intellectuals, they're not completely clueless, either, and this one might have tried to get a jab in.

Well, at least the rex-runners aren't clueless. The nursemaids are still mono-focused on Puck. He's redoubled his efforts to escape, no doubt inspired by our timely appearance.

Once my first mount is down, I swing astride the next nearest runner-rex while it's still confused by its buddy flailing around on the floor. Muriel springs under another, coming up on its other side while it's still poking its bill, snapping its jaws and wriggling its stinger, after where it thinks she should be. That gives her a chance to hobble it. When it stumbles and falls she dangles a bit of ribbon over its head. "Snap!" goes the T-teeth around the lure and, in a trice, Muriel has wrapped the rest of the ribbon round the jaw, snugging the knot off with a snazzy bow.

I do my rodeo routine once more and this time I *do* need to tear a strip off my nightdress, but that's because Dandycoot has joined in our riotous round-up. He's dropped his floppy cap over the head of one of the remaining T-runners, and while it's trying figure out where the light went, he sets about tying the beak shut right around the hat.

With our team of three and opponents who grow increasingly more befuddled by our evolving tactics, we manage disable the guardians. I'm not going to brag that we manage without a scrape or scratch – there're plenty of those – but Puck's still alive to be rescued once we lay the last of the road-rexes down to complete an orderly line of thrashing indignation.

Between adrenalin and anxiety, I'm nearly insane by the time I go rushing across the chamber to where Puck is encased in just about the most delicious, enticing, gut-ripping confection of a cage that anybody could imagine. I don't bother with the nursemaids, who are looking back and forth between me, Puck, and the line of trussed guardians, their eyes flashing white with confusion. I figure I can have Puck out of that cage before they figure out what to do next.

Open-armed, I barrel full-body into the cage. My goal is to knock it off the green amber pedestal, but it's firmly cemented into place. Nonetheless, with a cracking that I'm not sure is my bones or the bars of the cage, I slam into the cage once more. Up close, it smells like the best combination of a candy store and a bakery. The last is what gets me. After being immersed in the odor of the nectar, I'm almost immune to the lure of sweets – I guess there is some truth that there can be too much of a good thing. But fresh bread and cinnamon rolls and butter cookies, that nearly undoes me.

Ironically, it's one of the nursemaid birds finally deciding that I'm a threat and coming at me that saves the day. When she stabs into the fleshy part of my upper arm, sudden pain proves to be a wonderful way to clear a befuddled mind.

Puck takes advantage of the cracks I've made in the bars and batters a hole in the side of the cage. Then, hauling his sticky feet out one by one, he splats to the floor. Once there, he's so incredibly happy to be free that he's like kung-fu bunny. I'm astonished that he's not even pausing to grab a sticky paw of nectar or lick a glob off his toes. I guess, for once in his chubby life, he's full.

In a trice, we have all the nursemaids incapacitated. Puck's bouncing about doing a moon rabbit victory dance, and I realize that Dandycoot has vanished. It doesn't take us long to find him, though. The sound of weeping draws us into one of the side chambers.

He's standing next to a pedestal upon which rests a hybrid between an aquarium and one of those pricy paperweights in which various things have been encased so they seem to float. The shape of this one is a cylinder crossed with a Dali dream – weird curves where you wouldn't expect them to be. The color is that of the golden-amber nectar but denser, more concentrated.

I'm trying to figure out why my brain keeps saying "aquarium" as much as "paperweight" and chiming in with "a fly in amber," when I suddenly, gut-twistingly get it – and wish just as quickly that I hadn't. There's something in the cylinder, something moving slowly but purposefully. This is a cage like the one we rescued Puck from, a cage that has been woven around a little child ratling. But in the ratling's case, no one had gotten there before the cage had been finished, before the nectar had been poured in, before the honeybird eggs had been inserted into the hardening sweet goo, before...

And now the eggs are hatching, and the honeybirdlets are devouring the nectar around them, which accounts for why the cylinder has such an odd shape. And they're homing in, by instinct or scent or some combination of sensory inputs I can't begin to imagine, on the pathetic little rat in amber.

So, here's why Dandycoot had been hanging about, and why he knew so much about the honeybirds and how dangerous they can be. If I'd thought at all, I'd assumed he was an opportunistic nectar thief, hoping we'd create a diversion. This is far better... and far, far, worse.

"Can we do anything to help her?" Muriel asks, her voice all choked up. "Maybe? Surely?"

But Dandycoot is shaking his head, rat ears (no longer hidden by his cap), drooping, all of him drooping. "It's too late, it is. The nectar drowns and preserves..."

But I'm not having any of it. I remember our journey to Heka Egypt, and the story of Isis and Osiris. Well, this isn't nearly so bad, is it? I mean, the little rat is all there, not cut into pieces.

"What's her name?" I ask Dandycoot.

"Abby," he replies promptly, though he needs to swallow a sob to do it. "It's short for Absinthe."

"Absinthe?" I repeat, not quite believing my ears.

"That's right," Dandycoot says," as in the old saying 'Absinthe makes the heart grow fonder.' 'Twas one of her late grandmother's favorite sayings."

My brain hurts, as I find myself imaging an alcoholic rat clan matriarch rocking in a corner, knitting (probably a floppy cap) spilling over her lap.

"Right!" I say, refocusing. "Abby. Now, I've been thinking. From what I know about parasitic wasps and their ilk, I seem to recall that in most cases they don't kill their host creatures. They immobilize them or numb them or suchlike. Why shouldn't it be the same with these honeybirds? The nectar might nourish the captive just as it does the unhatched eggs. If that's the case, then..."

"Then we're not too late?!" Dandycoot's voice shrills with that most horrible of all emotions: Hope.

"That's right," I agree. "We may not be too late to save Abby."

Muriel has been inspecting the amber pedestal and the Dali-bed in which Abby is encased. Suddenly she turns and makes a frantic gesture, indicating that we need to look more closely. It doesn't take me long to figure out what has Muriel so worked up. Some of the honeybirds have worked their way quite close to the encysted ratling.

One thing that all forms of the honeybirds have shared has been a wickedly sharp beak. These not yet differentiated hatchlings are no exception. And less than an inch or so separates sleeping Abby from the closest of those probing proboscises. If Abby is still alive – and despite my encouraging words to Dandycoot, I'm not completely certain – then before long she's going to be a pincushion.

Who knows if those hatchlings might inject some sort of liquefying agent to make their dining and digesting easier. Seems to me I'd read about some types of spiders doing just that. If I'd felt pressured before, wondering just when more adult honeybirds might enter these chambers, now I feel positively frantic. And, yes, I'm still hungry, though, if contemplating the honeybird's probable eating habits has had any positive side effect, it's that I'm feeling markedly nauseous, too. Thank heavens for small favors!

I decide I'd better concentrate on the matter at hand.

"Dandycoot, how does the nectar react to water?"

He may have odd ideas as to how to name a child, but Dandycoot's not a dumb bunny – or rat. "Meaning, will these blocks melt in water? Maybe, if there was enough of it. Little drips and streams won't do it, and that's all there is in these tunnels."

I stare at him in surprise, realizing that as a tunnel dweller he has no idea what lies above. "Can you get us back to where you found us? I know where there's plenty of water."

Dandycoot looks nonplussed, even unsettled, but he nods. "I can. I even know a short cut from here so we wouldn't need to go back through that flock of nectar gatherers. Didn't use it before because I wanted to get to that overlook. But how will you move Abby? She's all but cemented to that pedestal. It would take someone far stronger and much larger than any of us to move her."

He's right, but I'm not giving up. Had Isis given up? No! Even when she couldn't find Osiris' phallus, she'd worked out a substitute. I glance over at Muriel and see from the worry line between her brows that she's also trying to figure out how we can make this work.

"Don't worry about getting Abby loose, Muriel," I assure her. "I'll manage that. You and Dandycoot go back to where we left Lady Bug and the boys. I'll leave it to you to figure out who's going to be able to fit down here."

"Eyebright at least," she says in the sort of voice that means she's convincing herself as much as me. "But will you be safe?"

"I'll be fine. Puck and I will stay right here. He'll guard me while I work on how to distract the hatchlings and get Abby's block off the pedestal. Now, go!"

And Muriel does, although she doesn't look any too happy about it. I hear Dandycoot asking her questions about the "boys" as he hustles along in the lead. I don't even try to listen, but focus all my attention on the curvy, wavy-shaped block of nectar.

"Puck," I say. "I meant it when I told Muriel that I trusted you to stand guard so I can focus on figuring out what I can do for Abby. Got that? No wandering off, right?"

Puck replies with an indignant squawk that sounds very much like, "As if!" Then he hops over and, to my great consternation, begins to gnaw at the block of solidified nectar around Abby.

"Puck! This is no time for a meal!"

He makes a muffled sound, unintelligible because of his occupied mouth. When he spits, I realized that he's doing his best to chew without getting any of the crystalized sweetness into his mouth. He manages pretty well, maybe because he's doing a sort of beaver chisel-tooth thing, working the amber off the block in long curls.

Closer and closer to the first hatchling go the cuts, then Puck stops. Wriggling his nose and scrubbing at the edges of his mouth with his paws, he seems to be waiting for me to do something. When a long hatchling leg pokes out of the tooth-carved crevice, I get it and, as I get it I'm horrified.

I'd been concentrating on keeping those sharp beaks out of Abby, but I hadn't thought about what was going to happen to the hatchlings when we ruined their nest. When they'd been nothing but inexorable motions within the block of solidified nectar, the hatchlings had been the threat and, as the threat, easily translated into the "enemy." But now, flailing around, knobby joints all awkward, peeping in frantic awareness that something is wrong, but too young, too stupid to be able to figure out any more than fear…

This isn't an enemy, it's a lost and probably dying baby bird. The entire time my horrified brain is working through this, my equally horrified fingers are squeezing into the crevice Puck had cut with his bunny fangs, easing loose one gawky leg, then another, then a wing, finally the remaining wing and lastly that big-eyed, baggy-eyelidded head with those tiny but already needle-sharp teeth. Yep. Teeth. When this baby grows up it's going to be a rex-runner, a warrior, a guardian.

If it grows up. Can it, now that I've taken it from nest and ersatz breast in one? Puck beeps at me and I realize that he's telling me I can pull another nestling out, away from Abby. At the same moment, maybe responding to Puck's high-pitched voice, the nestling in my hands cheeps and I'm short of hands and, if Puck's foot-slapping urgency is any indication, I'm short of time, too. Without really thinking about it, I shove the hatchling inside my nightdress.

Its claws grasp the fabric, and that gives me a moment to tighten the sash at my waist so that the bodice becomes a sort of bag. Then, feeling decidedly corseted, I hurry to slide my hand into Puck's newest incision. I'm groping about, seeing if I can haul – well, rather more like ease – the second nestling out of the block of nectar, noticing as I do that this one was scarily chose to Abby, when I feel a sharp needle stab into the flesh of my left breast. The sensation is sort of like a bee sting, sort of like… and then I don't feel it and I wonder if the honeybird nestlings can numb their captives.

Intellectually, I realize that Baby #1 has solved the dinner problem, at least for now. Emotionally, I'm seriously grossed out. Balancing the two, I decide that I can live with this, even as some small corner of my brain is worrying that pure human blood, unadulterated by an infusion of nectar may not be the best diet for this little opportunist. But there's no changing that and there's no pain and the little thing is *so* small that I can't imagine it will do me much harm.

In fact, I'm – well, it would be going a bit far to say "pleased" – but I'm at least relieved not to have a murderous slapgap as the only answer to the question of what to do with the hatchlings when I get them away from Abby. When I get #2 free – this one looks as if it has a nascent nursemaid's nectar-holding pouch – I put it inside my nightdress, too, making sure it snags a grip on the fabric before letting go. There's the pretty-much expected needle stab a few moments later, then numbing, but I'm already off to delve into Puck's latest crevice.

By the time Muriel reappears with Danycoot and a rather squashed-looking Eyebright, between us me and Puck have removed the hatchling threats to Abby. She's still incased in nectar, though, and hacking her loose would be incredibly dangerous to tiny limbs and whiskers. Puck's looking cross-eyed from resisting eating even one of the slivers of nectar and my stomach is growling so much that I don't even hear it anymore. I feel it though and, in a weirdly abstracted fashion, wonder if all that rumbly-tumbly stuff is going to shake loose the dozen or so honeybird nestlings we've removed from around quiescent Abby.

Welcome as she is for bringing Eyebright and assurance that there is indeed a faster way back to the surface, Muriel is even more welcome for another reason: She's brought food! There are a bunch of carrots for Puck, complete with healthy greens. For me, there's a peanut butter sandwich on thick slices of seeded dark rye bread, a banana, and a bottle of what tastes like mango-pomegranate juice.

"Turns out Lady Bug has a well-stocked storage compartment," Muriel says casually by way of explanation, though her eyes are snapping with pride. "We'd just never thought to ask."

I start to hug Muriel in thanks, then an annoyed cheeping from inside my baggy bodice stops me.

"Jessie! What have you got in there?" Muriel asks in a fashion that makes pretty clear she has some pretty serious suspicions.

"I'll explain later," I prevaricate. "We'd better get out of here while the going can be got, then see if salt water will melt Miss Absinthe out of the block."

The short version is that we do get out, though the longer version contains some really scary parts, like where the nectar block gets stuck and blocks the passage, and we need to get it loose. But we do get out. When we reach the passage to the desert island, Horatius reaches down and hauls the block up and onto the sands beneath the interestedly swaying saguaros.

Salt water doesn't exactly melt the hard candy nectar, but it does soften it enough that we can peel bits off Abby's exterior. When we melt Abby loose from the block, she starts trying to cough but not managing.

"The nectar's in her lungs!" Muriel whispers, eyes wide with horror, because it's looking like we're going to get Abby free only to cause her to die a whole lot more painfully than she would have as food for honeybird hatchlings. "And it's too solid for her to cough out."

She's hardly finished talking when I have one of those intuitive leaps that come so suddenly and so clear that they make you believe that some unseen being is whispering in your ear.

As we'd rushed through the shortcut, I'd checked out my little hitchhikers, and decided they seem to be doing pretty well. Now, without giving anyone opportunity to even think about what I'm doing, I pluck out a nursemaid type fledgling, then set it right up against Abby's ribcage. Bam! In goes the needlebeak and before you can say "Bob's your uncle" (why anyone would has always puzzled me), the nursemaid has filled its little belly and little bag, too. Then I drop it back inside my dress.

While Horatius restrains the kicking and squirming Dandycoot, I repeat the process with hatchlings grabbed at random. Soon little Abby is beginning to wheeze and cough, then to cough and breathe. There's no sign of lung collapse, so I'm betting that the nectar acted as a sort of patch, like the stuff you can put in a bike tire to seal small punctures.

Why not? It makes as much sense as most of what has gone on since we touched down on this saguaro-crowded island in the midst of this wide salt sea. Actually, as much as just about anything has since I awakened in the chamber atop that rosy tower.

So, at long last Abby stops coughing – or at least mostly stops because she's got a lot of goo in there and in the manner of goo it's going to take a while to get out. Have I ever mentioned how wet stuff multiplies when you spill it where you don't want it? The same is true of broken glass. But I've probably already been there. What's important is here.

So, when Abby stops coughing (mostly) and Dandycoot stops struggling (mostly), we learn how Abby got herself captured by the honeybirds. Turns out that Dandycoot had mentioned having a hankering for nectar, much the way that you and I might mention wanting some nearly impossible delight – like visiting an exotic land or a distant planet.

(Remember those credit card advertisements that encouraged people to go into debt so they could gift their loved ones with something "priceless"? Like that.)

Well, Abby had gotten herself into one of those scrapes that seem insurmountable to a child. She decided that if she got her daddy – because that's what Dandycoot is to her, in case that hasn't been clear – some of the honeybird nectar, he'd be so happy that he'd overlook her fall from grace. But things don't go as she planned, and that led to Dandycoot going looking for her, suspecting, but not knowing what had happened. And so he was there to help us and us him.

When Abby finishes her story, stopping every so often to cough or sniffle tears that seem pretty sincere to me, she says, "I'm sorry I didn't get you any nectar Daddycoot, but it really isn't all that great."

Puck wriggles his nose and quivers his whiskers, and Dandycoot looks thoughtful.

"Smells better than it tastes, especially when you've had a bellyful?"

Puck nods and bounces agreement, looking more like a bobble-head bunny in the back window of a car going down a dirt road with a serious case of washboarding than any live creature should.

And now that Abby's story is told, Dandycoot turns his mind to ours. The sun is setting, making the sky flame with long fingers of orange and red and yellow flared around with pink. Though part of his and Abby's way home will take them through tunnels where night and day don't matter no never mind, apparently there are ways that are better travelled when the sun is high and bright.

I wonder why this should be, but Dandycoot says he doesn't want to scare little Abby. Though she's pretty much asleep, snuggled up next to her daddy's legs, with his tail wrapped around her protectively, as if it's some killer snake, we respect his desire. I guess we've all been the kid who is almost but not quite asleep and hears what maybe she shouldn't.

"So, what brings you here?" Dandycoot asks. "Not down into the tunnels – that was Master Puck's doing – but into these lands."

Again, it's on my lips to say that I'm searching for a miracle, but I can't quite do it. And when I don't speak up, Muriel begins the tale. After all, it's her story, too, as I'm too often in danger of forgetting. Dandycoot listens with rat ears wide as satellite dishes listening for star song, soaking it all in.

Eventually, I help out here or there, adding details about our journeys to various of the window realms. As I do, I get powerfully homesick for those places that I've left behind me. When we get to the part about me being Jessie, and learning what happened to put her/me into the situation she is/was in, Dandycoot blinks and his whiskers curl in startlement and wonder.

"You're sure?" he asks. Then he catches himself and says, "Of course you're sure. You just explained why this must be so. Still, what an incredible tale!"

There is something in how he says "incredible" that makes me uneasy. I find myself thinking about what that word really means. It's come to be a synonym for "astonishing" or "fantastic," but it has its roots in "credo" or "to believe." Basically, "incredible" means "unbelievable." "Unbelievable" is another of those words that we've come to use outside of its literal definition. When we say "unbelievable," most of the time we mean, "I want to believe it, but it's a stretch."

Don't believe me? Think about how often when someone tells us something "unbelievable" our automatic response is "Really?" Does that mean we're calling that person a liar? No. But that's what we're doing. It's all too weird…

But for some reason when Dandycoot says "incredible" what I hear is what he's saying – that what I'm telling him is beyond belief. That my story is something that can't be believed as having really happened. That makes me really uneasy because ever since I learned that I'm Jessie and what has happened to Jessie, I've been looking for a miracle.

Miracles are another of those things that happen to other people. When something flat-out miraculous happens – like the spontaneous remission of a cancer or recovery from a horrible accident – then the first thing most people do is start looking for a reason to explain away the miracle. The one in a million treatment worked. The injuries weren't as bad as were originally thought. Stuff like that.

Why do we go there? Why don't we want to accept miracles *can* happen? Because if we don't feel that way, then we've got to wonder about all the people who *don't* get miracles. All those people the cancer kills. All those who don't come out of a coma. Those who wear out at seventy (that good old Biblical three score and ten), when someone else wears out at ninety or sixty. It's easier to dismiss the possibility of miracles, because the reality that miracles might just happen is too horrible to contemplate.

Or at least that's how it seems to me as I sit there in the sand on this oh, so literally desert island. I think about all those stories about resurrected gods, the ones that had made me decide to deny the horrid doom that seemed to have been decreed for little Absinthe, daughter of Cooter.

Are those sorts of stories meant as an exemplar, an encouragement that even if the miracle doesn't happen for you and yours, they do happen? Or is the fact that these are the ones who Came Back what makes them gods? And here's the real weirdness. Even the ones who Do come back rarely come back for good and real, not just to pick up their lives where they left off.

Jesus gets to hang out with the apostles and his other pals for a couple of days, then he Ascends. Osiris is brought back by his loving wife, the Mistress of Magic, but he doesn't get his old job back. Instead he gets a new one as the judge of the dead, presumably because he now really gets where they're coming from, what they've been through. Persephone's fate is decided as a shared custody deal between Mom and kidnapper-hubby. Baldr gets a comeback, but has to wait until after Ragnarok has scoured most of the other gods out of existence. Myriad vegetation gods die with the season, came back in the spring. Then there are all those heroes who wait sleeping until they'll be needed – after which they politely go away again, job done. "You kids get on with the rebuild. The Age of Heroes has ended. The Age of Daily Grind has begun."

The more I think about this, the more scared I get. I want to go back home. I really do. At least, I think I really do – but I think I've been, well, let's be really honest about it – my body was kept going, even encouraged to get itself fixed, sort of like when Isis did her jigsaw puzzle bit on Osiris – but I think that basically I've been dead.

Asphodel.

That was the word in my head when I came around in the rosy tower. And while Asphodel certainly is the name of a flower, it is also one of the ancient Greek names for where the dead go, a place that isn't heaven or hell or purgatory or anything like that, just a place where the souls of the dead get parked.

And getting back from being dead – well, the one thing the stories make clear is that just walking out isn't something that is easily done. Even for gods. Even for heroes. And me. I'm not either. Am I? Or *am* I?

"Am I a hero?" I say aloud, only realizing I've done so when the others swivel their heads around to look at me.

"Be-peep!" squeaks Puck in a way that sounds a little like "Of course!" flavored with wider notes of "duh."

Dandycoot is more articulate. "You are to me," he says firmly. "I never would have managed to free Abby without your inspiration."

Abby nods and giggles around a sleepy yawn. "Daddy's clever and sneaky, but he's not brave."

Those words may look mean, but they're not. They're all about true love, which means accepting a person for who they are – or he or she is – not for who you or they or he or she would like to be.

Muriel doesn't say anything, just rolls her eyes and smiles in a way that reminds me a lot of how Dandycoot's little Absinthe had looked at her ratfink daddy.

So everyone (except possibly me) agrees on the hero thing. For a brief delicious moment, I consider asking about what their opinions might be regarding the god question, but I back off, tasting bile. These are my friends, my confidants, my partners in this mad venture. If they said "no" or laughed or whatever, I'd have done myself no good. And if they said "yes," well, then I'd have done myself seriously worse, because I'd have robbed myself of my friends, my confidants, my partners, garnering worshippers instead.

So I stopper up my vanity and ask instead, "So, shall we all get some sleep?"

And we do, some of us in Lady Bug, some pillowed up against Eyebright and Horatius. As camping goes, it's pretty comfortable. When twilight shifts into full dark, the prickly-armed saguaros gather around us in a protective circle, raising their arms as if caught mid-way in the step of some complicated dance. Though we rest in peace and comfort, we all wake up as dawn is hardly more than a dream of light on the horizon.

Lady Bug serves us breakfast. Over rolls spread with thick, creamy butter and thicker mixed-up fruit jam that go very well with a dark, pineapple-mint tea, I ask Dandycoot what he's doing next.

He swallows a large swig of tea, then says firmly, "I'm going to get my adventurous ratling safely back to our nest. For now she's scared enough to have lost any taste she might have gotten for honeybird nectar, but that might not last. Best get her clear away."

He rises, then shuffles his feet, making a gesture with his forepaws that I realize is adjusting a floppy-topped cap that isn't perched atop his ears any longer. "You'd be very welcome – all of you, even the dragon and the giant – to come home with us. The tunnels would be a tight fit, but I think we could manage with a detour or two."

I'm tempted. It would be fascinating to see whatever strange rat warren in which Dandycoot and his family dwell. I'm considering suggesting that we take Dandycoot up on his offer, when Muriel speaks up first.

"We'd really love to take you up on your enormously kind invitation, but we have a mission of our own, one that we were diverted from by this mad moon rabbit who is more gifted in tummy than in good sense."

"Puck's brave though," says Abby, shyly lisping the accolade so that "brave" comes out more like "bwave."

"No one doubts his bravery," Muriel agrees. "We only wish he'd find fewer excuses to display it."

"What might your mission be?" asks Dandycoot. Then he slaps himself on his furry forehead. "But how could I forget? Of course, it must be getting Jessie back to where she can be a comfort to those she left behind."

"I don't suppose," Horatius rumbles, "that you have any thoughts where we might go from here."

Dandycoot shakes his head. "I've never been even this far into the world above."

Abby surprises us all by lisping, "East. Go east!"

For a moment, I mishear her, thinking she's said, "Eat! Go eat!" and I think she's telling her dandy daddy that she's still hungry despite the two enormous rolls she'd eaten. Then I sort out the syllables and so I ask, "East? Why east, Absinthe?"

The little rat fans out her ears with pleasure when I use her full name, but she answers with adult seriousness. "When I is in the block of nectar, I am so feeling that I needs to go west, that when the little birds wake, they will take me there. And when I go there, then never, ever, ever again will I be wiff my family just like now, so I thinks…"

She trails off, her store of conversation apparently exhausted. I give her a grin that's braver than I feel. "And since I want to find my way back to my family, then I should go east. That makes a curious sort of sense. Thank you, Abby."

The ratling wriggles in undisguised pleasure and whispers, "You's welcome, Jessie."

Then, with many protestations of friendship, as well as repeated thanks to me, to Muriel, to Eyebright, even to Puck (who is becoming far too pleased with himself once more), to Lady Bug for supplying breakfast, and to Horatius, just because, father and daughter rat take their leave.

Watching them vanish down the hole, I say, "I wonder if we should have made certain they get safely home."

Muriel sighs and shakes her head. "Time comes when folks need to look after themselves, without relying on heroes. Otherwise, they become less than they could be, when real heroes would want them to be more."

She looks really noble as she says this, and I realize that she's classifying herself as among the heroes. Again, I wonder why this should startle me so. After all, Muriel is a mere slip of a girl and yet she's done so much, up to and including going off alone with a strange and possibly untrustworthy rat through dim, dark, and dank tunnels for the purpose of bringing back a many-eyed dragon who is among her boon companions.

Who elected *me* as the main character of this tale anyhow? Maybe I'm the princess who needs to be rescued from a tower. Maybe from Muriel's point of view I'm only slightly less trouble than Puck. Certainly, I've gotten us into more scrapes than Puck has, and many of these without the excuse of impulsive curiosity. A couple of times, now that I consider it, my only excuse for leaving the tower and its comforts had been boredom.

I'm still immersed in uncomfortable contemplation of just how Muriel might see me and what role she might have cast me in our shared drama, when Eyebright, who rarely speaks except to prompt someone to draw the next card or move a piece on game board (although again, I find myself wondering why I'm so sure of this; who knows what he and Horatius have discussed in the solitude of the Rosy Tower when Puck, Muriel, and myself were off gallivanting about) says, "East is nice, but before we go, what are you going to do about those baby birds bloodsucking you under your nighty?"

I start because, believe it or not, I'd pretty much forgotten about the nestling honeybirds. I take a tentative peek and there they are. A careful count comes up with something between eleven and thirteen. Most of them seem to be prototypes of the nectar gatherers, but I'm figuring that only because they don't have the pendulous pelican pouch of the nursemaids or the brawny T-rex in training look that I associate with the guardians.

Now that I consider, there must be other types of honeybird. I mean, someone has to produce the eggs, right? On the other hand, I have no real reason to dismiss the nursemaids from that role. Or maybe the guardians lay the eggs and only guard when they're not. Or maybe…

Muriel nudges me and I realize that I've been standing there staring down the front of my nightgown.

"Sorry," I manage. "Umm, what to do with them? Well, I really don't want to go back to the hatchery. As it is, we lucked out with managing to escape the first time. Maybe we can – uh – put them in a basket and leave them for the nectar gatherers to find? If they can't carry them, then they could bring one of the guardians."

It isn't a great idea, but everyone agrees that it's the best option we have. Lady Bug (who we now know to query about supplies) has a picnic basket of sorts in her storage bay. We line this with a couple of folded cloth napkins, trying to make a cozy nest. Puck adds a couple of the larger blocks of the more or less solidified nectar that we'd pried off of Absinthe.

When these preparations are concluded, I hitch up my nightdress (Horatius and Eyebright turn all their eyes politely away) and reach for the nearest nestling. It releases its hold easily, with only a few sleepy cheeps of sated indignation. I hand it to Muriel, who gingerly accepts it and puts it in the basket.

Puck is waiting, pristine paws held up when I detach the next one. Remembering that he'd nearly ended up chick-food, I hesitate before giving the nestling to him, but he looks up with such wide-eyed appeal, begging to be trusted, that I give in. Puck lives up to my trust and so we set up a relay: Me to Puck to Muriel to basket.

We're about to move chick six when Muriel cries out, "Oh, no! They're climbing out of the basket!"

And they are, fluttering fledged wings in the finest fledgling fashion. (Had they had feathers before? I don't remember more than wisps. Maybe the feathers had been too damp to show. Maybe they just grow really fast.)

I'm about to say, "Well, put them back in the basket and this time close the top,"when two simultaneous realizations merge in my eyes and ears. With that, my reality takes a serious rocking. The hatchlings, nestlings, maybe better called "fledglings" now, aren't just randomly escaping captivity the way, say, kittens do when you try to put them in a box or whatever. They honeybirdlings are very direct in their course of a destination. They're all making a beeline – or maybe that should be a "birdline" – for *me*.

The first one has already reached the tattered hem of my nightdress and, with flapping wings and pickaxe strokes of its needlebeak, is starting to climb Mount Jessie. Or, as my ears are now telling me, "Mount Mom." I can't tell you how I know that's what they're saying, but I'm absolutely certain.

Muriel seems to understand them, too. She heaves a really incredible (that word again) sigh for someone so slender and apparently fragile.

"They've imprinted, Jessie. They think you're their mom."

I feel my eyes widen, but there's no denying the truth of it.

"So what'll happen if we just stuff them all in that basket and tie down the lid and skedaddle?" I answer myself, "Probably they'll die, just as surely as if we practiced our overhand pitching skills and used the ocean as a baseball diamond."

"And we can't do that," says Muriel, but with just that note of indecision that says, "But that would be the sensible thing, the *easy* thing, to do."

"We can't," I state firmly, knowing that this has to be my decision because, at least until we figure out how to wean them, the little creepizards are going to be drinking my blood. Already one of the fledglings has collapsed in exhaustion across my foot and is feebly probing at my bony ankle.

I scoop it up and drop it back down the front of my nightdress. At least there I don't need to watch its grizzly dining.

"So we're taking them, then?" Horatius rumbles.

"It's either that or we wait here or down in the caves until they're old enough to un-imprint," I say. "And who knows when that would happen? We'll bring those bits of nectar candy, though. Maybe we can convince them to try something other than a diet of Jessie blood."

Muriel brightens. "That should be possible. After all, the nectar gatherers make the nectar, so it can't be the honeybirds' only food. Maybe it's mostly for the babies and that's why the flavor is so intense."

Later, after we've gathered up what remains of dear Abby's almost tomb, we make ourselves comfortable in Lady Bug's capacious interior. Puck takes the bow again, but this time Muriel firmly holds onto one end of a braided ribbon harness, just in case our darling moon rabbit forgets what happened the last time he followed his nose. Horatius and Eyebright spread the chess board between them on the rearmost bench. Eyebright lets his coils spill out around the stern so we have a many-eyed watch behind.

Muriel and me and somewhere between eleven and thirteen honeybird fledglings take the middle seat. I'm not certain if "fledgling" is the right word for them, or if they're still nestlings, but I can't ignore the serious tickle of those little baby feathers, so fledgling it is.

"East," I say firmly. "Lady Bug, can you keep us going east, even after the sun rises?"

She doesn't answer, not in words, but the confident way her wings buzz, and how she rises into the air, then turns until precisely oriented are answer enough. I look down and wave to the saguaros. I smile as they wave back.

Flying east has distinct disadvantages, especially when you start off first thing in the morning while the sun's still climbing high. The dawn colors are amazing but once the pastels finish their aurora dance, then you're left with the light right in your eyes. If we'd still been in the rosy tower, we might have been able to convince ourselves that we possessed eyes like those of the phoenix, capable of looking directly into the sun. At the very least we might have been able to imagine ourselves sunglasses.

But we can't manage either of these and, though Lady Bug proves to have an impressive larder – at least as long as we keep Puck from over-foraging – she doesn't have any sunglasses, not even a scratched up pair in the compartment near the bow that reminds me of a glovebox. So she tints her own eyes smoky smoldering, and the rest of us sit on the floor and play cards with Horatius.

Eyebright, who has to hunker down, then curl around and around to protect his myriad eyes from the glare, decides he'd better be the dealer, since there's no way he can keep from seeing everyone else's cards, and that's just too much of an temptation, even for an honest dragon.

I'd just finished making a set of the Queen of Shoes and was fishing for a three of Stars when Lady Bug slows, indicating that she needs further directions. We all hop up, aware for the first time that we'd slipped below the glare of the rising sun and are, in fact, leaving him far behind us. In front of us the ocean has ended in a slender beach that in turn ends in a wall of green that seems to stretch from earth to sky, effectively barring us from flying further east.

Obviously, our first thought is to fly over the forest, but the trees really did seem to reach up to the sky. There is no "over" in which to fly. Lady Bug isn't dumb, after all. Now that we're all watching, she gradually adjusts her course so that we can see the pointy tops of the tallest pines, the spreading crowns of the oaks and elms, maples and gums.

Above these is only a tight line of sky like you'd see in a child's drawing: cerulean, flecked with little bits of white that might be clouds but could as easily be gaps left by a careless colorist. No matter. We aren't getting through that way. So, if over is out, then how about down or between?

Lady Bug seems dubious about the latter, but admits that she really hadn't examined down. She takes us to where the white-gold sand of the ocean shore meets with drifts of pine needle rich forest duff. We pile out and spread out to search for a path. At first it seems as if finding one will be easy enough, for where the tree line meets the beach is nothing more than the sort of small growth that is common along waterlines: little scrubby shrubs; bent and twisted evergreens; grass tufts randomly thrown about, like forgotten hassocks.

As I figure it, we'll work our way through this, then maybe through a tangle of vines along the margins, then we'll find ourselves in a cathedral wilderness where those (literally!) sky-brushing trees crowd out the light and water to the understory, creating an open area suitable for strolling. After that, it will be like a walk in the park, hushed and verdant.

Except that it isn't. Sure the scrub gives way to the expected tangled margins, but no matter how we push, we can't find our way through, not even Puck, not even after Muriel takes him off his leash on his sworn promise that he'll help, not just gallop off after the first interesting distraction.

"What we need is an axe," I muse, gently repositioning one of the little honeybirds who had fallen asleep and started slipping. "Lady Bug, would you happen to have one?"

Lady Bug flutters her wings in a mixture of apology and regret. I can tell she thinks she's failed us and hasten to reassure her. "You can't fly where there's no sky. Maybe we can make an axe. Are there any sharp stones or shells on the beach?"

But the stones all prove to be water-rounded, as pretty as can be, especially when the waters splash over them and bring out their hidden veins of contrasting colors. Most of the shells are tiny, elegant sculptures in miniature. The ones that aren't wouldn't make good axe blades. Muriel and I let ourselves get distracted collecting enough shells to make matching bracelets. Then we make a collar for Puck, and something like crowns for Horatius and Eyebright.

Lady Bug has gone small enough that she can now fit in my pocket and declines our offer to make her some sort of adornment. Indeed, when I ask, I sense that she's becoming impatient with this pause for play. She's spent our craft break trying to slip her much smaller self through the foliage barrier and is having less than no luck.

While I finish stringing the shells for Eyebright's crown, I consider the implications of this aloud. "As I see it, there are several interesting interpretations of our current situation. One is that this is, in fact, East. After all, the problem with directions like East and West is that they are relative.

Earlier we were *both* east and west, and this changed as we moved, east becoming west with every inch we moved. Only now that we can't go any further are we truly East."

Muriel considers this. "So our situation is rather like that bit someone said about East being East and West being West, and the two not meeting up. Here we're East of everything except for those trees and since we can't get through them, we're as east as east can be. Still, what does that mean for us getting you back to your family? Have we come to the wrong place? Was Absinthe wrong?"

"I don't think so," I reply. "I'm remembering all those stories my dad told where heroes" (or "gods," I think, but don't say) "came back from whatever version of the afterlife they'd ventured into. Finding the road was only part of the challenge. The other was defeating or tricking or otherwise overcoming those set to block commuter traffic between life and death."

"So we're going to need to fight someone?" Muriel asks hesitantly, while Puck bounces around in a fierce (or at least *he* thinks it's fierce) moon rabbit dance.

"It doesn't need to be a fight," I say. "In fact, I think fighting is probably the worst way to manage it. Orpheus charmed the denizens of the underworld when he went down to beg for his wife to be returned to him, but he screwed up in the end by looking back and showing that he didn't trust Persephone and Hades – or Pluto or Dis, pick your tag – to keep their promise. Virgil had a golden bough that gave him safe passage – at least I think it was Virgil. Or maybe that was Aeneas. Anyhow, whoever it was had safe passage. Hercules tied up Cerberus; he didn't kill him. And that's just a couple of the stories. When Gilgamesh went after Enkidu…"

Muriel raises both hands in mock protest. "Okay! We get it! We get it! You minored in Classics! I bet your dad would be amazed at all you remember from his rather weird choice of bedtime stories."

"It's not so weird," I protest. "Glory and I both really liked his stories because they were usually about winning through, even when your opponent was something as inevitable as death."

Horatius has been turning both faces to study the fringes of the forest while I'd rattled on. Now he shakes his head as if disappointed.

"What's wrong?"

"Oh," he says in that slow, rumbly way of his, a way that doesn't make him sound in the least stupid, more like he's carefully considering all the alternatives. "I was looking to see if there was a golden bough or suchlike hidden amidst all this tangle, but no such luck. I thought maybe we were supposed to find it, so you could use it as a talisman."

"Talisman, guide, helper..." I muse. "Well, I seem to lack the first two, but I'm amply blessed with the last."

And then, I realize that once again I'm setting myself up as the sole hero of this tale, when I'm beginning to think that I'm more like the princess in need of rescue. That I might be the princess is incredibly disturbing, because I've always secretly despised the Snow Whites and Sleeping Beauties, preferring my princesses to have at least enough sense to get themselves out of trouble or to at least help with the process. I mean, just one example, if Rapunzel could lower her hair to bring witches and princes up and down, why didn't she hack those golden locks off and get down herself?

Chewing on one thumbnail, I find myself remembering another story – not a myth or a fairytale, but something like.

"We've tried above and below," I say slowly, "and we've tried one sort of between – going between all these shrubs and such, but what about the other between?"

"Other between?" Muriel asks.

"Did I ever tell you about Tarzan?" I ask by way of reply. "He was a human raised by apes. Don't ask how or why; I'll tell you later if you want. But one thing I always loved about those stories was how when he was in a hurry he didn't go on the ground, he went through the 'middle terrace,' the branches of the trees. These trees here are too dense for Lady Bug to fly between, but that should make them perfect for traveling from branch to branch."

"What about Horatius and Eyebright?" Muriel asks. "They're pretty big."

"Damn! I hadn't considered that."

"We could stay," Horatius says. "We're good at waiting."

"No," I say. "That wouldn't be right. I feel like we have a puzzle to solve and when we do, we'll know what to do. There's something mazelike about this situation. I don't know how else to put it. We're East. Great, but that's just the first step in solving the maze."

Pursing my lips, I walk backwards so far that the surf licks around my ankles and pretty much finishes ruining the shoes and socks I'd donned back in the rosy tower in preparation for this journey. Sitting on a convenient rock, I take off shoes and socks, absently shaking off the sand and damp, then set them in the sun to dry. All this time, my gaze hardly leaves the swaying green forest, hardly leaves leaves and branches, tossing and fluttering, branches oriented to capture the uncapturable sun.

A idea sneaks through the edges of my thoughts and I'm back on my feet again, toes curled in the sand that shifts and slides with every rise and fall of the waves, toes curling, balance shifting in minute degrees so I feel part of one great dance in which forest partners with waves, one capturing light and transforming it into rich green leaves and needles, the other bouncing light from ripples, earthborn stars, more ephemeral than those now hidden above, trading permanence for sparkle and delight.

A larger wave knocks against my ankles, setting the honeybirds to shrill complaints but, though my toes curl to steady me, I am hardly aware of being off-balance. I am caught in unraveling the amazing maze that is this East. We've tried to find a path in at ground level without luck. Even if we could craft axe or hatchet, I would now be reluctant to take recourse to that course. A forest that bars someone as small as Puck or mini-Lady Bug isn't going to take kindly to someone (or someones) who think that ripping and tearing is the best course of action.

I still feel there's something to my idea about the middle terrace, but Muriel is right. Even if we could get up into those spreading limbs – something I'm seriously beginning to doubt is possible, how would we manage to get Horatius and Eyebright through? Abandoning companions for no other reason than they are not conveniently sized doesn't seem very heroic to me.

Despite my egotistical inclination to keep casting myself in the role of hero, the others are more than sidekicks. I'm determined that all of us will have the choice to go on. To do otherwise is to surrender to defeat and retreat.

So... Not through. Not between. Under doesn't seem an option. Puck's the only digger among us, and it's impossible to imagine him digging a tunnel under a forest the extent of which we do not know. Does that leave only up? I let my gaze travel up and further up, shifting from point to point, trying to find evidence of a ladder we might climb. But wouldn't a ladder just take us higher and higher on a wall that already bars us? This continues to trouble me, even as I determinedly seek a path.

Then, as is so often the case with inspiration, between one breath and the next I have the answer. I'm not saying I *like* it. That would be pushing any defined definition of "like." But the answer is there in the rise and fall of the waves, in the rooting of my toes in the sand, in the way the trees impossibly but undeniably go all the way up to the sky.

"Puck!" I call. "Want to help me dig a hole?"

The moon rabbit comes tearing over, bouncing up and down in the frantic eagerness with which he greets any opportunity to do something that involves action, the one thing he may love more than he does eating. Muriel looks more concerned. Like me, she's been studying the possibilities. From the little line of puzzlement and concern between her finely drawn brows, she hasn't reached the same conclusion I have.

"Jessie? Why are we digging a hole?"

I press my lips together before offering a partial answer. "We're going to plant a seed. The seed will grow into a tree that will carry us up to the sky. That will be my route back and your conduit – all of you, you, not just Muriel-you – to remain connected to me."

"Seed?" Muriel says, but Puck's already started digging and I use the need to give him directions to grant me a moment's grace before I must explain more to this all too dear, all too perceptive, friend.

"Not there, Puck! Over there, closer to the forest. How about where that little streamlet is trickling out, on the sunny side. That way our tree will have plenty of light and water."

Horatius and Eyebright have stowed their cards in Lady Bug (who got big again while I was wading) and now stomp and glide over to join Puck.

"How deep, Jessie?" asks Horatius. And Eyebright, who may have seen more than the rest, adds, "What dimensions?"

And I say, "About six feet deep is traditional if we can manage it. And about this long and this wide" I continue, sketching my own dimensions and a bit more.

Muriel stares at me both appalled and reluctantly understanding.

"Don't ask," I say, "how I know. I just do. Maybe it's all that about vegetation gods or maybe it's about world trees, but I know this is right. I'll be the seed of the tree and the tree me will be able to come back to life, to make a path out of Asphodel."

I expect Muriel to protest, to need convincing, but all she does is pick up a big bivalve clamshell from the sand, break it in two, and hand me half.

"It's not much of a shovel," she says, "but then you're a very strange seed."

Digging the hole goes by in a haze of repeated motion. Before I can comprehend that it's done, we have a tidy trench, just the right size for me. We stopped shy of six feet deep, which is something of a comfort but, even four or five seems deep enough when I step in and start to lay myself flat. As I am doing so, I feel the shift and wriggle of the eleven or thirteen honeybirds under my gown. They certainly can't go with me, so I detach them one by one and set them on the upper edge of the hole.

They've gone from hatchlings to nestlings to fledglings to miniatures of the weird dino-bug-birds they will grow up to be (that is, if a diet of my blood and crystalized nectar hasn't completely warped them). Now the nectar gatherers flutter and buzz. The guardians and nursemaids flap their wings and try their legs, stumbling on knobby knees, but clearly ready to become the ground patrol of their little flock.

This time when separated from me they don't twitter "Mama! Mama!" and race back to the safety of me. I'm pretty certain I'm happy about this, but I'm a little sad, too.

"I'm not saying goodbye," I announce as I recline in the hole. "Because I'm not going away from you. I don't know how long until I sprout, but I have a good feeling it won't take long. As soon as I'm big enough, grab hold and we'll be up and out. Now, go on, put the dirt back in the hole."

I close my eyes and make sure my lips aren't parted, though I try to make sure I'm smiling, not grimacing. I fold my hands across my under-occupied chest, hoping I look tranquil, like Sleeping Beauty, not, as I suspect, like a ratty, tattered castaway corpse. Then the dirt starts coming down and I don't have energy to worry about anything but not bolting up and out and giving this up as a really bad job.

Then it's dark and squished feeling and I'm left with the task of becoming a tree. Turns out, when you're a seed, becoming a tree is as natural as earth, water, and impulse. Warmth helps, but file that under "impulse," because really all these things are interwoven so you can't do without the suite. Really, I guess for me, the only question is what sort of tree I'll be. As I shoot forth, bending and unfolding, pretty much like those bean sprouts you might have sprouted on damp paper towels when you were in grammar school, I consider what sort of tree I'd like to end up as.

My first thought is how nice it would be to be a peach tree like those the Lady of the Moon had had in her orchards. They'd been so elegant with their long leaves, branches strong but not overly heavy, and solid foundations. The flowers had been both delicate and elegant. Best of all, if I could manage it, Puck would love the fruit.

I laugh at the idea, a laugh that turns into a long trunk, spreading boughs, and a bursting forth into the light to the delight of my friends. I'm not yet strong enough to pick them up, so they dance a wild frolic around me: girl, dragon, moon rabbit, lady bug, giant, and a buzzing swooping, long-legged baker's dozen (or maybe a few bites less) of various shapes of honeybird.

Muriel is singing something about poems lovely as a tree and Puck's beating out the bass with his big feet. I soak in their happiness along with dirt and water and warm sunshine. As I had anticipated, my growth is rapid. What I had not anticipated was that myself as tree would be rare and wondrous beyond comprehension.

There is the peach tree, most certainly, but there are also limbs and leaves borrowed from the unicorn's forest. There are sturdy maples and determined elms such as grew among the buildings of the gargoyle's city. There are palm trees, or at least a few fronds, right out of Heka Egypt. There is a bough just like that of the spreading old oak from which my impractical father had tried to hang a swing for me and Glory – a swing later rehung by our more practical mother.

As my limbs multiply and spread there are dogwood and redbud blossoms, there are leaves of brilliant aspen gold from an autumn trip into the mountains with my college friends, there are broad catalpa leaves, spring-fresh and accompanied by clusters of orchid-like flowers. As I grow I add even more varieties, in fruit, in flower, in all of autumn's varied colors. Evergreen needles have their place as well, snapping not only with their natural sharp scent but with those borrowed from anise and sage.

I grow and grow until I become what I know myself to be: ImpossibiliTree!

I am launching toward the distant sky. As I do, my friends leap onto the limb or bough of their choice, rather as children might run for their chosen mounts on the dizzily swirling platform of a carousel. Puck chooses a limb of peach overhung with apples, underswept with fat damson plums. Muriel surrounds herself with the flowering tufts of a Japanese cherry blossom. Horatius chooses a sturdy oak limb, and Eyebright twines around and between the branches of a white flowering pear.

The honeybirds, like young children everywhere, cannot make up their minds. Lady Bug, large again, makes herself both chariot and charioteer for the guardian honeybirds, who do not seem comfortable flying, although from time to time one launches forth and runs up and down my trunk. The prickling of their claws gives me a touch of nostalgia, but even that becomes fertilizer for my ebullient surge up and up, reaching for the sky with upswept arms that nonetheless are the branches of an eternally optimistic ash, touched with old magics and pink flowers.

And then we are there, to the sky and beyond, moving at escape velocity into a reality that will enfold Jessie. And the rest? All but the honeybirds tumble into Lady Bug's capacious interior. They will be around but not bound to follow me, heroes in their own right, not sidekicks, aides, guides. They will probably take up residence on the Moon, because we have friends there. No doubt they will visit many of the places where we have friends, as well as going forth and making new friends and having new adventures.

Sometimes I will join them, although whether I will choose to believe this only a dream will be up to me. After all, I have a journey of my own to make, a journey back to health and strength and, hopefully, happiness. I will need to learn to be a full participant in a family that never gave up on me, even when I came terrifying close to giving up on myself.

Before joining the others in Lady Bug's chariot, the honeybirds spread themselves out over the vast span of my ImpossibiliTree. In concert they drive their beaks – no longer only needle-sharp but like nails or at least like pins – into the knots and bends in my tree, choosing places that will be my joints when I go back to being human. Like practitioners of some bizarre form of acupuncture, they open up areas that had been crushed, making it possible for Life's energy to flow cleanly again.

This won't save me from pain, nor from having to work hard to rebuild atrophied muscles and strengthen damaged bones and tendons. What it does do is assure that, if I work hard, healing will happen. I won't be saved from either pain or effort, but I will be from despair. And really, when you think about it, that's quite a lot.

A cheat? An easy out? Maybe so but, nonetheless, after everything has healed that's going to heal, I still feel pinpricks upon my breasts and deep within various joints. The docs can't explain why, but I know and smile.

What they can't see is that when the moon is full and the rabbits dance, those pinprick wounds weep tears that mingle blood and nectar, and I sway to winds only I can see.

The End. Or Maybe, Just the Beginning.

71195011R00104

Made in the USA
Middletown, DE
20 April 2018